Taste of Air
Cassie Sweet

Dreamspinner Press

Published by
DREAMSPINNER PRESS

5032 Capital Circle SW, Suite 2, PMB# 279, Tallahassee, FL 32305-7886 USA
http://www.dreamspinnerpress.com/

Taste of Air
© 2014 Cassie Sweet.

Cover Art
© 2014 Brooke Albrecht.
http://brookealbrechtstudio.blogspot.com
Cover content is for illustrative purposes only and any person depicted on the cover is a model.

ISBN: 978-1-62798-934-3
Digital ISBN: 978-1-62798-935-0
Library of Congress Control Number: 2014943208
First Edition August 2014

Printed in the United States of America
∞
This paper meets the requirements of
ANSI/NISO Z39.48-1992 (Permanence of Paper).

# Chapter One

ESTOBÁN MEDOVIN studied his visitors. Though they sat at his table by his invitation, he was not easy in the association. Every time his gaze landed on the scarred face of his former lover, Theodyne Thespacian, guilt lodged like a lump of coal in his stomach. His food did not want to stay put, and he was too quick to reach for his wine. At this rate he would be well into his cups before the next course.

At least three years had passed since they had seen each other. Estobán tried to avoid Theodyne as much as possible—anything to not have to look at the horrible disfigurement that Theodyne wore like some fleshy medal of honor. If Estobán hadn't heard disturbing news coming out of the holy city of Gusan, he would have forgone this meeting as well.

Estobán took another sip of his wine, fortifying himself. "My contacts in Gusan tell me the *demigoge* is on his deathbed and the *cardgrans* are preparing to choose a successor to the Throne of Heaven."

Theodyne and his current lover, Count Nicodemus de Valencia, exchanged glances.

Nico put his arm on the table and leaned forward. "And you want to know where the alchemists sit? If we have any thoughts on who should fill the position?"

Estobán shook his head. "No. You misunderstand my reason for calling this meeting. I have heard your reasons in the past for not getting involved in ecumenical matters, and I admire your resoluteness; however, my contacts also express a certain level of anxiety over the choices being put forth as those in the running for the *demigoge's* seat."

Theodyne rubbed his hand over his chin. "Are any of them believed to have ties with the necromancers?"

A remembered scent of death filled Estobán's nose. He almost gagged on the thought. He picked up his wineglass only to realize he had emptied it. A servant rushed to pour more. After Estobán took a sip to wet his parched throat, he said, "Not that we've been able to confirm with any degree of reliability."

Nico gave a sigh. "And it is going to take an alchemist to discover if any of the *cardgrans* up for the vote are under a necromancer's influence."

Estobán's throat tightened around the word. "Yes."

"Tell me what you need?" Nico's face showed that same determination Estobán noticed three years ago when the Count and Theodyne had taken on the necromancers in the *prolatial* court.

Now that the request was out in the air, Estobán relaxed. "I will need a liaison with the authority to speak for the alchemists in matters that concern your order. One who can detect a necromancer."

Theodyne picked up his own glass of wine and swirled it. "You need an elemental."

Nico nodded. "One who has felt the evil touch of the death dancers."

Estobán felt a hand, cold as the grave, move over his skin as if the necromancer had not been cast out completely. Yet he knew the fiend had been. In the deepest hours of the night, memories filled him so acutely. During the day, when governmental business kept his mind occupied, he was able to forget the sense of violation caused by the necromancer.

"It might be helpful if it is someone who knows the intricacies of such a...." Words failed Estobán. He did not want to call it a relationship, since it more resembled a parasitic infestation than anything else.

Theodyne's golden eyes softened. "I know what you mean. You don't have to put it into words when there are none."

"Not that fit," Estobán agreed.

VISIONS CAME from some hellish place inside Estobán's soul. All night long he fought dream demons too cowardly to show their faces during his waking hours. In the mornings, without memory of doing such, he'd find his hands covered in tempera and oil paints.

The first time it happened, he'd woken in the morning to find the walls of his bedchamber filled with the mindless doodles of an untrained hand. Believing his illness only temporary and brought on by his ordeal with the necromancers, Estobán soon realized his nocturnal artistry had a deeper, more permanent meaning.

As the months passed, he had an easel and canvases brought in to capture the wild images from his darkest nightmares and save his walls from destruction.

He sat on the edge of the bed and stared at his fingers—once again stained with crimson and midnight. Candlelight only afforded him a skewed view of the latest painting. Not enough of the scene had been completed to determine a subject. Then again none of them ever made any real sense. All seemed to represent places so dark that no light dared penetrate.

When would this torment cease? It was as if he'd lived with the horror an eternity. Hard to believe it had only been a few years.

A light knock sounded on the door.

Estobán leaned back on the bed and hid his paint-spattered hands under the covers. "Enter."

The door opened, and light from the hallway flooded the floor. A dark silhouette of a man stood just inside. "Sorry to wake you, Your Grace. The Holy See is here and wishes to speak with you. He says it is urgent."

"Thank you, Silas. Offer him some of our best wine, cheese, and bread, and inform him I will be down in a few minutes."

The servant exited, closing the door behind him.

Nothing good ever came of a late-night visit from the Holy See. The head of the local archdioceses had recently given over to delusions where he ran the city-state rather than Estobán. It was a very delicate situation that caused Estobán more than a few headaches.

He rose and hurried to clean the evidence of his creative side from his hands. He dressed carefully in a robe of state and descended to the small sitting room where he entertained church officials and dignitaries.

Desan Karis sat at the small round table. In his right hand, he held a goblet of expensive red wine. The bulk of his abdomen stood out, as if he hid a barrel under his cassock. His narrow eyes disappeared under rolls of fat that hung from his upper lids. The room filled with arrogance, radiating from the self-important being who sat in a chair inscribed with the insignia of the Medovin family and reserved for the *prolate*. It did not escape Estobán's notice that the *desan* waited for the command to move out of the chair.

It would be a long damn wait. Estobán was in no mood to play pissing games with a fat fuck who probably hadn't seen his own cock since the seminary. Instead Estobán approached the table and poured a glass of wine and remained standing to look down at the *desan*.

"What brings you to the *prolatial* palace at this time of night, Your Eminence?" Estobán did not even try to mask the annoyance in his voice.

"I thought it best if you heard the news directly from me. The *demigoge* has passed. May his spirit live in the eternal bosom of the Gods." Desan Karis bowed his head as if in holy prayer for the soul of the church patriarch.

Estobán knew better. The man was probably praying that all the bribes and gifts he'd paid to the Council of *Cardgrans* over the last few years might begin to bear fruit in the form of an appointment to the basilica in Gusan. A move Estobán had taken great pains to block at every turn.

Estobán waited until the *desan* had finished his act and then gave an appropriate condolence. Honestly, there wasn't one that quite covered the moment. The late *demigoge* had been a strong and capable church head. He'd managed to keep the city-states in check with regard to unification. Some members of the Council of *Cardgrans* were not so sympathetic to the city-states or their concerns.

"Are you traveling to Gusan, then?" Estobán swirled the wine in his glass, then took a sip.

"I leave at first light," Desan Karis confirmed. A beat of silence passed. "Are there any messages or correspondences you wish to relay to anyone there? I will be more than happy to deliver them in person."

"Holy See, that is most generous and accommodating of you, but I plan to make the journey as well."

Desan Karis opened his eyes a bit wider. "Is that so? Quite fascinating."

"Not in the least." Estobán poured a bit more wine. The Valencia red was an exquisitely balanced vintage. "Medovin *prolates* have attended the selections since the founding of Sadonia and Lancor in particular. By doing so, I am following in the traditions of my ancestors."

A thought occurred to Estobán: none of the cathedral bells had chimed. There should have been a solemn toll of the largest bell. One strike for each year the late *demigoge* had served as a vessel of the Gods on the Heavenly Throne.

"Have you decided to forgo the traditional death invocation?"

Desan Karis shook his head. A telltale blush spread across his cheeks. "I only postponed it until you were notified, out of respect for your office."

Estobán believed the reason went deeper but decided not to press the matter. "I will not keep you any longer, then. My servant will show you out. If you will excuse me, I have much to prepare before I leave for Gusan."

The Holy See merely nodded and made the sign of the five-pointed star over Estobán as if granting him a blessing to leave.

Offense boiled under the surface. In another life and time, he'd have been more like Theodyne and not given a flying fuck about niceties and decorum. He'd have told the Holy See where he could stick his blessing and been done with it. But politics and matters of state did not work that way. More could be gained by diplomacy and underhanded deals than all the rants in the world.

More was the pity.

On his way back to his suite, he passed Silas. "Have the carriages readied and the horses put in harness. We leave for Gusan after morning meal. Also, I'll need a messenger to take a missive to Villa de Valencia."

"Yes, Your Grace." Silas bowed and started away to do his master's bidding.

Cool air traveled through the palace from open windows. Estobán's shoes made lonely sounds against the mosaic tiles as he walked. No one else was awake at this end of the house. Good, this time of the morning— the hour before the first light of dawn began to break over the horizon—

was more conducive to thinking than all the other hours of the day combined.

He opened the door to his office and lit the lamp. A few things needed to be made official before he left for Gusan—the order of succession for one.

Without an heir, the succession was open for a power struggle should anything happen to him. He should have resolved this matter after the infection by the necromancer, but he had not been sure at the time which members of his family had also been under the death dancer's influence. Time and observance had to take place before he could make a final decision.

Estobán sat down and began to write the letter to Count Nicodemus before he prepared the succession documents for the church and *prolatial* magus.

Silas stuck his head in the door and knocked as he watched his master. "Your Grace, the messenger awaits."

"Thank you." Estobán took his seal of office and melted wax to affix the folded parchment together. His choice for successor was also going into the hands of the alchemists. If they could not keep his heir safe, no one could.

He handed the paper to Silas. "Wake the magus and tell him I need him and his clerk here immediately."

"Yes, Your Grace."

# Chapter Two

THE ENTIRE Medovin family gathered in the *prolatial* court. Morning sunshine poured through the windows, a welcome visitor after the demons of night. After the events of three years ago, Estobán had moved the official court to another part of the palace. This room was larger, open on three sides, with ornate columns and painted ceiling.

Estobán gazed down over the assemblage, retaining an austere and commanding expression. The news he meant to impart was of the most serious nature, capable of shaking the very foundations of the mansion.

The magus stood behind and to the right of Estobán's chair. As the official councilor of the *prolate*, tradition stated he must not be a member of the ruling family. The thought behind such an appointment was that without blood ties the magus could give a wise and unbiased view to his *prolate*.

Since that dark day in the court when the necromancers showed their hands, Estobán had found himself relying more on the magus and less on the advice of his cousin, Cesare. The rift was beginning to show along the main branches of the family. Demarcations were evident and battle lines drawn.

Estobán would not lose.

The magus struck his staff against the marble floor three times, heralding the beginning of court. "His Grace, Estobán Medovin, *prolate* of Lancor-Sadonia calls this court in session."

Estobán waited for the murmurings to quiet before he spoke. "The death of the *demigoge* requires my presence during the congregation of *cardgrans*. In my absence, I am appointing my sister, Viola, to run the business of state."

As he knew it would, the announcement caused mutters to erupt in the chamber. His gaze sought and found Viola's wide eyes. Her surprise was only surpassed by that of Cesare.

The magus banged the staff again. "Silence!"

The Medovins quieted on command.

Estobán continued. "I am henceforth naming her my heir and the next in succession to take the *prolate*'s robes upon my death. This request is on file with the church officials and in the hands of trusted nobles solely unconnected to the family. This is my final decision on the matter. Court is adjourned."

Estobán stood and left the room through the door located behind the dais. As expected, Cesare was hot on his heels. Estobán made it to his office only a step or two before his enraged cousin.

Cesare slammed the door, closing them both inside. Estobán walked to the drink cabinet and poured a goblet of wine. He did not acknowledge Cesare's anger. After all, Estobán had anticipated it. He'd have been more alarmed had Cesare taken the news in a magnanimous manner.

"You can't mean to do this? Not only do you throw the Medovin dynasty into the sewers by naming a woman as heir, but you name one who is no more than a weak child." Cesare stood with his hands on his hips, his face red as the surplice on his robe. "I *will* challenge this."

Estobán shifted so Cesare could note the raised brow he gave his cousin. "You do, and it is at your own peril. I will not turn this into a familial war because you feel slighted. Naming you as heir was never guaranteed. You've just always assumed."

Cesare took a few steps forward, closing a bit of the distance between them. "With your proclivities, it seems unlikely you'll ever father a child. Not unless the Gods see fit to change the natural order and some of your *lovers* get with child."

Cesare had never mentioned Estobán's love for other men with such venom. Segments of the nobility accepted such unions by turning a blind eye. Others denounced it as anathema for the simple reason it muddied the lines of succession. To Estobán he'd never seen a problem with being able to work around such things. Any issue from Viola would have Medovin blood. The line would continue—of course the provision of naming a child of hers to the *prolate*'s office was dependent on the child keeping the surname Medovin.

Estobán eyed his cousin and took a slow sip of wine. "I have yet to see a problem with either my choice of heir or my choice of bed partners. It's not as if I haven't caught you sucking Ignatius Agia's cock more than once."

Cesare's face turned puce. There didn't seem to be any breath going in and out of his body.

Estobán smiled. "What, Cousin? Did you think I didn't know? That your frequent trips to Delaneux were more about fulfilling your carnal lusts than diplomatic obligations? You've underestimated me very badly."

Cesare stood there in stark silence as if he didn't know whether to storm out of the office defeated or pour himself a stronger drink than the wine in Estobán's hand.

Estobán let his cousin decide, holding out the silence until he could read the pain of it across Cesare's face. Even now the man had plots and intrigues rampaging through his mind. He didn't try to hide the evidence of it from his eyes.

"In time you'll see this for the mistake it is, and you'll regret it."

"Cesare, I've regretted a lot of things in my life, but I doubt this is one of them." Estobán used the hand holding the goblet to indicate his cousin. "Even before this outburst today you've proven to me you haven't the temperament required of a *prolate*."

Cesare finally gave in and poured himself some wine. "This is about Theodyne Thespacian and his accusations three years ago. You've never quite absolved me of being in the same room with the necromancers."

That strike was too close to the bone. That statement held more truth than Estobán cared to admit. "This is about doing what is best for the city-state of Sadonia."

"A woman? How is giving the local government over to a woman the *best* for Sadonia?" Cesare didn't even attempt to conceal his contempt.

"Would you dare call Queen Razell of Danvic weak? That woman rides into battle at the head of her troops." Estobán was never one to assume another's strength or lack thereof on merely their sex. Personally, he knew an awful lot of weak men.

"She is the exception."

"And what about the long line of Danvicon queens who have ruled that country for centuries. Are they all exceptions?" Estobán waved his hand in the air. "Sorry, the only thing weak is your argument."

"And who do you think to leave behind while you travel to Gusan? Someone will have to counsel the woman."

"*The woman's* name is Viola, and she is your honored and beloved cousin. Do not forget that again." Estobán wanted another glass of wine but refrained. He needed to appear in control and capable of restraint. Even if the situation felt as if one strong breeze might tip him past the point of amendment. "Actually, I am leaving Gaius behind. He is more in touch with the running of the city-state than anyone else."

"You are leaving your magus? Very risky." A secret smile accentuated the comment.

"I will do well with the magus's clerk." Duard had proven to be efficient and knowledgeable in all aspects of a magus's duties. He might someday make the leap to hold his own post in that exalted position.

A knock on the door stalled the conversation.

"Enter."

The door opened, and Viola started to step inside but withdrew slightly when she spotted Cesare.

"Don't leave. Cesare is quite finished dressing me down." Estobán flicked his hand at Cesare, a clear dismissal.

Cesare slammed his goblet on the table and stalked out, nearly knocking Viola off her feet in his haste.

Viola turned, staring after their arrogant and difficult cousin. She closed the door, hesitating with her hand on the wood. "He will feel the need for vengeance, Essi."

"And I'll be ready." Estobán held up the decanter. "Drink?"

She waved her hand in refusal as she faced him. "Too early in the day for me."

He set it back down, having lost his thirst for it. "As I've told Cesare, I'm leaving the magus here should you need him."

"You've placed your faith in the wrong person."

"No, my dearest, I haven't. You have more strength and foresight than you give yourself credit." He took a place behind his desk and unlocked the bottom drawer. "You were the only one who cautioned me of my folly when I had Theodyne arrested."

"Advice you disregarded," she pointed out.

"Much to my own painful regrets." Estobán removed a copy of the article of succession. He held the sealed document out for her. "There are many ways to rule with strength that have nothing to do with gender or brutality. You've always been rational and even-tempered."

She took the paper and rubbed her thumb over the seal. "There has never been a choice. Living my life within the confines of the mighty Medovin clan, surrounded by males who always believed their way is superior or they are the only ones allowed to think and feel...." Her voice trailed off. "I'm sorry. I'm railing against the wrong man. You are the one person in this clan who has always treated me as if there was more to me than the obligation to produce the next generation."

"You need never hold your tongue with me, Viola." Truly she had never said a cross word about anyone in her entire life. He was a bit surprised and relieved she had said as much as she had. It only reinforced he'd made the right decision.

The smile she bestowed took him back to their childhood. A bit of the devil lay beneath her serene countenance. Just enough mischief to intrigue. "I hope you haven't decided to marry me off now you've made me your heir."

Estobán frowned. "I've let you languish without a husband longer than most women are allowed. You will need to marry and soon, but it can wait until things are more settled. I've too much in front of me with the *demigogal* election to worry about a suitable husband for a very beloved sister."

Viola moved around the desk, then leaned in and placed a kiss on her brother's forehead. "He will have to be an extraordinary man to hold up to your scrutiny."

Estobán took her hand and pressed his lips to her fingers. In all the world, he loved no one more dearly than his sister. She knew everything about him. All the darkness and pain had been laid at her feet. They had no secrets between them. Her arms had held his body, wracked with sobs when Theodyne left. Her hands had dried his tears after the necromancer's infection. For all that she was so many years younger, she had always been the stronger.

Viola had spoken true. Any man to whom Estobán gave her hand had to be truly exemplary. The problem had never been in finding a man who would take his sister to wife—she was beauty and gentleness personified. What he often wondered in the wee hours of the morning when his bed was empty and cold was if he'd ever find anyone to share his life.

# Chapter Three

MASTER ALCHEMIST Jolen Meripen tried very hard not to stare at the sights around him. The holy city of Gusan was as splendid as it was profane. Not even the Gold School itself could match the glittery edifice of the Basilica of the Heavenly Throne. The white walls were composed of a stone rich in crystal fragments that reflected the sunlight into a million tiny prisms. The experience reminded him of walking through interrupted rainbows.

Energy pulsed through the square. The clerics would call it the presence of the Gods. Jolen knew it to be nothing more than the voices of the elementals still embedded in the stones. They did not appear very contented in their tasks. Perhaps they perceived a dark future and wished to warn the residents. He'd have to speak with them later and discover the source of their distress.

Jolen had never imagined his life would lead him to such a pass. The fact that Master Nico handpicked him to aid the Medovin *prolate* was an honor and privilege. Still he was honest enough with himself to realize he might be out of his depth. How was he to discover if the *cardgran* candidates were tainted by the will of the necromancers? The exercises practiced at the school were not done with real necromancers but spells used to mimic the feel of a death dancer's influence. Applying what he'd learned to a real-life scenario would be the delicate part of the operation. Even with the training, he had not had many occasions to practice the fine art of detection.

Fear of being clumsy or inept in his attempts made his stomach clench.

A fact he'd keep to himself or risk looking the fool.

Jolen was not one to shy away from a challenge. No one who was schooled in the art of alchemy could claim cowardice. It took a brave soul and stout heart to walk such a path. However, not a lot of time had passed since his mind was filled with infection by the necromancers. Three years was not long enough to recover from such an intimate invasion.

The bastards had controlled his mind and used his body to spy on the alchemists. For this Master Nico trusted him with such an important mission? Unbelievable. Unprecedented. He was so unworthy of the honor.

Pilgrims from all over the city-states of Dominicál converged on Gusan to witness the selection of a new *demigoge*. Their ranks of nobility and city-state of origin were visible in the colors and finery of their garments. Vocations were recognizable only so far as the clerics were dressed in robes of their calling. All the others wore their wealth as a badge of honor. The display of wealth enough to make Jolen sick.

Headmaster Oberon had warned Jolen to dress humbly and forgo his formal adept's robes. He was not at Gusan as a representative of the alchemists—and truly the likelihood of being welcomed by the clerics with open arms if Nico and Oberon had insisted on a contingent was slim to nil.

Jolen looked down at the map in his hand. He needed to gain his bearings or risk wandering through the holy city for the duration of the congregation. The Medovin's private villa was located on the far side of the square overlooking a structure called the Divine Causeway and the *demigoge*'s private residence. The location was a prime one in a city where everything was about status and position.

Not very Gods-like.

But then Jolen had observed long ago that not much the church did kept with the teachings of the Trinity. Instead they were more interested in the politics of power than saving the souls of their faithful. A ripe harvest for the necromancers, indeed.

He crossed the square, careful to stay to the walkways reserved for visitors to the holy city. Other paved areas were marked for only clerics of the higher echelons to walk. If someone not of the faith or correct order touched the stones, it was said the square had to be closed and the walkways cleansed and consecrated anew.

The massive basilica complex was like stepping into a different world where all the rules comforting and familiar to Jolen had been tossed by the wayside. Headmaster Oberon had gone over such laws and protocols with him since Master Nico had sent the notice. Jolen doubted he'd ever remember all the rules and only hoped he'd not disappoint or embarrass the Medovin *prolate* he'd come to aid.

Finally Jolen reached the bronze doors that led to the Medovin's Gusan residence. He took the large knocker into his hand and banged it against the special platform used for such a purpose. A vibration rang through the square, echoing off the neighboring buildings. He shuffled and lowered his heat-washed face. Sneaking into this residence was never going to happen.

The doors opened, and a stone-faced guard wearing full armor plating over his short tunic and hose looked Jolen up and down before dismissing him as unimportant. "Servants' entrance is around back."

Was he considered a servant? In this capacity it was questionable.

"I was sent for by the Medovin *prolate*." Jolen held out his hand. A signet ring with the seal of the Adepts of Delaneux circled the middle finger of his left hand.

The guard's gaze shifted from the ring to Jolen's face. "You look too young to be an adept."

Jolen cocked his head. "Have you known many?"

The guard narrowed his eyes and jerked his head to the left. "Get on with you. Around back."

Jolen hefted his pack higher on his shoulder and started the way he was instructed to go. Apparently the alchemists were needed but not held in high regard. Resentment boiled up Jolen's throat. He'd spent long enough making his way up the ranks of his order that he'd learned humility. Had learned how to take orders from those who were above him. He glanced back at the closed door. One guard wearing the colors of the Medovin house was not now nor never would be above Jolen in status.

He found the back entrance off the kitchens. Heat from the ovens boiled out into a garden that appeared well tended. He wondered briefly if the Medovin kept a staff at the residence at all times to care for such things. Not that it mattered for his mission.

A woman clad in a flour-covered dress and apron stepped out onto the small tiled porch. She looked up, startled at Jolen's presence. "Why are you skulking out here? Get in there and get to work. We've been waiting on you for hours."

Jolen raised a brow. "I'm afraid you might have me mistaken for someone else. I was sent from Delaneux to meet with the Medovin."

A knowing look came into her eyes. "Oh, you're one of those. Come this way."

Jolen had no idea what she meant, but her tone did not sound encouraging.

They entered the kitchen to the yeasty scents of baking bread and roasting meat. Dirty boys in grease-stained clothes twirled a whole pig on a spit.

"Wendro! Come. You are needed." Her voice carried through the kitchen with the resonance of the tolling of a loud bell during a coastal fog.

A boy of no more than ten years, with scrawny legs and gangly movements came down the hallway at a run. He held a red cap in place on his head as he skidded to a stop in front of the woman. "Yes, Linka."

"Show him to the gallery rooms."

"Yes, Linka."

The boy glanced up at Jolen and smiled shyly. "You don't look like the others."

At a loss, Jolen asked, "What others?"

Linka gave the boy a clout on the back of the head. "Shush and do as you're told."

The boy, Wendro, rubbed the back of his head and frowned. "Follow me."

Jolen had no choice but to do so. They moved through the back hallways to a long corridor that looked more like a breezeway. Pillars separated and supported the upper stories at precise intervals. The square structures were decorated with realistic and beautiful paintings, sculptures and carvings. Jolen wanted nothing more than to stop and study the priceless artwork but thought it more prudent to get settled before he attempted to send word to the Medovin of his arrival.

A bath and change of clothes would not go amiss.

Wendro stopped in front of a room. "This room isn't being used." He pointed to a panel on the wall. A blue stone was placed in a small niche. He picked up the stone and changed it for a yellow one. "There. Now no one will try to put someone else in here with you."

"Thank you." Jolen stepped into the room, and the lad followed him.

"When do the others arrive?"

Jolen set his pack on the bed. "That's the second time you've mentioned others. Why don't you tell me what you mean now we're out of Linka's reach?"

Wendro took off his hat and held it in front of him. "There aren't going to be any others coming? I thought at least the carnival players."

Jolen made a sound at the back of his throat. "Sorry to disappoint, but I know nothing of any players. I'm simply here to meet with the Medovin about a matter he'd discussed with my superior."

"You aren't a performer, then?"

"No." Though most people regarded alchemists as no more than stage magicians and charlatans, the truth was so much more fantastic.

"What do you do, then?"

Jolen dug into his pocket for a *gint* and handed it to the lad. "Close your hand tightly around the coin."

Wendro did as asked. His knuckles white with the action.

Jolen moved his hand over Wendro's closed fist. "Now open your hand." Where the brass coin had been, now sat a copper *slew*.

"Oh." Wendro's dark eyes rounded. His gaze shifted and landed on Jolen's ring. "You're one of *them*." The disappointment had turned to awe. "I've heard of your kind. My mama used to tell me stories of the alchemists and elementals."

Not many lay people told their children such tales unless to frighten them. "Did she? What did she say about us?"

He backed up and shook his head. "I can't repeat it. Not in this town. When she came here looking for work, she made me promise never to mention the stories again."

Jolen did not point out the boy already had. "Very wise."

Wendro gave an awkward bow. "The room key is in the cupboard. If you need anything at all, pull the bell by the bed."

"I will need some water. Both to bathe and to drink. Can you see to that for me?"

"Yes, sir."

The boy left, and Jolen sat on the bed. He'd walked for miles and his feet hurt. After the last time he'd taken a horse across country, he had not wanted to sit on a saddle again for a great distance. Truth of the matter, his last experience had given him a healthy fear of horses, or at least being in the saddle for long hours. Though Gusan was not as far away as Lancor, it was still a two-day ride from the school. This time he'd taken a postal caravan and ridden as one of the paid passengers.

When they had reached the city gates, he'd decided to walk the rest of the way. His feet were not going to let him hear the end of it.

Jolen dug through his pack and took out his clothes to hang in the wardrobe. Perhaps some of the wrinkles would fall out. He'd hate to present to the Medovin looking like he'd slept in his garments.

The fabrics were of good quality—granted not excellent. Headmaster Oberon and Nico had decided that Jolen needed to maintain a certain level of humbleness or risk drawing more attention to himself. Therefore the clothes were more befitting a very minor nobleman or successful merchant. Nothing too bold or too plain.

His dark blond hair had been trimmed in the latest style—shorter than he was used to, and he still felt a bit bald.

A knock at the door sounded before Wendro entered to place the water near the washbasin. "Is there anything else?"

"Not at the moment. You've been very helpful."

It was a dismissal that was lost on the boy.

"You may return to your duties. I'm sure Linka will be looking for you."

"Oh, she isn't my direct superior. She just runs the kitchens. I sneak down there every now and then to steal a pastry or two. She pretends not to notice, and in exchange I do extra errands for her in between my duties." Wendro took off his hat and twirled it in his hands again as if gearing up some courage.

Jolen couldn't help but smile. "That's very accommodating of her. Most cooks get very angry when their pastries go missing."

"I've heard her say she thinks I need meat on my bones. And I told her that I stay skinny so she can't put me on her spit."

Jolen laughed. "I don't think you have anything to fear there."

A bell began to toll somewhere in the house. Wendro stuffed his cap on his head. "I have to go. The servants are being sent for."

"What does it mean?"

"It means someone is in trouble and the Medovin is not happy." Then Wendro was off like a shot, and the door banged closed behind him.

HOURS PASSED and Jolen could no longer pretend his stomach wasn't empty. None of the Medovin's servants had been along to tell him where or when the meals were served, and he wondered if he was supposed to find his own sustenance while in residence. However, given the staff had been called together for some transgression, there probably wasn't anyone to assist him. The Gods above knew he wasn't about to get involved in any household problems.

Dressed in a black velvet doublet over a white shirt with black hose, boots, and leather belt, he set out to find the dining hall. He stopped midstride. What if he was supposed to dine with the servants? He supposed he'd find out.

Servants were all dour faced with their heads down as they moved along the corridors. Jolen stopped one of them, a young woman with a pretty face and kind eyes. "Excuse me. I have no idea where I'm supposed to be."

"Who are you? And what rooms are you staying in?"

"My name is Jolen Meripen, and I'm staying in the gallery."

"If you will take a place in the red salon over there, I will check and come back to guide you."

"Thank you." He stepped into the red salon and was immediately assailed by a heavy dose of elemental energy. The power almost knocked him off his feet. He searched the room, trying to discover the source. The essence of a fire elemental permeated the air. The feeling reminded him of the sensation he got while standing in the presence of the immortal form of Anjufer, though in this case there was also a definite presence of earth.

Jolen moved to a large display case with glass panels and gold fittings. Inside, on a bed of ermine was a piece of ruby about the size of Jolen's palm, inscribed with symbols he'd only seen in the *Eye of Truth*.

His breath stuttered and held. Exhalation stalled. He was afraid to even move. What was such a piece of sacred alchemical stone doing in the hands of the Medovin family at a little-used villa in the holy city?

Master Nico needed to know about this as soon as possible. When he turned to leave, the woman he'd stopped in the hallway greeted him. She gave him a curtsey. "If you will follow me, Master Jolen, the Medovin awaits you."

He almost told her he needed to return to his room but decided the artifact had been in the hands of the Medovins for only the Gods knew how long, he doubted it would go missing during the span of one meal.

Jolen set the need to contact Master Nico aside and fell in line behind the servant. She led him through the house and down into a large formal garden, lit with paper lanterns and swathed in white silk shot with gold strands.

Diners were already seated around the table. Laughter and music floated up to the top of the stairs. He started down with his heart pounding in his throat. Jolen preferred for first meetings to be held in private. Placing him at a dinner with other guests made him unsure of what the Medovin had shared with his family and guests and what he'd kept secret.

"Ah, Master Jolen Meripen. Glad you finally decided to join us." The voice was deep and sensual, the brush of a lover's hand over his senses.

Jolen looked to the man seated at the head of the table. He gave a slight bow to acknowledge the greeting. "Thank you for the invitation. It is much appreciated."

Estobán Medovin was younger than Jolen had expected. Certainly more handsome. A world-weary sadness filled his eyes and put brackets around his mouth that suggested he might have once been given to frequent smiles but the world had shown much disappointment and thus now he knew only frowns.

Jolen sat down, and a servant poured him a glass of wine. He nodded in thanks.

"I apologize for your welcome today. The guard who sent you to the servants' entrance has been dealt with."

Jolen stalled the drink halfway to his mouth. "That wasn't necessary, Your Grace. You see, I am here and have a nice room and clean water." He gestured with his glass. "Wine and food. I have all I need. There was no harm."

He was not about to mention that as an adept he could have gone into the yards, picked pieces of the lawn and transformed it into fruit and had a private banquet.

Medovin narrowed his eyes. "You are not at all what I expected."

Jolen let a smile crack the corner of his mouth. "What *did* you expect?"

The Medovin's eyes darkened, and his gaze dropped to Jolen's lips. Heat exploded low in Jolen's belly. Even sitting perfectly still, the Medovin was a dangerous man. "Someone a bit more... seasoned."

Jolen felt the warm rush of shame bathe his cheeks. "I assure you, I am more seasoned than I appear. At least for what you need."

Laughter exploded around the table.

"He's got you there, Estobán," said a man with the seal of Devani around his neck. He was not the *prolate* of that city-state but perhaps another functionary.

Estobán Medovin gave Jolen a smoldering glance. "I cannot wait to find out."

# Chapter Four

SOMETHING WAS wrong with the air in the garden. All of it had been sucked out and vented into a void. Estobán's throat was parched; his heart hurt as if he'd been punched in the chest. And all through his pain and agony, he could do nothing more than stare at his guest.

Damn Count Nico and Theodyne for sending someone so damaged in spirit that Estobán felt the effects all the way to his end of the table.

Master Jolen might be all of twenty-five—about the same age as Theodyne when he'd been released from prison. Estobán hardly remembered being that young. Not that he was old now. He'd only passed his thirtieth birthday in the winter. He just felt so much older.

The meal progressed with quiet conversation and laughter. Estobán had a feeling a summons to appear in front of the *cardgrans* would arrive in the morning. The selection of a new *demigoge* was a solemn occasion, and the sound of laughter filtering from the garden and into the square was cause for penalty. Usually that came in the form of an excised tithe paid directly into the basilica's coffers.

Estobán would let the revelers continue for a bit longer, and then he'd put a stop to the boisterous direction the dinner had taken. For now, he had other business to conduct.

He stood. "Master Jolen, if you will follow me, we have much to discuss."

The alchemist gazed down at his unfinished meal and dipped his hands in the cleansing bowl. "As you wish, Your Grace."

Master Jolen rose with a fluidity that could only be described as elemental. Estobán narrowed his eyes at the man. He knew Count Nico meant to send him an elemental, but had not been fully prepared for the experience. To his knowledge he'd not met with one in private and at the full height of their powers. Theodyne notwithstanding.

Estobán guided Master Jolen through the apartments and to the private offices located on the upper floors overlooking the square. The room was not as grand as his sanctum in Lancor, but adequate enough to impress.

A guard opened the door for them to enter. Estobán stepped to a drink table and offered Master Jolen some wine. The alchemist waved it off with a hand. Instead of pouring the wine, Estobán switched to water. He'd be better served to keep his wits about him when dealing with the alchemists, especially one unknown to him.

"Has Count… rather Masters Nico and Theodyne discussed your exact reason for being sent to join my retinue?"

Sky-blue eyes rimmed with dark lashes regarded Estobán in a sideways glance. "My mission was relayed by the Gold School's headmaster, Oberon."

"And you feel you are qualified to ferret out any *cardgrans* who may be under necromanical influence?"

Master Jolen gave a scoff of disbelief. "I was *appointed* to this post. I did not seek it out. If Master Nico believes I am qualified to fulfill such a duty, then I am beholden to his confidence."

Estobán laughed. "More a diplomat, I'd say."

Master Jolen gave a subtle shrug of a muscular shoulder. "These days alchemists serve many functions."

The longer Estobán observed Master Jolen, the more he wanted to know about the man in front of him. Mystery and a fair bit of aloofness surrounded Master Jolen. Estobán wanted very badly to break through.

"How will you go about testing the candidates?"

"It is a relatively easy process but will require me to be in close proximity of those you wish me to check for the influence." Master Jolen folded his hands in front of him in a humble gesture.

"Hum. That might be rather difficult, but we shall endeavor to arrange it." Estobán lifted a hand. "Do you need to meet with them alone?"

"There can be others present." Master Jolen's gaze shifted, landing on the water. "May I?"

"Yes, of course." Estobán poured a goblet full and handed it to Master Jolen.

"Traveling is a thirsty business." Master Jolen lifted the glass in salute. He took a large drink, leaving Estobán to watch the alchemist's throat work. How could such a simple action feel if it was part of some arcane ritual? How was it possible that an action so mundane had the power to fascinate?

Estobán cleared his throat. The conversation stalled. No words came to him. He had nothing to say. He'd never been a man who was at a loose end for a topic or observation to share, but he found himself unable to speak to Master Jolen.

"Would you care for some more?"

"A bit."

Master Jolen held up his glass as Estobán poured. "I would expect the waters around the school to be quite refreshing."

"Yes. The mountains provide many streams and rivers rich in drinking water." A sexy smile played along Master Jolen's lips. "Even if they did not, alchemists have ways to glean water from unexpected places."

Estobán wanted so much to ask what that meant and the locations of said places, but refrained. The secrets of the alchemists had to remain that way for now.

"Tomorrow there is to be a general meeting to convene the Council of *Cardgrans*. All *prolates* and their retinues are obliged to attend. You may be able to do some preliminary work to single out those under influence."

Master Jolen placed the goblet on the table and rubbed his thumb across his bottom lip. "I should be able to tell how many are in the room, but not who they are."

"That will be sufficient for a first day."

Master Jolen looked to the ground for a moment, and then those piercing eyes rose and connected with Estobán's. A sensation came over him, as if he fell from a great height. Estobán ground his back teeth together to keep the disquieted thoughts at bay.

"I wonder, Your Grace, if I may ask a question of you?"

Estobán twirled his hand. "Go ahead."

"Earlier while I waited to be brought to dinner, I noticed an artifact in one of your salons that would be of great interest to the alchemists. I wonder if I might study the piece while I'm in residence?"

"Of which trinket do you speak?" Estobán gave what he thought was a charming smile. "My apartments hold many treasures."

"To be sure." Master Jolen made a circuit of the office, inspecting various baubles. "This is a fragment of a carved ruby tablet."

It took Estobán a moment to recall the exact piece Master Jolen mentioned. "Oh, yes. I found it on a pilgrimage to the far-off lands of Ruanathe."

Master Jolen had an odd look on his face. "Found it? Where?"

Estobán gave a shrug. "I really don't remember."

It was so long ago, and he hadn't thought of that trip since he'd returned some fifteen years before.

"Was it in a bazaar or a shop? Did you find it in the home of a friend? Was it given as a gift?"

Estobán held up his hand to fend off the verbal cannon blasts. "I swear I do not remember. However, if it is that important to you, Master Jolen, I will think on it and see if anything comes to me."

"It would help if I knew the context in which it came to you." Master Jolen came back around so he faced Estobán. Those cool blue eyes seemed to penetrate Estobán right down to the bone. "And may I study the artifact?"

"If you wish."

Master Jolen gave a decisive nod. "Is that all you wish to discuss with me this evening?"

*No.* Far from it. Estobán wanted to keep Master Jolen there speaking with him all night long—to hold the nightmares at bay with conversation.

That did not mean that Estobán had become more at ease. If anything he was unsure of what subjects to open with the alchemist.

"I would like to get to know you better, Master Jolen. If we are to work together, I think it imperative I know where you stand."

"On what?" Master Jolen folded his arms in front of him in a defensive stance. It was the only outward sign that he was enjoying neither Estobán's company nor the conversation.

"How do you feel about a united Dominicál?"

"Master Nico believes it is not for the alchemists to become involved in political wrangling."

"I know Master Nico's stance on the matter. What I want to know is yours?"

"It all depends on the reason for the unification. If it's to fight a foreign enemy, then a limited scope is for the common good." Master Jolen leaned against the desk. His face impassive. Eyes unhappy. "Coordinating so many city-states when they fly their own banner is problematic and confusing. Every *prolate* working under their own agenda and brokering secret deals with each other when they should concentrate on our foe. It is nothing more than an excuse to make a power grab."

Anger flashed through Estobán's blood. An inferno ignited through the onslaught of harsh words and blatant misconceptions. "You have a very low opinion of government."

"I have a very low opinion of men who seek ways to fill their pockets when their minds are better occupied by helping the poor and destitute." Master Jolen's cheeks filled with color. His eyes sparked to life in the heat of the argument. "We alchemists do what we can to help. It is nothing to us to bring food and clothing to those in need. Those who their government—their *prolates* have forgotten."

Estobán's heart gave a kick at the sight of Master Jolen so impassioned. "I hope you do not extend that assessment to me."

Master Jolen closed his eyes as if finally realizing what he'd said. "You are not responsible for the crimes of the Agia."

The Delaneux *prolate* was notorious for his greed and selfishness. Estobán suspected that was how the necromancers gained a foothold in the city-states. "With any luck that line will be allowed to die out and the *prolatial* seat passed to another family."

Surprise widened Master Jolen's eyes. "I thought they were allies of the Medovin House?"

Estobán smiled. "And yet you chose to voice an objection of his governorship to my face."

"I only spoke the truth. If that gets me into trouble, so be it." Master Jolen straightened. "I have been up against worse in my experience and survived."

Estobán decided to keep his comments on that quarter to himself. "What about your stance on the church? It was thought the clerics might try to extend another alliance with your order."

"Yes, I have heard those rumors. I doubt it will come to pass at this time. We are still not over the loss of our former headmaster who dared to cross the clerics in league with the Agia."

The death of Headmaster Donando had been cause for speculation. Rumors of murder at the hands of the Agia's guards continued to circulate. No wonder the alchemists did not trust their local *prolate*.

Estobán dug a little deeper. "Is it not possible that the clerics have also been infected by the necromancers as have the alchemists and *prolates*? How, then, can you paint all clerics with the same brush?"

Master Jolen cocked his head. "Isn't that why I'm here? If I find evidence that they have been infected and aren't just pushing their own agenda to make this country a theocracy, then, of course, I'd be all for an alliance if it comes to war with the necromancers."

Estobán gave a rueful smile. "And he speaks of war."

"It might be the only way to rid ourselves of the death dancers."

Estobán waved his hand. "I've kept you too long from your own amusements. I bid you good night and will see you in the morning. The first session is at nine."

Master Jolen tipped his head and left. "Good night, Your Grace."

Alone, Estobán sat down and put his head in his hands. That did not go as well as he'd envisioned. Somehow he'd thought that once he had Master Jolen in private, they would find much to discuss. He'd not expected so much anger.

Estobán rang for Silas.

The servant entered the office and bowed. "Yes, Your Grace?"

"In the red salon is a glass cabinet. Locked inside is a piece of carved ruby about so big." Estobán held up his hand to indicate the approximate size of the artifact. "I want you to take that piece to Master Jolen's room with my compliments. He is to have free access to it for as long as he is here in the villa. Also, if he wishes to make use of our library, he may do so at his leisure. Please extend the invitation when you deliver the relic."

"Yes, Your Grace."

Silas left to do Estobán's bidding. By rights Estobán should have walked to the red salon and delivered the piece himself. It would have given him an excuse to see how his guest had settled in and if the room was suitable.

Estobán frowned. He had no idea where Master Jolen had been lodged. What if the room was inadequate? Granted, no guest suites in the villa were without comforts or even a few minor amenities. Even the servants' quarters were not without their small luxuries.

He'd always been a generous employer, except when the guards decided to do as they pleased and embarrassed the house. A month mucking out stalls at the villa stables would keep the man in check in future.

Estobán left the office but did not return to the garden. He climbed the stairs to his room overlooking the commons and studied the canvas that sat by his bed.

The oils were still wet from the night before. Splashes of red came out from a black central core. The perspective was off slightly, as if the viewer stood a bit right of center looking at the subject from an angle. No clues were visible in the painting to detect what he saw in his dream or how it impacted his sleep. He never remembered the theme of his dreams or what spurred him out of his bed. If he could only find a way to guide himself through his labors while still in his trance, he might be able to glean some useful information.

Truthfully he thought naming a successor would bring him some peace, but it only increased his worry. Viola was going to be the focus of family scorn and jealousy. He doubted that Cesare would make a move to remove her from the line of succession, no matter what bluster he made or challenges he imposed. However, he wasn't so sure the other members of their vast clan wouldn't make a play for his sister.

Estobán had left strict instructions with Magus Gaius to not let her meet with anyone alone for any reason. Food testers were to sample her food, even if she should pluck a fresh fruit from a tree in the *prolatial* gardens.

Worrying that an assassin might take his sister so young was not going to quiet his mind before bedtime. If anything, he feared it would keep him awake into the wee hours of the morning.

Estobán frowned. He moved to the side, looking at the painting from where the viewer might. What was that in the upper left corner, hidden behind a small projection of color? He grabbed a lantern from beside the bed and held it up to the painting. It appeared to be a small symbol but not like any he had ever seen. On closer inspection he realized he'd painted the infinity sign with a triangle on either side; one pointed up and the other down. Did the alchemists use such a sigil in their equations?

At the bottom of the picture was the same device but in reverse as if seen in reflection. Each character was painted in gold, then scratched into the surface of the paint, giving it the appearance of being chiseled into rock.

The mystery was almost worth going to sleep to see if the meaning became clear. Since waking from the necromancer's influence, this was the first time he actually looked forward to bedtime.

Slowly and methodically he set the paints on the palette and put the brushes where they were within easy reach. He changed out of his clothes and put on a nightshirt. He had no need to call a servant for assistance. The fewer people who had access to his room the better. Servants were notorious gossips when anything out of their sphere of understanding or superstitions was presented. He'd be damned for a fool before he'd become the center of speculation from his own staff.

Estobán pulled the covers back and slid into the bed. Visions of Master Jolen filled his mind. Had the alchemist received the piece of carved ruby yet? What was his reaction?

Estobán stacked his hands under his head and lay against the pillow. It did not take long for sleep to claim him.

THE FRAGMENT was the most remarkable thing Jolen had ever held. Oceans of energy swam through the artifact as if it were caught in a cross current where river met sea. All the answers of *aerothancy* were written on that stone. Correction, it wasn't only the principles of *aerothancy* but that of the other elementals that were inscribed on the lost tablet. History told tales of the *Elementica* broken up and scattered during the dark times—the Great Purge—when the elementals were under direct attack by foreign forces.

Where the *Eye of Truth* unlocked the mysteries and codices of the alchemists, the *Elementica* told the story of the elementals. It did not hold as many words or characters as the *Eye of Truth*, but what it lacked in heft it made up for in wisdom. This small piece, able to fit securely in the palm of his hand, held more power than all the spells of the alchemists combined.

Jolen tried not to let the knowledge of his elemental blood take him down the road of arrogance and pride, but it was a difficult task. As an adept he was superior to most men—as an *aerothant* he rose higher still. Yet he had a long way to go on his journey of self-discovery.

*No man is complete until he truly knows himself.* So read the Third Principle of the *Elementica*. This spoke of not only knowing the powers that dwelled within the blood but the hidden truths of the mind and soul. The point of the principle was as much about seeing faults of self and embracing them while working toward the goal of perfection. Jolen knew a lot of alchemists and those of the elemental persuasion, and he'd yet to find even one who came close to that ideal.

What was perfection anyhow?

Jolen turned the broken piece of tablet over in his hand, studying the back of it. The chunk of ruby was so clear the carved cartouches were visible from behind. Now this—this was perfection.

Where were the other sections? Were they all lost in some foreign desert, buried by sand and eroded by wind? Had they been disposed of during the Great Purge, when his kind were slaughtered like animals? If that were the case, then was there some way to call to the elemental forces inside the ruby—to summon the pieces to find him? What if he did and the brethren decided he was not worthy of such a task? That due to the taint of the necromancers, he was not fit to bring the pieces of the *Elementica* home?

Still this was only one piece, and it did not even belong to the alchemists.

Jolen rose from the bed, where he studied the exquisite artifact, and grabbed a pot of ink from the desk. He went to the water pitcher and filled the bowl halfway, then added the ink. The water turned gray but gave enough of a reflective surface to call forth Master Nico.

It took some moments before the heir to the founder of the Gold School came into view. When he did, he looked extremely troubled. Jolen did not let Master Nico's mood deter him from his purpose.

Jolen held up the piece of the ruby tablet to show Master Nico.

*"Where?"* Nico's voice was faint traveling over the vast distances between scrying bowls.

"Medovin's Gusan villa."

*"We need to negotiate to obtain the artifact."*

"Indeed." Jolen had every intention of finding a way to procure the item, even if he had to smuggle it out on his way back to Delaneux.

*"Have you found any others?"*

"No. But I have only just arrived this afternoon. I will scout for more, but I doubt there is any other in his possession."

*"Why do you think that?"*

Jolen had no solid reason, only that he had hoped when asked about it, Medovin might have divulged he owned more than one piece of the broken tablet. Wishing something was so did not make it thus.

Estobán Medovin was nothing like Jolen had imagined. From the stories he'd heard of the Medovin clan, Jolen had thought he'd see a man whose face was as riddled with the disease of his indulgences as surely as his soul had been scarred by greed. What Jolen saw was a man of average height and sturdy build. The Medovin did not have an ounce of fat on his stocky frame. His dark eyes were full of mystery and intrigue.

A heady mix of spice and man had covered the *prolate* as clouds covered the moon—dark, inviting but infinitely romantic.

Jolen shook his head to clear his thoughts. Master Nico had said something that Jolen missed. "I'm sorry. I did not catch that last bit."

Master Nico frowned. *"Obtaining that piece has just become your secondary mission. I do not care what it takes, but do not leave that villa without it."*

"Yes, Master."

The image in the water cleared. Master Nico had broken the connection.

Damn, the last thing Jolen needed was for his possession of the tablet piece to become a mandate, but that's exactly how Master Nico had worded his request. As an order.

Jolen moved back to the bed and tried to sit in meditation to connect with the being in the artifact. After a few moments, he determined there was no longer any life left in the ruby. Whatever being had resided inside the gem's depths had been released when the tablet was broken. Maybe it would return if the fragments were reunited.

Melancholy settled over Jolen. So many elementals had been lost during the purge. Bright minds and brave souls to the last—they had tried desperately to protect the alchemists and gave their lives to do so.

This one needed protecting. After he studied it, he'd seal it away in a hiding place and place energy shields around it. One that would alert him if anyone touched, moved, or meddled with the fragment.

Jolen lay back on the bed with the chunk of ruby in his hand, holding it firmly between his palms, and appealed to the Grand Matter. An image of all the pieces coming together and reuniting burned in his brain. The vision that stayed with him well into sleep.

# Chapter Five

THE ASSEMBLED *cardgrans* were dour-faced men of ill humor and bad digestion, if their expressions were any indication. Jolen sat in the private box seating reserved for the Medovin family. Estobán Medovin was on his left. To the left of the *prolate* was a man introduced as Duard, the Medovin magus's clerk. People were still filing into the large circular chamber where the initial meeting would take place.

Across the rotunda were a row of empty chairs. The candidates for the position of *demigoge* would sit there as the rules for the election were read. The process was all a matter of formality. Those who were elevated to the council knew the rules set down in their canon since the founding of the church.

Jolen scanned the crowd. The Agias were sitting across the way from the Medovins. Rage sprang to life in Jolen. Ignatius Agia sat in his robe of state, as if he owned the world. Perhaps he did, but the bastard had bought it with the blood of the alchemists.

The Medovin glanced over at Jolen. "You really do not care for the Agia."

"Is it that apparent?"

"You are seething."

Jolen turned to the Medovin and noticed a smile lurking in the corner of that sensuous mouth. The effect was like a punch to the stomach. He let his gaze linger on the curve of Medovin's lips and the flash of white teeth.

"This amuses you?" Jolen raised a brow. "You have an odd sense of humor, Your Grace."

"I have no sense of humor, Master Jolen, especially when it comes to the Agia. I only find it reassuring to have met a like-minded person."

"Look around you. There is probably not one person in this room who feels an ounce of respect for Ignatius Agia, and that includes his staff." Strong words, but they were the truth.

The Medovin leaned closer. "His staff is composed of family members. Of course they lack respect for him. They all wish to take his place when he dies."

Jolen frowned and considered the Agia. "He has not named a successor?"

"Yes. That would be his son, Flaxton." Medovin nodded to the man sitting on the Agia's right. "Believe me, he is worse than his father."

How did the alchemists not know that the Agia had named his heir? It did not seem to be common knowledge in Delaneux. Jolen didn't like being made to look as if he did not have a grasp on a given situation. Going down that path was how he'd gotten into trouble before—and how he managed to do all he could to stay out of it. At the first sign that he was no longer operating under his own faculties, he was going to kill his human vessel and release his elemental soul. Hell would have to be under a glacier before he allowed his mind to fall under the control of the necromancers and their lackeys again.

A side door off the chamber opened, and the *cardgrans* entered the room to take their places for the opening ceremony. Jolen started the scan, sifting briefly through each of their minds. One or two of them didn't feel right, but it wasn't anything overt. Nothing to pinpoint with any degree of accuracy.

Medovin arched a brow in question.

Jolen gave a subtle shake of his head in answer. He'd have to delve deeper into each of them, do a search while in extremely close proximity. Not only was it going to be a challenge, but also quite the undertaking.

"I'll need your contacts, Medovin."

"Anything you need."

A hush fell over the crowd as a man dressed in the purple robes of the *demigoge*'s prior stepped up to the altar. "Let us pray."

The faithful bowed their heads as the prior read the benediction and consecration of the sacred chamber where the election was to take place. While the prayers wound into familiar chants that the audience spoke along with the prior, Jolen studied his quarry.

Each of the *cardgrans* had his head bowed in respectful contemplation. Jolen got the impression it was all for show. He sensed no sincerity coming from that direction. As a matter of fact, he felt none in the entire audience. Not one person—including himself—was there with any emotion even close to piety. The overwhelming emotion flooding the hall was greed, avarice. The greatest concentration of this came from the galley where clerics of various tiers sat in humble silence, listening as the prior began another prayer.

Jolen scanned the galley. While others here were not up for election or elevation in the order, plenty had ambition and dreams of greatness. It stood to reason that those who might labor under the influence of the necromancers might not be the ones in line for the holy throne. They could just as easily be the clerics who served the *cardgrans*. What better line of influence than to whisper in the ear of those with power? Whoever the new *demigoge*, he would no doubt elect new *cardgrans* to the position.

An event of this magnitude had to draw the attention of the alchemists, and the necromancers knew the magicians would be watching and waiting for any indication that a new infestation had begun.

One mind in particular stood out from the rest. Wicked and evil, it oozed with the slimy remnants of the necromancers. Jolen leaned to the side to try and get a line of sight, but from this distance and in the crowd, it was hard to pinpoint the exact location.

Silently he cursed his skills. He was not as well versed in this as Master Oberon. Why could Master Nico not have sent him? The Gold School would have run quite smoothly for a few weeks under Master Rhone's direction.

Feeling attention on him Jolen turned and looked into the eyes of the Medovin. The *prolate* frowned in question. The prayers continued around him. Whispering his suspicions at the moment was inappropriate, especially when another might hear.

The opening ceremony stretched on into the late morning. Choirs sang and more prayers were sent up to the deities. The consecration of the sacred space with incense and water came after another chant. At last the faithful were asked to ground the ceremony with the simple feast.

Jolen did not want to accept the offering since his alchemical beliefs did not run in line with holy writ; however, he saw no way out of it. The grounding ritual consisted of only a crust of bread and a sip of juice. The drink wasn't even fermented. Church doctrine forbade the drinking of any fermented juices or distilled spirits on holy ground. He doubted in most cases that particular tenant was followed.

After a closing prayer and the pageantry of the releasing of the late *demigoge*'s soul, the ceremony was closed, and the *cardgrans* on trial were locked inside. One member of that congress would be elevated to take the Heavenly Throne.

Jolen walked with the processional from the Medovin villa back to the garden where a feast was laid out. A few guests were already seated around the table. Laughter and drink were flowing. A hush settled over the small gathering as they noticed the Medovin enter the area.

"How did it go, Your Grace?" said a man who was dressed as a noble but bore no distinguishing mark of rank.

"Boring and long-winded, like most of the church rites." The Medovin waited for a servant to pull out his chair, then sat. He waved his hand for another servant to pour him a drink.

Jolen watched the scene, disconnected from the action. He stood at the fringe, not wanting to engage in the merriment when the possibility that an agent of the necromancers roamed the holy city.

The Medovin turned and looked over his shoulder at Jolen. "Come sit and have a bite to eat."

There came a time in every man's life when he needed to make a stand. That time had come.

Hunger gnawed on his insides. It would be foolish to forgo a beautifully placed meal in order to prove a point, but he was going to. If it angered his host, then so be it. More important issues were at stake than the celebrations and libations of choosing a new *demigoge*.

Jolen bowed. "I thank you, no. I have much work to do and very few days to accomplish it. If you will excuse me?"

He turned and started away from the diners when he heard the scrape of a chair across the patterned bricks. No power under the heavens would make him turn around to see if he was being pursued by the Medovin. He didn't need to. He could feel it.

A hand grabbed his arm, turning him around.

Jolen lifted a hand, three fingers outstretched and pointed at his assailant. An arc of light—a tiny storm in the palm of his hand—flashed. "I wouldn't do that if I were you."

The Medovin's eyes went wide. "You'd refuse my hospitality?"

Jolen leaned in, his lips almost grazing across the Medovin's tanned cheek. This close he could smell the man's skin like a punch to the gut. Desire was there and a dose of fear. "There was someone in the galley under the direct influence of the necromancers. It was not one of the candidate *cardgrans*, but nonetheless here in the holy city and allowed access to the rites. Now I can either sit at the table and feast as if I know nothing of this latest infection, or I can go perform the duties that brought me here. Which do you suggest?"

Estobán Medovin glanced back at his guests, then lifted a hand indicating that Jolen should precede him up the stairs and into the villa proper. Once under the archways and enclosed in the marble hallway, the Medovin held Jolen's gaze. The *prolate*'s had grown troubled, intense. "Do you know from whom you felt the influence?"

Jolen shook his head. "No. I can't be sure. It came from the direction of the galley of clerics. No one of any higher rank than a Holy See."

An odd expression came over the Medovin's face.

"You know something, Your Grace." Jolen folded his arms and prepared to wait.

The Medovin looked around them. "No. We can't talk here. Let's step into my office. We can speak freely and privately there."

As the night before, Jolen followed the Medovin to his office. The *prolate* rang for a servant who appeared as if on the wind. "Please, bring us some food and drink. We will be working through the meal."

The servant bowed and left the room.

"Please have a seat and let me fill you in on my suspicions."

With a lead-in like that, Jolen never even thought to refuse. He sat in the chair across the desk from the Medovin, who had his hands folded across the black lacquered wood.

"The Holy See of Lancor is a greedy, power-hungry bastard who thinks nothing of throwing away church doctrine and making it appear as if it were of no moment."

Jolen frowned. "Is he so open about it?"

"Yes." The Medovin narrowed his eyes. "I've long since suspected his only true calling is to serve himself from the clerical coffers."

Jolen loved the irony of that statement. "There are those who believe the same of the *prolates*. You have people charged and thrown into prison and their lands and possessions confiscated to pay for their incarceration. I have it on good authority that these material goods once seized are never seen again."

The Medovin had the good sense to blush, though anger flashed in his eyes. "There is precedent for the seizing of property from the convicted."

"That doesn't make it right." Jolen dismissed his words with the wave of a hand. "But continue. We are not here to debate law and policy."

The Medovin started to open his mouth, then closed it again. His expression changed. Regret pulled his mouth down at the corners. "Despite what you might have been told, I did love Master Theodyne. He broke my heart when he left."

Jolen swallowed. Erotic thoughts pushed their way into his brain, imagining Estobán Medovin as a lover. The man had more raw, potent sexuality than Jolen had ever seen. It cascaded off him like a waterfall.

Quiet filled the place between them. Their gazes were locked in a timeless struggle—neither one able to admit defeat and look away.

A knock on the door broke the unexpected tableau.

The servant spread the meal out, poured them wine, then left them alone. Jolen picked up his glass and took a swallow. Despite telling the Medovin the night before that he preferred not to drink, Jolen didn't think he could stay in the room with Estobán Medovin and remain without some form of liquid courage.

When Jolen found his voice again, he asked, "What specific complaints do you have against the Holy See?"

"I have no evidence, only a strong sense of intuition that tells me Desan Karis would like nothing more than to see the city-states turned over into church keeping and make this a theocracy." Judging from the expression on the *prolate*'s face, the Medovin did not care for this idea.

No wonder the Medovin had been interested in Jolen's opinions on the matter the night before.

Jolen leaned back in his chair. "If that is the case—and he is only one man—I doubt his plans will come to fruition. However, that same man with the promises of the necromancers behind him, and we of the Dominicál city-states have a very real threat."

"Damn him!" The Medovin slammed his fist on the desk. Plates rattled and silver shook. "I have never trusted him and even less so now."

Jolen held up his hand. "We are getting way ahead of ourselves here. I have no idea where the influence came from. It could have been any one of the clerics sitting in the gallery. It could also have come from the *prolatial* retinues seated behind them. Don't assume because the Holy See of Lancor is an ambitious man that he is under the necromancers' influence. Greed is often a character flaw that needs no outside manipulation to see manifest."

"No. You're right." The Medovin narrowed his eyes. "Still it will not be remiss if I were to send an invitation for him to dine with me while he is here in Gusan. We are, after all, from the same city, and it will only appear as good manners."

"Meanwhile you want me to scan him and see if he is infected."

The Medovin shrugged. "You did say you needed one-on-one contact to be sure of a diagnosis."

He had Jolen there. "Yes."

"And then what?"

Jolen smiled. "It is your plan. You decide what comes next."

The Medovin's gaze dropped to Jolen's mouth, and his eyes grew dark. "You should not leave these things up to me. I've been unwise on such matters in the past."

The heat in the room seemed to intensify. Sweat broke out on Jolen's back, and his undcrarms grew damp. He held the Medovin's gaze. "Are you sure you aren't a fire elemental?"

Surprise rounded the *prolate*'s eyes. "Me? No. I don't believe so. The Medovins have no elemental blood in their lines."

Jolen rose and came around the desk. He held his hand under the Medovin's chin and turned his face to the sunlight streaming in the window. "How can you be sure?"

The Medovin grew still. "Because we can trace our lineage back to the founding, and if we had even a drop of elemental blood, it would have been exploited long ago."

Jolen scoffed and released the Medovin's face. "And yet there is something about your eyes that tell me you can call fire."

"And what can you call, oh great and wise adept?"

Jolen turned and sent a breeze, laden with exotic scents over to the Medovin. "I am the Air."

# Chapter Six

*I AM the Air.*

The words haunted Estobán for the rest of the night.

He tossed and turned and beat his pillow into submission. Sleep was an elusive lover that never quite tucked him into that sweet, nocturnal embrace. Tonight it was more of a vindictive persuasion, sent to torment him until he wanted to shout his frustrations to the heavens. Every time he closed his eyes, he saw the alchemist standing like a magnificent fallen god calling the wind with a turn of a powerful hand.

Oh, to have those hands caressing his body. Those sensual lips placing kisses down his belly and taking him into that hot mouth.

Estobán let out a growl and sat up on the bed. His cock was hard, throbbing. He needed attention. It had been too long between lovers.

His gaze caught the easel by his bed. With things the way they were, he didn't dare. Not until he finished the painting and learned its significance. The risk was too great. What would happen if word got out that the Medovin—once infected by the necromancers—painted in his sleep? Though he loved his sister dearly and wanted nothing more than for her to ascend to the seat of *prolate* on his death, he did not want that day to come too soon.

And yet….

That face. That angelic, knowing face of Jolen's seemed to see inside him. It would not surprise Estobán at all to discover Jolen knew about the dreams and nightly additions to the canvas. For such a young man, he saw more than an old one. Perhaps that was part of the training, or it ran in his blood as an *aerothant*. Whatever the cause, it rattled Estobán at the very foundations.

He lay back against the pillows and ran his hand down his furred midsection to his thick erection. He lowered his lids and immediately saw a pair of sky-blue eyes staring at him from the depths of his imagination.

Estobán wrapped his hand around his cock and began a slow, hard stroke that made him bite his lip in pleasure. Blood pounded in his ears. His heartbeat thundered.

*"Jolen."* He whispered the name to the darkness, liking the taste of it on his tongue.

Wind blew in the window and caressed his warm skin like a lover's touch. It ruffled the bed linens and tightened his flat nipples. He lifted his hips, imagining driving into the alchemist's lips. The wet slide of his wicked tongue over Estobán's length.

The room filled with tiny eddies and gusts. They sent the chimes dancing and curtains buzzing. The harder he pumped, the more frantic the world around him became. Harsh breath filled his ear, as if his lover were breathing into it, taking that last gulp before plunging into the chasm of release.

Estobán arched his back and kicked his hips upward into his hand. A vision flashed in his mind: Jolen lying in bed, looking up at the ceiling, calling Air, his hand wrapped around his own cock pumping away.

Estobán held on to the scene, not wanting to let it go for fear of missing Jolen's orgasm.

*"Please Gods, not yet."* The words tumbled from vision Jolen's lips. His head went back and his jaw tightened. A spray of white rose between his fingers, raining down to paint his belly and thighs.

Seeing that erotic display, Estobán could no longer hold back. He let himself fall, feeling as if he had just made love with the wind. The night. The *aerothant*.

The orgasm seemed to go on forever.

When it finally finished, he covered his eyes with his arm. His breath the only sound in the room. He wondered if it was all just a dream or if the alchemist had the power to invade his mind and make love to him though they were separated by several floors and tons of marble.

As he drifted off, the words *"Now sleep"* were a gentle caress across his brow.

ETHICS WERE ground into every student of the Gold School as they grew, matured, and came into their full powers. Jolen pushed the guilt that swamped him from the little sexual mindplay the night before. Estobán Medovin might not admit to having the blood of an elemental, but he did possess some form of power that had allowed Jolen into his nighttime musings.

It didn't make what Jolen did right. He should have let go when he realized he'd slipped into the *prolate*'s fantasy. Instead, Jolen had lapped it up like a man thirsting for a drink in the middle of a desert.

Jolen ran his hand through his hair and started out of his room. A walk around the streets might do him good. He needed to get out of the villa and mingle with the locals and those in town for the election. Interactions with the populace might be a good way to see if any others suffered under the necromancers' influence. Knowing what he did about the past infestation, it was highly probable more than one cleric was walking around with a death dancer in his mind.

Footsteps slapped on the tiles behind him. Judging from the cadence, the person came at him in a run. Jolen turned in time to find Wendro skidding to a stop.

"Where are you going, Master? Can I go with you?" The words tumbled over one another as if falling off a cliff.

"For a walk along the promenade and town center." Jolen hitched his pack higher on his back.

"Why are you taking that with you? Looks like you're running away. Did His Grace throw you out?"

Heat rose to Jolen's face at the mention of *His Grace*. "No, not yet."

Wendro canted his head. "Is he going to?"

Jolen gave Wendro a grave look. "I sincerely hope not. I have some work to attend while I'm here, and I can't do it back in Delaneux."

"Can I help you?"

"What about your duties? Won't Linka be angry if you take off with me for the day?"

"Not if you tell her you need me to show you around."

"How can I argue with such logic?" Jolen pointed in the direction of the kitchens. "Hurry and tell her you'll be with me."

Wendro took off as fast as his skinny legs could go. He turned and yelled over his shoulder, "Don't leave until I get back."

"I'll be at the front gates." Jolen made his way to the portal and stood outside on the cobbled steps that led to the promenade. As the morning grew later, he stood more of a chance of running into the Medovin, and he didn't think that was the best situation—not until he worked up a bit of courage.

Desire swam in his veins with the thought of the Medovin. Truly he was damned by his lapse in ethics. Curiosity had gotten the better of him. It made for a very poor excuse. When the Medovin had mentioned loving Theodyne, something inside Jolen had shifted—changed so he might never be the same. Jolen knew then he'd give anything to have the Medovin feel even a fraction of that emotion for someone like him.

He gazed off into the distance. It seemed his life had been plagued by a host of bad decisions and indiscretions that buried like a chisel in his soul, cleaving it in two until he held the pieces together by nothing more than sheer will. No matter how good a man he tried to be, his passions always led him astray.

And he'd paid.

Gods and spirits how he'd paid.

The gate opened with a creak of hinges. Wendro exited and mashed his cap down on his head.

"Where did you want to go first?"

Jolen squinted as the sun crested the villa's roof. "This time of day I think we will find most of the people in the market square. We'll start there, and if I do not find what I'm looking for, we will go someplace else."

"This way."

Wendro began walking in a northeast direction, out toward the commerce district. Jolen fell into step beside him, scanning those they passed for the touch of the necromancers.

They tucked down an alley that was partially bathed in shadows. A shortcut by the looks of it—and a well-used one at that.

Wendro's lanky form moved with all the grace of a new foal. He kept looking around as if he thought they were being followed and didn't care for the fact.

Jolen glanced over his shoulder as well. "Did you not tell Linka where you are going?"

"I told her." Defensive in both tone and posture, Wendro did not convince Jolen of the truth in the statement.

Jolen let the boy get away with a small fib this time. He would have plenty of time later for instruction and correction. "Then why do you keep looking behind us? People will think you've stolen something."

"Not me. I only nick pastries from Linka. Swear." Wendro held up his hand in a gesture that meant he had witnessed before the Gods his sincerity.

"Then tell me."

They came out the end of the alley and into the open air and sunshine of the commons. Already the square was full of people. Scents of roasting meats and fresh citrus filled the air. Jolen took in a deep breath. His stomach rumbled in hunger.

Wendro frowned and shook his head. "I can't."

"Why not?" Thinking the boy merely had no words to describe what he felt, Jolen pushed. "Are you forbidden?"

The boy grew more uncomfortable. He rubbed his hands over his stomach. "I promised my mother before she died. She was afraid I'd be sent away."

"What about your father?"

"I never had one of those." Wendro turned to the left and slipped in between two carts. "I don't think my mother liked him very much. She never talked about him."

Jolen flinched. He'd not meant to lay the child's shame bare. Perhaps she had been raped or used by her employers. Either way no man had stepped forward to claim the child and give him a name.

"How long has your mother been gone?"

"Two years. She left to go to the late market and never returned."

Little pieces of his heart fell away for this child without name or family but with a layman's knowledge of elementals. What else had his mother told him?

Wendro stopped and took a deep breath in, his face a study of sublime and innocent pleasure. "Oranges."

Jolen capped the boy's head with his palm and steered him in the direction of the fruit stand. "The least I could do for you showing me the way here is to buy you an orange."

Wendro's dark eyes sparkled. "Really?"

"Really."

They waited in front of the stand while the proprietress helped another customer. Wendro massaged the oranges, searching through the fruit to find the best ones. "These two."

Jolen chuckled. "Are you sure? I think there are a few over on the right you haven't handled."

"No. These are the ones. I promise."

The proprietress glanced down at Wendro and winked. "So you've found some poor soul to buy you oranges? What sad story did you give him?"

"None." Wendro looked offended. "I just showed him to the market."

Jolen dug into his purse and dropped a couple of coins into the woman's hand. They exchanged knowing glances. She had heard Wendro's story, the pity was there in her eyes.

He tipped his head in thanks, then turned to Wendro. "Let us find a place to sit and enjoy our fruit and watch the crowds."

"I know just the place."

Once again he followed Wendro through the streaming people. Everywhere they walked Jolen felt eyes on him, watching, dragging him slower with their will. The influence of the necromancers surrounded him as surely as the air.

A knot formed in his throat, making it hard to breathe. He nearly stumbled on the uneven paving stones but managed to keep his feet by sheer luck.

Wendro led them to a small wall that bordered an herb garden just outside of the communal fountain. They sat and peeled the oranges, tossing the rinds to the birds that circled, hoping for a treat. Jolen stayed vigilant, listening for the voices of the necromancers.

"You hear it, don't you?" Wendro spoke so softly Jolen almost missed it.

He studied the boy for a moment, trying to sense if any necromancers nearby might put the child in danger. The immediate area was still. "Hear what?"

A frown knit Wendro's brows together. "The sun."

Jolen held his breath. He knew there was much more to this slight boy than first appeared.

"On days like this, when the sun is bright and paints the grass and stones in gold, the sun makes music when it hits the buildings."

"And you hear this?"

Wendro nodded. "Different stones make different notes. Not all of them are the same."

Astonished, Jolen thought back during his training and if any of the tomes about elementals described this particular power. If he had heard of it, he'd forgotten.

"Can you hear other things the same way?"

Wendro stuck out his bottom lip in a considering manner. He shook his head. "Nope. But I can hear what happens when air feeds fire or water takes fire." His eyes grew troubled. "It's bad. Very bad."

Jolen separated a wedge from his orange and stuck it in his mouth. It exploded sweet and cool down his throat. "Oh, that's good."

"Paeda always gets the best oranges. Her brother owns a grove on the other side of Maypool."

Maypool was a tiny berg halfway between civilization and nowhere. He'd passed it on his journey from Delaneux.

Jolen put another piece in his mouth and chewed slowly.

A wind blew in from the east. He closed his eyes and rode the ether, calling on his *aerothant* blood. Foul, rancid thoughts brushed up against his. They searched for him, looking for one they had touched in the past—one where they had a foothold.

Jolen stood. "We need to return to the villa."

Wendro glanced up unsure. "You've gone pale."

"I'll go a lot more than that if we don't hurry back."

"I know an even shorter cut. This way." Wendro clenched the remainder of his orange in his fist and pushed off from the wall. He wended through the press of bodies to find what amounted to a rabbit hole.

It was easy for a skinny child to fit through, but Jolen had a harder time with the width of his shoulders. Stones on either side pressed in like a marble coffin. Uneven bits of the rock face tore at his clothing. He touched the elementals in the buildings and requested clear passage. The stones moved and shifted a bit to allow him through.

All along the path, he felt the fetid breath of the necromancers hot on his neck. He increased his pace, placing his hand in the middle of Wendro's shoulder blades and urging the lad to move faster.

Jolen no longer had any doubt—the necromancers had returned to Dominicál, and they were armed for war.

# Chapter Seven

ESTOBÁN RUBBED his brow. A letter lay open on his desk, sent by special messenger. News from Lancor was not encouraging: Cesare had made his move.

The clerics refused to recognize Viola as the legitimate heir. According to the articles of succession, he did not have to pass the *prolate*'s seat to a male heir. Only tradition made that so.

He needed to contact Masters Nico and Theodyne and insure they kept an eye on Viola. As long as Cesare was in league with the clerics, Viola was in danger. It did make him wonder who approached whom. Did Cesare go to the clerics as soon as Estobán was away from town? Or vice versa?

Truly the move by the clerics surprised him. He'd think they would stand behind the appointment, believing Viola would be easily manipulated by their machinations. The magus would not let anything happen to her—of that Estobán was sure.

How was he supposed to take care of problems in Lancor and help Jolen to entertain a host of necromantic puppets? By the Gods, he was only one man and one who hung by a very thin thread at the moment.

Estobán cradled his face in his hand, rubbing his brow. Over the years he'd heard some wild rumors about the alchemists and how they used stones or water to speak with each other on opposite sides of the city-states. He needed to find Jolen and discover if there was any truth to the tales.

Heat speared him through with the thought of Jolen. Proud, beautiful Jolen.

The air in the room changed. Thickened—as if the very essence of life altered when the adept walked into the office. As if it took the mere thought of him alone to bring him to Estobán's side.

Estobán longed to look up and drink him in, but the only thing he could see was the memory of the sublime pleasure on Jolen's face as he came.

A distinct throat clearing came from the doorway. "Your manservant said I could find you here. If you are otherwise engaged, I can return later, but this is rather urgent."

Estobán lowered his hand and looked up. Time suspended, caught between one heartbeat and the next. Then everything clicked into motion again. A distinct appearance of disquiet settled over Jolen. Something had happened after he'd left the villa earlier that morning.

"Is something wrong?"

"I did use the word *urgent*, which implies that all is not well." Jolen pushed off from the doorframe and came into the room. Arrogance rolled off him as a sharp scent that bit Estobán's nose.

That unnamed presence tightened like a noose around his neck. The alchemist was in quite the temper. Was it possible that he only grew handsomer the angrier he became?

Estobán used his foot to kick the chair across from him out. The move was both casual and deliberate in its rudeness. "Then by all means have a seat and tell me."

"I made a slight miscalculation in my last report." Jolen pulled the chair out farther and sat. "The necromancers have not just sent those affected by their vile touch here, but are now ensconced in the holy city."

Estobán really didn't need this at the moment, but he had expected it. "Any indication of their intentions?"

Jolen paled. He turned his face away. "They search for those who wear the stain."

The implication was unmistakable. How did Jolen know about one of Estobán's greatest shames? Had Nico given Jolen such delicate information? Of course he had. The alchemists probably kept some great list written in ancient script with the names of all those infected and decorated with sigils for protection.

Uncomfortable with the way Jolen stared at him, Estobán turned to look out the window. The bright sun had given way to murky clouds. They rolled over, churning and wheeling, a mirror to a storm-tossed sea.

"How do you know this?"

Jolen's jaw tightened. A muscle twitched in his cheek. "Because I fell victim."

Estobán knew that small fact about Jolen. It had been discussed in his initial contact with Master Nico and Theodyne at dinner.

Common ground. That one elusive element to bring them together had been there all along and from so unlikely a source. "I knew that from Master Nico, but it doesn't answer my question. How do you know they search for their past victims now?"

Jolen rubbed a hand around his mouth, then dropped his arm to his side. "It's hard to explain. When they brushed across my mind I felt their intent more so than their thoughts."

Such an intimate touch from evil had to be disconcerting. "Do you feel you are in danger from falling victim again?"

Jolen's hand tightened into a fist. His knuckles blanched white. "I was younger then, a journeyman and not at my full strength. I had no defense against the infection. Truly, from what I was told later, not even Masters Nico and Oberon believed the attack had come from that quarter. At first they thought I was an agent of the Agia."

Estobán scoffed. "And no doubt wished it were the case once the truth was known."

Jolen gave a graceful shrug. "It no longer matters. They have returned in full. We must flush them out and discover why they've come to Gusan."

"I think it is obvious why they've come. They wish to tilt the election to their advantage."

"For what purpose?" Jolen stood and paced to the window to stare out at the angry sky. "They have to realize that we will not allow them to gain a foothold. Their kind was banished once from Dominicál. I mean to see it done again."

"How do you purpose to do that? You are one man."

Jolen turned. His nostrils were flared in umbrage. "I am an *aerothant*."

A chill of desire swept over Estobán. The man was simply magnificent. "Be that as it may, we must be prudent with this matter and discover their exact plans."

"How do you propose we do that? Go up to one and say, 'Excuse me, your decomposedness, but I understand you wish to take over the Dominicál city-states. How do you plan to do it?'"

"Sarcasm is unhelpful." Estobán glanced down at the letter on his desk. It gave him an idea of how to take care of both his problems. "Theodyne accused my cousin Cesare of being the instrument for the necromancers' introduction to the Agia. I wonder how true that is?"

Jolen turned and folded his arms over his chest. His brow was cocked in speculation. "Not meaning to besmirch your cousin's name, but *is* that a possibility?" He held up his hand. "Before you answer that, know I *do* believe it of the Agia."

"I am going to divulge a confidence to you that may make you think less of me for revealing the content. Do I have your promise it will not leave this room?"

Jolen pushed off from the wall. He nodded. "Of course."

"Cesare and Ignatius Agia have been lovers for many years. If Cesare thought to bring the necromancers into the country, he would start there, I'm sure."

Jolen frowned. "Why start there? Why not in Lancor?"

"If the deal went sour, he risks only his lover, not his own family. You see?" Estobán rose and poured himself a drink. "He might wish to take my place and see my sister deposed as heir, but he'd never risk the entire family. That would be too great a price to pay."

"Ah. So he tests the waters far away in Delaneux to see how it goes and monitors the rewards and returns via his lover." Jolen took up his pacing again. He tapped his chin with his finger, his face a study in concentration. "Is Cesare here in Gusan?"

"Currently no. He told me he was to travel here, only to stay behind and stir up trouble for my sister with the local clerics."

"How much influence do you hold over your family?"

"I am *the* Medovin. They live and die by my command."

Jolen leaned over the desk and placed his finger on the blotter. "Send him a missive, and demand he attend you here."

Estobán let out the breath he'd been unaware of holding. This conversation was akin to laying bare his weaknesses, and that just didn't sit well. "What are you thinking?"

"If he is the original instigator as Theodyne suspects, then the necromancers will be very interested to bring him back into the fold—provided he ever left their service."

A shudder ran through Estobán. Would he have even known if his cousin remained infected after Theodyne had driven out the unholy essence? That a small piece had been left behind to germinate and grow? "What was it like for you?"

"Terrifying."

Estobán had been lucky. He didn't remember much. Most of it was a dreamlike haze and a subject best left for another day. "I need to speak with Master Nico as quickly as possible. Can you arrange that?"

"Of course." Jolen walked over to the water pitcher. "I need some of this and a bowl."

Estobán emptied a shallow crystal dish filled with sand used for dusting missives. "Will this work?"

"It will do. The visual will be smaller, but it will still conduct sound." Jolen poured water into the bowl, then dropped a stopper full of ink onto the surface. It swirled and mixed in a ribbon of color, dispersing and fading from black to gray.

Jolen tapped the side of the dish a few times. Musical notes tinkled as bright as a bell. "It will take a few minutes to summon Master Nico."

Estobán gazed into the water and marveled at the complexity and ingenuity of the device. The items were simple, everyday props used for mundane tasks, and yet here they were, working in concert to aid in long-distance communication.

If the alchemists could turn such things into objects of power, no wonder the clerics were eager to gain their confidence and backing.

Clouds shifted in the bowl, forming the face and shoulders of a man. Slowly the image began to coalesce. Master Nico looked weary, haggard.

*"Master Jolen?"*

"The Medovin needs a word, and it is too imperative to wait on courier."

*"Your Grace?"* Master Nico's image nodded in greeting. *"What can I do to assist you?"*

"There is a motion before the clerics to remove my sister from rightful ascension as my heir. It is spearheaded by my cousin, Cesare. I mistakenly believed he would let others do his bidding, but that is not the case. He's decided on a frontal attack."

Master Nico gave a cold smile. *"Say no more. You have my assurance that I will do all I can to ensure your sister is not meddled with and your writ stands as filed."*

Estobán gave a nod of thanks. "I am twice in your debt, Master Nico."

*"Is Master Jolen still with you?"*

Jolen moved closer, bending to look into the water. "I am here."

*"Have you found anything more?"*

"The necromancers are here in the holy city. Do a sweep for them in Lancor. Make sure you warn Theodyne. They search for those of us who know the touch."

Master Nico turned to someone out of the scrying bowl's range. His expression was a mix of love and worry. He said something to whoever was in the room with him—Theodyne no doubt—but the words were lost to water and distance.

When he turned back around, his gaze sharpened, grew more intense. *"Theodyne says the elementals here are not restful. There is something in the air they do not like."*

Jolen gripped the side of the table where the bowl sat. "It's the necromancers. I know that without having to taste their foulness on my tongue. They will most likely use the question of ascension to renew their association with Cesare."

*"It is a strong foothold,"* Master Nico agreed. *"We will do our part here. Remain diligent in Gusan."*

"Yes, Master." Jolen bowed in a show of respect and cut the connection. He glanced up at Estobán, those sky-blue eyes roiling with angry purpose. "We have much to do to discover those infected and drive the necromancers out."

Out of his depth, Estobán heard himself ask, "How can I help?"

Without missing a beat, Jolen answered, "Get me into the conclave."

# Chapter Eight

THIS WAS not what Jolen had meant.

If it was the best way in, then it had to count for something, though the stench was about to see him embarrassed. The kerchief tied around his nose and mouth did little to filter the noxious smells of rot and decay. Spiderwebs hung in clumps, streamers festooned on a parade route to welcome the dead.

Catacombs were not for the faint of heart. Admiration for the Medovin grew exponentially as the *prolate* traversed the dark, dank environs, a demented explorer looking for the back way into hell. He slashed at webs, those invisible threads that clung with such tenacity to skin and hair, some so strong they snapped, unleashing a soft *crack* as they broke.

Jolen followed behind, offering no complaint or commentary on their journey. He dared not. He'd asked for this, and the *prolate* gave it to him, even went so far as to personally show him the way.

They passed by row after row of dead clerics. Bones that looked as old as the dirt that surrounded them lay in state. Their burial robes long since turned to dust along with flesh and blood. Rats scurried along the floor heading back to the surface in search of a meal. They'd find none down here. Not unless they wished to feast on bugs, worms, and other sort of small creatures. Jolen was not of the squeamish variety, but he had to admit not enjoying the insects that had hundreds of legs growing from their scaly bodies.

The Medovin stopped at the archway into a deeper chamber. Darkness spilled out from the room, painting the floor in inky black. The absence of light wasn't what troubled Jolen about the area beyond the opening; it was the way Estobán stood as if entranced that sent a warning to pierce through him. Jolen laid his hand on the wall, connecting to the stones on an elemental level. The essences within were disturbed over something that happened quite recently—though Jolen knew that most stones did not mark time the way humans did.

Jolen stood beside the Medovin, gazing up at the strange golden symbols carved into the keystone. "What is it?"

Medovin frowned and shook his head, coming out of his private thoughts. His dark eyes were troubled. Brackets cut grooves around his mouth. "This is new."

Jolen raised his brow. "You come down here often enough to know if this is new?"

"No. Not in years, but look at how raw the chisel marks are around the area. The gold leaf didn't hide that from detection."

Jolen had no idea what the *prolate* meant. "Is this perhaps the place where the *demigoge* will be laid to rest?"

The Medovin shook his head. "These catacombs are the oldest of the passages. They haven't used these to lay *demigoges* in state for over a hundred years."

"Then what would someone want with it? Why mark it in such a fashion?"

"You don't recognize the sigil?" The Medovin narrowed his eyes, as if doing so might make it easier to gaze into Jolen's mind.

"That is the symbol for infinity, but the arrows used with it are odd. It is most certainly not one used by alchemists. Not even in our most ancient texts." Jolen put his hand on the Medovin's shoulder offering comfort. "If you like, I will contact Master Oberon at the Gold School and see if he or one of the scholars can trace it. Just because I don't recognize it, does not mean it is unknown to one of my brothers."

The Medovin rubbed his hand across his forehead. "It isn't so much the symbol but the location that worries me."

"Why the location? Because people are using the catacombs for things other than burying the dead?" Jolen gave what he hoped passed for an ironic smile. "Like we are using it to gain access to the conclave?"

The Medovin shook his head. "You don't understand."

"If you believe the necromancers have come down here and are placing their symbols on chambers for some unknown purpose, you need to let me know." Jolen closed his eyes and let the fetid air fill his head and lungs. Though the atmosphere was stale and awful, he did not find a trace of the necromancers at present. That did not mean they hadn't been down here, only that their invasion was not evident.

Layers of age and decay would blend well with the taste of the necromancers' taint. The bodies of clerics from centuries past hid the stink in the folds of their rotting robes. A more perfect place to hide they'd never find.

Jolen raised his torch higher and started into the chamber to investigate.

The Medovin grabbed his arm. "Where are you going?"

"I want to see what's in there. If the necromancers have kept their presence in the holy city underground, we need to know."

For the first time since meeting Estobán Medovin, the *prolate* looked afraid. Hesitant. He moved his torch along the walls, looking at the strange paintings etched delicate as lace along the walls. He lifted a blunt-fingered hand and touched the symbols. Aversion passed over his face in a grimace.

"Can you feel them?" Jolen placed his hand on the wall next to the Medovin's. A trace of essence remained, yet too dim to distinguish anything definite.

Their fingers brushed, barely a sensation of touch, yet a spark ignited. Memories from the night before tore through Jolen in a powerful gust of emotion. He wanted the touch to linger, to spread. However, other more important things needed to be accomplished. Jolen slid his hand away and started into the chamber.

Stakes in the ground every few yards marked out the way. Each one contained an oil-soaked globe of cloth with a wooden wick at the top. Jolen picked up one of the globes and sniffed it. The oil remained in its liquid form, which suggested that the bulbs had been placed recently. If any time had passed, then the dirt and dust in the catacombs would have dried it up or reduced it to a residue. Someone had been using this path quite frequently if they thought to light it in such a manner.

Jolen continued on, lifting his torch to study the walls for clues as he walked. Behind him came the soft shuffle of the Medovin's shoes. He wasn't near as assured as he'd been in the other passage. Seeing the sigil over the archway had undermined a fundamental part of the *prolate*. Made him wary. Jolen intended to solve that mystery before they reached the surface.

This part of the catacombs wended along an odd path composed of ninety-degree angles that shot right and left with a couple of switchbacks thrown in for the sake of confusion. Other corridors led off from the main passage but did not have torches planted in the ground. Jolen avoided those and continued following the trail left by the unknown visitors.

At one such intersection, he came to a halt, the design finally dawning on him. "It's a maze."

The Medovin stepped close, looking into the dark over Jolen's shoulder. Heat from his body coursed through Jolen's shirt, threatening to ignite his skin as surely as if he'd been kissed by flame. He closed his eyes and tried to push the erotic sensation to the furthest reaches of his mind.

"There are legends," the Medovin began, "that say a great labyrinth was constructed to hide the remains of the first *demigoge* from his enemies. Still others maintain it was built centuries before the founding of Gusan as a place of worship for the older religions, before the Gods were split into many, and there was but one supreme godhead."

"I've heard the legends but never heard they were in Gusan. I always heard they were farther south in the city-state of Dharakhan."

Jolen felt rather than saw the Medovin shrug. "I guess all regions have subscribed to the myth, making it part of their histories."

"You knew this was a maze all the time." Jolen turned to study the Medovin's face in the torchlight.

"Of course. I simply had no reason to believe it had been used so recently."

Jolen gave the prolate an incredulous expression. "With necromancers on the loose, and you didn't believe they'd go to ground with so attractive a hiding place available to them?" He shook his head and traveled along the path of the torches.

Tension radiated off the *prolate* as they continued on.

"Why am I leading if you know this place?"

"Because you took charge. Who am I to dissuade an *aerothant*?"

Jolen couldn't help but give a self-deprecating laugh. "Who indeed? My elemental nature does not make me a natural leader."

"Perhaps not, but you are one, despite how you may see yourself."

"A leader?" Jolen tried not to scoff at the notion. He didn't see himself as a leader of men, merely one who tried to navigate his way through the storm-tossed waters of change.

"If you are not a leader, even as an adept and master of your craft, then how do you see yourself?"

It was an odd question, considering their current location and where they were headed. "I see myself as a servant to the gifts I've been given, to the blood that flows in my veins."

"So humble an answer, Master Jolen."

They came to an intersection. Posts went off in both directions, indicating the passages had been used recently and repeatedly.

"Which way?"

"Right." The Medovin slid by Jolen. "There is a slight incline in about a hundred feet. Watch your step."

The walls narrowed until both men were forced to turn sideways to get through. "You didn't warn me we'd be crushed to death in the process."

"It's only a bit farther. We'll come to a small flight of stairs and then a door." The Medovin held his torch in front of him, the light illuminating the passage completely. The same strange sigils were present here as they had been at the archway.

Jolen lifted his torch higher. Gold leaf rose up the walls to the ceiling. The markings were so unique he knew not if they were for protection or evil. Sacred or profane. He lifted a hand to touch the curious marks only to have the Medovin wrap his own hand around Jolen's.

"I think it unwise to do that until we know who placed them."

Mute with desire at the connection, Jolen stood there, wanting nothing more than to twine their fingers together, but denied himself the pleasure.

He cleared his throat. "I need to determine if this was placed by the necromancers. There's only one way to do so, and that's to commune with the elementals in the gold."

"Would they still be present?"

"I won't know until I summon them."

"Will they talk to you if they've been corrupted by the necromancers?"

"I *am* a master of the Gold School."

The Medovin gave him a speculative glance. "But you might not have mastery over these particular elementals."

"It doesn't work that way, Medovin."

"Estobán," the *prolate* whispered.

Jolen stared at the Medovin. It was a horrible breach of protocol to call a *prolate* by his given name. Did the Medovin want their association to become more intimate?

He swallowed. "Jolen."

Estobán released Jolen's hand but remained close. The first touch across the metallic tint indicated nothing more than a few flecks of gold leaf that came off onto his fingertip. The procedure was delicate, one that he need not rush. Finding the elemental in gold leaf was like discovering the origins in beach sand, it was elusive and changeable, as ethereal as a spirit.

A minutia of an essence brushed against his. It had been so suppressed it was hard to feel, impossible to trace. Is this how the necromancers had learned to manipulate the alchemists with elemental blood? They took smaller entities that were unable to protect themselves and manipulated them into compliance. From there it was not such a leap to learn the ways to do so on the human descendants of elementals.

"Do you detect anything?"

"There is a presence, but it's very weak. I doubt I'll get anything useful from it." Jolen rubbed his fingers together to release any residue contained in the smudges. "But there might be another way."

Jolen placed his hand against the wall over the strange writing. Tiny sparks of energy crackled along his palm. Life thrummed in the tunnels, it was just hard to find. The connection to the elementals in the walls was very faint, barely a whisper. The entities had not used their voices in years, perhaps centuries. Their thoughts were sluggish, confused.

He shook his head in defeat. "They won't connect to me."

Estobán held his torch higher over the area. "Are they being controlled by the necromancers?"

"No. They haven't communicated with human-elemental hybrids in so long they have forgotten how or are sleeping. I'll give them a few days to wake and try again. For now, I suggest we press on."

The stairs were harder to navigate while walking sideways, but the passage was too narrow to face forward. Even Jolen had to suck in his breath to make it through. He worried Estobán with his stockier build might become permanently lodged.

Suddenly a loud pop sounded, preceding a shot of air, and the room opened into a sizable vestibule with a domed ceiling and eternal flames near a glass casket set high on a dais.

Jolen chafed at his body where the tight tunnel had pressed in on him. "Who is that?"

"Akabar Kolhen."

Jolen approached the deceased, who lay in a perfect state of preservation, even though he'd been dead for nearly five hundred years. This was the man whose wisdom and poetry had penned the rules that governed the city-states. He'd heard that the great man was buried in Gusan but had assumed it was a marble tomb.

"This is remarkable and a tempting target for the necromancers. It must be moved or at least altered." Jolen walked around the glass coffin, stirring the air as the wind does to the dust. Movement was small at first, a few particles here; a few dust motes there. Each grain of sand collided with another, combined, and began the process of building a sarcophagus around the glass tomb.

Through the veil of transformation, Jolen felt Estobán gaze upon him. Curiosity was a golden caress along his skin. He didn't dare explain or forewarn Estobán of his plan, the *prolate* would see it soon enough.

Jolen worked for some time before the covering over the casket appeared as nothing more than a mound of dirt. Built-in protections would keep it safe from anyone who tried to access the remains for their own purposes.

"There. I think that will do for now. It might not be a permanent solution, but it will slow them down and alert me if anyone tries to remove the casing." Jolen surveyed the crypt. "Where to now?"

Estobán shook his head as if clearing his thoughts. "This way." He pointed to the left and a small niche between two elaborate columns. Upon closer inspection, the area hid a doorway. Estobán tried the handle. "Locked."

"Not to worry. It won't be for long." Jolen closed his eyes and concentrated on the Grand Matter, using it to feel the material from which the bolt was made. Metal. Iron: an element very easy to manipulate with a change of state. In this case, Jolen pulled the oxygen from the air and water vapor from the humidity to oxidize the bar and turn it quickly to rust.

Jolen's part in the procedure was nothing more than speeding up a process that naturally occurred. It took a few minutes for the transformation to take place and the bolt to fall into rusty flakes to the floor, but finally the door gave way, and they were within the halls of the holy palace.

After verifying the way was clear, they stepped out of the vestibule and into a common hallway.

"We are going to be recognized in these clothes. No one save the *cardgrans*, pages, and holy guards are allowed in this part of the palace during election. We need to find the armory and steal some uniforms," Estobán whispered as they took off down another hallway.

They were almost at a dead run when Jolen grabbed Estobán's arm. "The quickest way to see us caught is to call attention to ourselves. No matter what we wear. Walk slow and steady and as if we have every reason to be here. If we are challenged, simply tell the guard you have been summoned by whatever *cardgran* represents your district."

"Amasio," Estobán answered absently.

"Say it is on behalf of your sister and her ascension to office of *prolate*. Any guard will not question the importance of such a mission, even during an election."

Estobán nodded. "If it becomes necessary. However, that story will not get us into the very walls where the *cardgrans* are meeting."

"I am not worried about getting into the congress. I need to be close to their advisors and attendants. Those are the ones who have the ears of the *cardgrans* after the deliberations are finished for the day. They are the ones with the influence. The ones who carry messages and make secret alliances in order to get their candidate on the Heavenly Throne."

Estobán narrowed his eyes. "You speak as one who has seen this process close up on more than one occasion."

Jolen shook his head, denying the charge. He had never been involved in an election on so grand of scale, but he did know mankind and of what treachery most were capable. He also knew most men would do anything to gain favor with their masters, especially if the one in question was in a position to sit on the highest religious seat in the land.

Voices and the sound of boots on marble echoed from another side corridor. Jolen threw Estobán against a wall and lifted his arms in protection. He called on the Grand Matter to shield them from discovery. As far as being a sure method of hiding it was far from the best. Not when they were standing against marble without a way to change the state of their environment.

He placed his mouth on Estobán's ear and whispered. "Do not move. Do not even breathe, or we will be detected."

Estobán's body stiffened against Jolen's. The *prolate* held his breath as instructed.

*"Brothers of stone, protect us. Shield us from discovery."*

A groan of marble slabs grinding together came from the opposite end of the hall. The floor beneath their feet trembled.

"It's a quake!" one of the guards shouted.

"Hurry to the conclave. We must evacuate the *cardgrans*."

The floor continued to tremble and shake, but no cracks appeared in the walls, and no paintings crashed and broke.

*"Thank you, my brothers."*

Jolen peeled away from Estobán. He ran a hand down Estobán's back in comfort. "You can breathe now."

Estobán's dark eyes had gone round as saucers. "You can call quakes? Just like that?"

"No. I asked for help from the marble stones that compose the structure. They took it upon themselves to shift a bit." Jolen straightened his clothes and stepped back so he was no longer standing so close to temptation. "Come, let's hurry before there are more soldiers filling the hallways."

# Chapter Nine

ESTOBÁN REGRETTED ever suggesting he show Jolen how to get into the holy palace. He'd been shaken by the sigils painted on the walls of the catacombs. The scene verified that his dream paintings were prophetic in nature. He'd always considered himself a strong man, but this rocked him to the very foundations of his being.

They stopped at the main entrance to the guard barracks. The building had been emptied when the quake struck.

Estobán held the door open for Jolen as they sneaked inside. "Hurry. When the guards realize there was no real damage or aftershocks, they'll return."

"And be on edge for the rest of the day." Jolen slipped by Estobán and into the barracks. "Where are the uniforms kept?"

"I have no idea. Look around, and maybe we'll find some in a cubby." Estobán began to open cabinets and drawers. Across the room, Jolen did likewise.

"I'm not seeing any uniforms. Suppose they are made for the guards on demand and there is no stock on hand." Jolen opened a few more doors, then grew very still.

Estobán looked up from his search. "What did you find?"

"More sigils."

Ice ran through Estobán's veins. He hurried over to the cabinet where Jolen stood, gazing into the back of the wardrobe as if it were a foreign land. "Do you recognize these symbols?"

"In a way. It's murky. Like I remember them from a dream but not able to make the image clear." Jolen pushed on the back of the cabinet, and the wood gave way to another secret passage. He glanced over his shoulder at Estobán. "I really want to see where this leads."

"After you."

Objections screamed through Estobán's mind. He'd rather return to the catacombs than take a trip down a wardrobe passage to only the Gods knew where. No telling if a room full of rotting necromancers waited at the end of the journey like a council of the damned.

But he'd not complain. He'd not say a word to let Jolen see how uncomfortable this trip made him. Or how weak of will he felt since seeing the sigils from his nightmares painted on the walls of the tomb.

A passionate hate for the necromancers bubbled under his skin. He'd never felt so alienated from his own emotions before—never had a moment of doubt as to his path or power until the death dancers came into his life. They'd robbed him of his confidence. All he showed the world now was pure bluster. Fear of discovery kept him moving, even when he longed to curl up in a ball and hide away from the world.

Jolen turned and placed his finger over his mouth in the sign for silence. Estobán nodded. Muffled voices came from behind a wooden divider. The partition was not so sturdy a structure as to be called a wall and was makeshift at best.

Estobán closed his eyes and oriented himself to their location within the walls of the palace. They had stumbled upon the resident chambers of the *cardgrans* while in sequester.

He leaned forward and pressed his ear to the board. The words were hard to make out.

Those behind the partition were speaking in the address of the holy court: ancient Dominicán. Estobán was somewhat rusty in that area of language, especially conversational. Most rites and rituals were handed down through fifteen hundred years of practice and repetition. The words were known by all who attended the services in the cathedrals. The subject was taught by tutors to those in the upper classes. He knew enough, however, to get the gist of the conversation.

Estobán lifted a finger to Jolen. He didn't know how much or how well the alchemists taught the ancient language, but he motioned for Jolen to press his ear to the wall. They stood facing each other, gazes locked, and listened.

"…minor dignitaries and clerics. The guard will have autonomy to dispense justice as needed."

"And in the *prolatial* villas? Who will see to it that the house guards are not a problem?"

"May I suggest we take those more slowly? We must first win the *prolates* themselves over to our cause. After that, their guards will not be a problem."

A creaking and popping of wood, as if someone changed position in a chair came through the divider. "There is an adept staying with the Medovin."

"Are you positive?"

"Ha! That man has always had his cock in one alchemist or another."

"I can't say I blame him this time. I hear the man is as powerful as he is handsome. Quite the combination."

"And quite the problem. If this alchemist is the Medovin's new lover, the *prolate* will listen to his counsel. The alchemists as a whole are not inclined to unite the city-states."

Estobán held his breath. Already assumptions by those who had seen them at the opening ceremony that he and Jolen were lovers ran rampant in the city. There had already been talk in the basilica.

"We will force them to see our point of view."

The ominous words hung on the air as someone else entered the room and called them to attend their charges. Estobán motioned for Jolen to remain still until the others were gone. When he heard their retreating footsteps he leaned back against the outside wall and heaved a sigh.

"I need to warn the other *prolates*."

When Estobán started to turn away, Jolen held his arm in a tight grip. "This was not an accident. The sigils on the entrance guided you here for a reason. Do not play into their hands."

Acid burned his belly and throat. "I can't keep silent. The other *prolates* have a right to know they are being plotted against."

"Then send a message anonymously. Do not be seen stirring the waters. You already have enough problems with Cesare and I'm sure the Agia by association." Jolen's touch gentled. His gaze softened, pleaded for understanding. "Please, Estobán. I fear this will end badly for all involved."

For a song, Estobán would have leaned over and pressed his lips to Jolen's. Instead, he contented himself with dropping his gaze to the alchemist's sensuous mouth before turning away to lead them out of the passage.

They sneaked back through the short hallway. Voices filtered down the corridor, echoing like the rustle of leaves on the wind. A murmur of sound, warning them to stay put.

Estobán stopped. He held up his hand to block Jolen's way. They had to turn back. He pointed down the passage that led to the resident chambers. They'd have to move the panel that separated the hallway from the chambers proper. He doubted the flimsy wood would give Jolen much pause.

When they reached the partition, Estobán nodded in the direction of the panel. "Do your magic."

Jolen surprised him by simply lifting the panel out of the way and leaning it against the wall. "That magical enough for you?"

"I thought you'd turn it to leaves or some other appropriate part of a tree."

Jolen's blue eyes twinkled with mischief. "One of the first principles we learn is to not use our knowledge when other more mundane methods can apply."

Estobán didn't quite believe the validity in that statement. Maybe it was true, but he had no one to verify it at the moment, so he said nothing and stepped through the doorway.

They had to find the way back to the catacombs or out to the gardens and leave that way. The formal gardens supported enough foliage to hide their escape.

Resident chambers were broken up into small compartments where the *cardgrans* took their meals and slept in seclusion. Intrigues were carried on by way of clerks who scurried between the cubbies like mice. Not that Estobán had occasion to witness it first hand, but he'd heard stories, and after seeing the tiny, uncomfortable rooms, he was inclined to believe.

As they walked, Estobán glanced into the rooms and the cots tucked up neatly by the walls. The scene made him want to laugh. Most of the *cardgrans* who had advanced to the level of the council lived in palatial palaces paid for by the citizens of their respective jurisdictions. They were truly princes of the state and acted accordingly. Seeing the humble surroundings forced on them during election was quite comical, if not downright hypocritical. Estobán had never been one to suffer false piety gladly. As a matter of fact, it rather turned his stomach.

At the end of the chambers, two passages converged. Neither of them looked promising.

Jolen turned his head to look down both corridors before conceding to Estobán. "Which way?"

"To the left. It should circle us back around to another section of the catacombs."

Jolen raised a brow. "Without ever seeing the people we came to? I want to at least make some effort of contact."

"They are attending to their masters and won't return until later."

"Then get me closer to where they congregate." Jolen raised a shoulder. "If you'd rather leave me here, I'll find the way back to your villa alone. After all, I did only ask that you get me in, which you've done."

Offended that Jolen thought he'd cut and run now, Estobán gritted his teeth and turned right. By now the attendants would have led the *cardgrans* from the conclave and into a more secure location, though no more quakes rocked the basilica. Where would they go that was more secure than the conclave? The cathedral boasted vaulted ceilings. Perhaps they'd have removed the council there, believing the structure more secure.

Estobán avoided the processional corridor and used the one reserved for servants.

No warning came. One moment they were alone in the passage, the next they were surrounded by guards.

"You are trespassing, Your Grace."

Jolen put his hand out, a warning to not react. The main guard, a hideous creature with beady eyes and grotesque features, took exception to the movement. For a heavy man he was quick as a striking snake. His meaty hand grasped Estobán by the throat, lifting him off the ground.

Breath stalled. Blood beat up in his head. Darkness threatened. The muffled sound of an angry wail captured Estobán's failing senses.

Sparks shot out in all directions, fanning out like cannon fire. The guard's grip loosened. Estobán dropped to the ground like a sack of potatoes. He held his hands to his throat soothing the sore area. Coughs overcame him and his eyes watered. He watched in amazement as Jolen went berserk.

"It's the alchemist!" one of the guards yelled.

Jolen's graceful hand was raised as if he held a ball and blew. Wind filled the passageway, raging with the ferocity of a hurricane. Guards skidded and fell, crashing against the marble walls.

"Behind you," Estobán croaked.

JOLEN TURNED in time to feel the blade slice his outer tunic. He lifted his hands as if to surrender, but unleashed the power of transmutation, turning the sword from steel to shavings.

Shock did not reach the guard's eyes. Another unholy light had taken up residence there—the influence of a death dancer. Jolen had no time to eradicate the rotted essence from the man. Suddenly the guard lunged forward.

Jolen hadn't even seen the dagger until it was too late. Cold sliced into his side. Recognition of the material registered along his senses. Bone. Not just any bone, but one infused with the hatred and evil of the necromancers. He had no way to fight against the effects. Infection, immediate and consuming, filled his gut. It traveled through his bloodstream, corrupting every cell and system it touched. Cold sweat broke out along his forehead and upper lip.

The guard laughed, showing an amazing array of rotted teeth. A devil's mask in living flesh. A fiendish thing of nightmares. Jolen reached out with his right hand and twisted his wrist and yanked, calling on the forces of water to vacate the man's body. A split second of sheer surprise came over the guard's face as he crumpled to dust at Jolen's feet.

The remaining guard thought better of his life and turned to run. Ancient words once spoken to Jolen from a far-off dream came to him then. He repeated them, speaking through numb lips. The frightened guard collapsed.

Estobán was by Jolen in an instant. Though Jolen's eyes were closed, the *prolate*'s scent was strong, welcoming as he helped Jolen to stand.

Jolen grabbed Estobán's shirt. "Maybe we should have turned left after all."

What came out was a cross between a laugh and a growl. "What? And miss all this adventure? Not on your life."

"It might be so if we don't get back to your villa. That blade was made of necromantic bone. I have no way to fight the infection alone." Jolen glanced down at his hand where it held the wound. Blood seeped through his fingers. "It's a bad one. Deep."

"Lean on me, and we'll both pray we get out of here before more guards arrive." Estobán placed his arm around Jolen's waist. "Put your arm around my shoulder. We are going to have to move fairly quickly."

The room started to spin. He was going to lose consciousness before they ever managed to get out of the damn hallway. If that happened, his mission would fail. The necromancers would win, and the future of Dominicál would be forfeit.

Jolen wended his finger through the hole in his clothes, gouging at the slice in his flesh. He bit his lip to keep the pained cry at bay, but it did the trick. Agony kept him awake and moving.

Estobán led them to the next intersecting hallway. He leaned Jolen against a wall. "Stay here. I want to make sure there are no guards coming this way."

Jolen rested his head against the cool marble. Tremors began in his legs. He'd not be upright for long. Passing out was an extra burden he'd not place on Estobán's broad shoulders.

*"By the elements, I beg you to get Estobán out safely. See him guarded and protected so he may tell others what we have discovered here."*

Whispers came from the walls. The air fairly crackled with life around him.

*"Do you not wish to be saved as well?"* The disembodied voice spoke in his ear like the chime of silver bells.

*"I am but one man. If I fall, another alchemist can take my place and complete the mission."*

*"But the mission was entrusted to you, Jolen Meripen."*

He was losing his mind. This voice was that of his guilt, urging him forward.

A ghostly touch skimmed over his face. *"Wake. We will see to your safe passage."*

Jolen cracked an eye open and was amazed to be surrounded not by *aerothants*, but full air elementals. Their mist-like bodies shifted on ribbons of air, dancing sea grass on the ocean. Jolen held out a shaking hand, trying to feel if they had substance, but his finger passed through them with only a hint of atmosphere.

Estobán returned. He did not seem to notice the presence of the full elementals surrounding them. Perhaps they did not wish to be seen. "The way is clear, but it won't be forever. We need to hurry."

Jolen pushed off from the wall, slipping in his blood puddle on the floor. Damn, he'd end up leaving a trail all the way back to the Medovin villa. "Wait."

"We don't have time."

"We have to *make* time. I'm bleeding like a leaky rain barrel. It won't take a scholar to track us directly to your door." He spoke between gritted teeth. Between the pain and the fact he was only a shade away from succumbing to darkness, he had to force the words out.

"Gods and devils, man!" Estobán placed his arm around Jolen's waist, bringing him away from the wall. "I'm more worried about you bleeding to death than I am if the guards come to my door."

Jolen waved his hand over the blood, concentrating on the metals contained within, turning the liquid to a fine metallic powder. "The guards won't see that as blood."

As each drop hit the floor, it turned to that same shimmery residue.

"Oh, to have even half your abilities."

They hurried along the hallway as fast as Jolen could manage, which was to say not with any great speed. Each step vibrated through his body as if he were being stabbed anew. The finger he lodged in his injury no longer had any affect. The site had gone numb. They entered a short breezeway that led to the garden. Estobán tucked into a niche where a large statue of the first *demigoge* stood. He slid a panel behind the sculpture and turned a lever. A door popped open. Dank air swirled up from the pits of the catacombs.

Jolen thought he saw a stairwell, but it was hard to tell in the darkness. He had no more energy to call on fire to light their way. "I hope there are torches down there."

# Chapter Ten

ESTOBÁN CARRIED Jolen the rest of the way to the villa. By the time he reached the back door, he feared Jolen no longer breathed. Guards fell out of his way as he hurried to the kitchen entrance. This one was the closest to Jolen's room.

"Let me carry him for you, Your Grace." Fessen the guard captain held out his arms to accept Jolen's unmoving body.

Estobán shook his head. "I've carried him this far. Summon Duard. I have duties for him to perform."

Fessen bowed and hurried away.

Estobán continued on through the kitchens. Linka's eyes widened.

A lanky boy ran up to him.

"What happened to Master Jolen? Is he dead?" Large dark eyes filled with pain and fear. The boy worried a red cap between grubby hands.

"No. Not if I can help it."

The lad dogged Estobán's steps as he hurried to the guest rooms. He looked back at the boy. "What is your name?"

"Wendro, Your Grace."

"Please move in front of me and open the doors."

"Yes, Your Grace." Wendro wiggled between Estobán and the wall, then hurried on ahead. How did Jolen even know this child who lived and worked in the villa yet Estobán had never met? Obviously, Wendro knew Jolen enough to be concerned for his welfare. That spoke of a bond.

They turned down the hall that lead to the breezeway—a row of guest rooms that were reserved for traveling players, actors, and performers, when they were in house.

"Do we have any rooms prepared in the colonnade?"

"One or two aren't being used."

The child was also well informed. "Take me to one facing the garden."

"Yes, Your Grace." Wendro turned down another hall and to a set of doors that led to the ballroom. "It's quicker if we go through here."

Estobán's shoulders and arm muscles ached, his thighs burned. Jolen was not an overly large man, but he had decided mass. They entered the ballroom, crossed the expanse of the floor, and exited out the back of the room where a permanent dais sat.

Wendro opened the door where guards patrolled the hallway to the private staircase that led to Estobán's chambers.

"Hey boy, where do you think you're—" The guard's reprimand dropped off, and he bowed. "Your Grace."

"Find the house physician and have him meet us in the colonnade. Master Jolen is grievously injured."

The guard held his sword to keep it from bouncing and hurried away. Another approached Estobán, holding his arms out in a silent request to relieve him of Jolen's weight. He appreciated the gesture but again refused the offer of help.

A long flight of stairs came into view. The colonnade was located on the third floor. Estobán steeled himself for the climb. He hitched Jolen higher on his shoulder and started a slow trek up the stairs.

Halfway up, his legs burned so badly, he had to stop and rest. They shook under the strain of Jolen's added weight. "Not too much farther now." Estobán was unsure if he said that to his unconscious burden or to reassure himself.

He felt the curl of a fist along his back. "Are you with me, Jolen?"

Jolen mumbled something unintelligible. His skin was an inferno. A powerful fever had already taken hold. Sweat rolled off Jolen's body, soaking Estobán's clothing. Blood saturated his tunic, thick and sticky. The transformation from liquid to metallic powder had ceased when Jolen lost consciousness. The wound didn't bleed as much as before, but it hadn't stopped either.

Estobán made it to the landing. He really needed to stop and rest but was afraid if he did, he'd never make it the rest of the way. Sometimes it was best to just push on and not think about the journey yet to come.

He started up the last flight of steps. Jolen placed his hand in the middle of Estobán's back. Energy raced through him from the point of contact, giving him the extra boost he needed to finish the climb.

The colonnade was a set of suites reserved for visiting dignitaries and statesmen. The rooms were more opulent, spacious, and came with their own set of servants. Wendro led Estobán to a chamber at the very end of the row. This room stood out among the others as the best of the lot, reserved only for those visitors who ranked very high in Dominicál society.

It was perfect.

The bedroom was a separate chamber set back into the suite. A terrace ran from the salon all the way down to the bathing area. Estobán hurried to the bed and slowly lowered Jolen onto the mattress.

Wendro let out a gasp. Jolen's face was ashen. His lips pale. Sweat plastered his hair to his head. He was a shambles.

Estobán set about removing Jolen's belt and outer tunic. Undressing a man out of his head with fever was no easy task. Every time he rolled Jolen to the side, he got his hands batted for the effort. Pleased to see at least that much activity now, it didn't seem to help matters.

"Jolen, please. I want to get this shirt off you and assess the wound."

Ancient words fell from Jolen's lips. He reached out a hand and took Estobán's in a feeble grip. More of the same indecipherable ranting. It had to be something important for Jolen to try so hard in his state to communicate.

Estobán quit trying to undress him and leaned down. "You have to speak in one of the Dominicán dialects. I don't understand what you're trying to tell me."

Wendro glanced up from the bed and the struggling Jolen. "He said he doesn't know how the bone works."

"You understand him?"

Wendro nodded and scratched his head. "Of course. My mama used to speak it to me."

Estobán wanted to ask what particular language it was, but in the interest of Jolen's health, refrained. "Are you sure you translated that right? It doesn't make sense."

"It might not make sense, but that's what he said."

Estobán tapped Jolen's cheek a few times to attempt to make him focus. "What do you mean about the bone?"

Jolen opened his eyes and stared at Estobán much the same way a blind person searches for noise by turning their heads. His gaze never quite focused on Estoban's. That lovely lyrical language he'd spoken before came again.

Wendro frowned. "That makes even less sense."

"What did he say?"

"The blade is bone."

Estobán closed his eyes for a second as the words sunk in, and then he was in motion, ripping Jolen's clothes without thought to finesse or economy. "Go and hurry the physician along. Tell him if he is not here within the next few minutes, I will replace him."

Wendro's dark eyes widened. "Yes, Your Grace."

The boy took off like a shooting star, banging the door behind him.

The noise startled Jolen, bringing him off the bed. "No!"

Estobán took Jolen by the shoulders and pressed him into the bed. "Jolen! Listen to me. You are injured, but you are now in the Medovin villa. You do not have anything to worry about. I will take care of you. I promise."

Jolen's gaze finally focused, a moment of clarity. "Estobán?"

"I'm here. Let me look at your wound."

"Dead death dancers. Bones. Necromancers."

"I know." What else was he supposed to say? He was completely out of his depth and had a sick feeling his physician would be as well. What he needed was another alchemist to heal this illness of questionable origin.

He pried Jolen's hands away from the wound. Blood had dried and crusted on Jolen's fingers. Little specks of metallic dust glittered around the opening in his side. Already the area looked and smelled as if it had turned putrid. A foul stench of rotted flesh wafted up, turning Estobán's stomach.

A knock sounded on the door.

"Enter."

Duard came in and crossed the room to the bed. "You wished to see me, Your Grace."

"Yes. I need a message sent to the Gold School immediately. They need to send someone well versed in the healing arts." Estobán put his hand beside the wound and pressed. Dark green pus oozed out, foul and purulent. How did infection perpetuate so quickly? "As you see, we have quite the situation on our hands."

Duard stared at the wound. "Did he have that this morning?"

"No. It's fresh."

"Great Gods." Duard bowed. "I will contact the school immediately." He left Estobán alone with the ailing Jolen.

Not knowing what else to do, he continued to press the site, trying to milk it of all the infection. The horrific exudates continued to roll out as if a never-ending supply sat tucked within Jolen's body.

Sweat rolled down into Estobán's eyes. He gave an absent swipe across his forehead. "Where is this coming from? I've never seen anything like it."

Jolen spoke in his delirium. His eyes were glassy and hot. "Need me out of the way."

"Who does?"

"Necromancers."

The door opened again. This time Wendro came with the physician, Havero. He crossed the room and placed his bag on the bed and began pulling out vials of liquids and powders. He glanced over at the wound a few times and assessed the fluid Estobán had managed to remove. "We'll start with this. I'll need you to take these forceps and hold both sides of the wound open."

Estobán took the instruments and did as instructed.

Havero pulled the stopper from one of the vials and poured the contents into the gash.

Jolen came off the bed, shouting in agony. "It's burning me!"

Smoke began to rise. A scent of burnt flesh filled the room.

"Of course it is. That's how I know it's working." Havero flicked a quick glance to Estobán. "Hold him still, he's going to like the next step even less."

"What are you planning to do?"

"Stuff the wound with herbs. They'll help fight the infection."

Estobán didn't like that idea, but then he wasn't a healer. He had no idea what to do but as he'd been instructed.

"Continue to hold the wound open."

Estobán took in Jolen's appearance. His eyes were wild. Breathing erratic, fast. His face had gone from ashen to flush. Sweat dripped from his brow and nose. "Forgive me, Jolen, but I don't know what else to do for you."

Jolen's frightened gaze flicked to meet Estobán's. "Don't leave me."

His heart nearly broke at the desperation he heard in Jolen's voice. "No. I won't. I'll stay right here with you."

Havero grabbed a long bright green leaf and split it open. Clear jelly coated the center on both sides. He turned it inside out and pinched it between a pair of tongs. Gently he slid the plant, jelly side out, into the wound, repeating the process a few more times until the greenery peeked out along the edges. "Now we bind the wound and check the progress in a few hours."

At this rate, in a few hours, Jolen might be nothing more than a memory. Estobán didn't say it out loud, but the worry burned the back of his throat with acid.

Havero set a bottle of powder on the bedside table. "This dissolved in a full glass of water every two hours. Make sure he drinks it all."

"What is it?"

"Something to bring down his fever. I never give away my trade secrets."

"Wendro, can you bring us some water?"

"Yes, Your Grace."

As Havero bound the wound, Estobán sat by the bed and held Jolen's hand. Sometimes it was important for the ill to feel the presence of another person. It helped to know they did not battle the fever alone. That someone cared.

What was he going to do if Jolen died? No punishment in the mortal or afterlife was enough to expunge such a crime. He waited until he was alone before allowing his emotions to leak out. He raised Jolen's hand to his mouth and kissed the back of it. "I promise you, we will get through this. I owe you my life."

It might have been Estobán's imagination, but he swore a faint smile played in the corner of Jolen's mouth. Sweet, innocent, and hinting that he didn't mind the burden in the least.

"For what it's worth, I do repay my debts."

Though in all truth he owed more than he could ever repay. He'd been terribly blessed his entire life and had done nothing but amass more wealth and improve the station of his family. Theodyne had been right about him all along.

Hours passed as he sat there holding Jolen's fevered hand. The alchemist thrashed about on the bed, as if trying to climb out of his hot skin. Estobán forced fluids down Jolen's throat, hoping to stave off dehydration. It might very well be a losing battle, but he'd wage it all the same.

What Estobán didn't understand was despite giving the infusion as Havero directed and bathing Jolen in cool water, his fever continued to rage. With the amount of perspiration pouring off Jolen's body, either he should be dry as an old corn husk or the fever completely gone. Possibly both. But neither had happened, which worried Estobán immensely.

He mixed yet another glass of the special powder into slightly tepid water. He found the crystals dissolved faster that way, though it might not be the best for cooling a body internally. Gently, he placed his arm under Jolen's back and lifted him off the bed to a sitting position. "Drink."

Jolen turned his head away from the noxious scent of the herbs. The potent aroma was enough to turn a stomach. Shapes moved across the wall, catching Estobán's attention from the corner of his eye.

He turned to see the faint trace of shadows moving across the wall, growing larger, then smaller. At first he thought it was his shadow caused by the flickering candlelight. But no, these were flowing, ethereal. Elementals?

No pervading malice came from the creatures, only concern. They moved across the floor, their wispy forms wavering in the divide between this realm and the ether.

"Do not stand there and stare at him. Help him!"

He had no idea if they heard him or not. Perhaps their hearing was not the same as a human's and therefore his command went unheeded. The elementals circled the bed, bending low over Jolen's prostrate form. One lifted an arm as elusive as a puff of smoke and waved it over Jolen, who shuddered. The touch appeared anything but comforting.

Estobán sat again and took Jolen's hand in his. "Are they helping or hurting? I don't know."

Jolen moaned but did not answer in any manner consistent with an understanding of the question. He'd have to take it on faith that an elemental would not hurt one of its own. Sometimes healing meant pain, if only to drive the ills away.

The being that moved over Jolen drew back quickly and struck a defensive pose. It held its arm in a protective posture. Had the area of Jolen's wound hurt the elemental in some way? Impossible. Wasn't it?

Then again Estobán had crossed into a world of things he had no basis for understanding. He'd never so much as read an alchemical primer. His critics in the *cardgrans'* housing were wrong—he did not have a string of lovers indoctrinated into the discipline. There had been only one, and Theodyne had not been an alchemist when they were together.

Seeing the path the country had taken of late, he would rather throw in his lot with the alchemists and forsake all others. For a few centuries now the magical chemists were not favored with the aristocracy; Estobán intended to change that. It might very well be the only way to survive the coming conflict.

Unite the city-states! Gods forbid! He'd seen what happened when the country of Sorela had gone from territories governed by local rule to a centralized body. The wars had devastated.

Estobán rubbed a hand down his face as if the action would clear his head and soothe his troubled thoughts. One of the elementals hovered near him. It tilted its oddly hazy head in an attempt to study him. To say it was unsettling was not giving his emotions full credit. He'd never been so wholly evaluated by such a being.

Tingles erupted along the surface of his skin. The hairs stood up on his arms, legs, and along the back of his neck. The sensation of a cold breath blew along the top of his head, infusing him with an odd mixture of love and well-being.

Had he been found worthy by these amazing life-forms? The air elemental bowed solemnly and moved away. The others followed until nothing was left in the room but a vague feeling of a cool breeze.

Estobán checked Jolen's skin. He was only a bit cooler than before, the sweat dried to his clothes, hair matted. At least now he slept comfortably. Exhausted, Estobán laid his head on the bed next to Jolen's arm. Only a few minutes of rest before the next round of treatment.

He woke with a start. Disoriented with his surroundings, he looked for anything of the familiar. He closed his fingers around the long wooden stick in his hand. His paintbrush. The scent of pigments was sharp on the air.

Full night had fallen. The room was shrouded in blackness, save for the moonlight that poured into the balcony windows. Through the slice of pale light, he could make out the glow of the white canvas resting against the easel.

Had anyone seen him during his nocturnal wanderings? He turned toward the door. In the dim light, it was hard to tell if it was shut tightly or still ajar. No matter, he did not hear anyone stirring outside in the hall beyond his suite.

Curious as to what he painted, Estobán grabbed a candle and held it to the canvas. Red paint placed on the canvas in chunks with jagged edges filled the field—a puzzle with some of the pieces missing.

An odd knowing came over him. Nervous tension tightened his muscles as if readying for a fight for his life. He knew those pieces. As well he should. He owned one.

How could he have been so blind? To have held in his possession an artifact of such importance and not realized the significance until now? Both his homes, here and in Lancor, were filled with treasures acquired through travels and forfeitures from felons. So many pieces of consequence he didn't even realize what he owned.

Shame filled his heart. Jolen had been right that first night—the *prolates* acquired the belongings of those who were imprisoned and used them for selfish reasons. The acquisition of the items bore little difference in how he'd come to hold a fragment of great power he'd found in a bazaar on a trip he barely remembered. The piece had been nothing more than a pretty trinket to him.

Estobán lifted his hand, careful not to touch the canvas and smear the paint. Before now the idea of the fragment was merely an abstract—something one learned about in history. Clarity came with the jagged edges and chiseled words carved onto the flat, ruby surface.

His nightmare ability had brought him to his room to paint an image of the *Elementica*.

# Chapter Eleven

DAYS LATER and still Jolen showed no signs of improvement. Havero continued to press herbs into the wound without consequence. It seemed a futile attempt to heal a body that refused to be mended. Not even the visit from the elementals had turned the tide of illness.

Luckily there had been no news from the basilica about intruders, nor had the guards come to his door to demand his arrest. Estobán had cleverly begun to circulate rumors among the other *prolates* that they were soon to be pressed into service under a common flag. Invitations to attend secret meetings arrived fast on the heels of the news.

Estobán had taken a brief respite from sitting beside Jolen's sickbed. There were other matters pressing from all sides, and none of them were going to resolve if left unattended. He'd left Jolen under the watchful eyes of Wendro. Nothing seemed to get past that boy. For his age and circumstances, he was highly intelligent and amazingly intuitive.

Papers lay spread out across Estobán's desk. He shifted through the pile of correspondences Duard had indicated were most immediate. Third down in the stack was a letter from his magus. By rights it should have been directly on top. He'd have to speak with Duard on that point later.

He picked up the missive and scanned the contents, then gave a sigh. The news was encouraging. Not completely positive, but it appeared that Master Nico's influence as a count and one who had sponsored the building of the additions to the cathedral a few years before had gained him a sympathetic ear with the local clerics. No telling how long that might last, but they needed to press their advantage without delay.

What he needed was for Viola to face a challenge and be seen to handle the crisis with calm, composure, and strength. Then she might be seen as a true candidate for the *prolate*'s seat in the clerics' eyes. He'd have to consider the matter at great length before deciding on a way to proceed. Doubt did not lie with him, but others wholly unconnected to the running of the Medovin family. By rights the church had no say in who ascended to the *prolates*' seats. There had to be a precedence set. One that the church would not mistake for a show of power and strength.

The *cardgrans* did not allow the *prolates* to vote on who succeeded to the Heavenly Throne. Why should they dictate how the ruling families managed their ascensions? It would be a point he'd bring up when he met with the other *prolates.*

A knock on the door came a second before Silas poked his head inside the office. "Your Grace, Master Theodyne Thespacian is here to see you."

Estobán sat back in shock, unable to hide his reaction. It took him a moment to regain breath and calm his thoughts. He'd not sent for Theodyne—as a matter of fact he'd instructed Duard to send for help in the opposite direction to avoid such a pass.

Silas's impassive expression never changed. He awaited his instructions as if the visit was of no importance to him. It had to be. This most faithful servant had been with Estobán when he and Theodyne had been lovers. Silas knew the implications.

Finally he nodded. "Send him in." With those words, he braced himself to receive the man who wore the depth of Estobán's sins on his face.

Not one to mix words or observe the pleasantries, Theodyne did not even bother with a greeting or sit down before he began. "Where is Jolen?"

"In his room. I'm afraid he is in no shape to be anywhere else these last few days." Estobán rose. "Judging from your greeting, I will assume he is why you are here. Come, I will take you to him."

Theodyne gave a curt nod. Something about that paired with the expression in his golden eyes shamed Estobán, as if the injury to Jolen had been inflicted by Estobán's own hand. Though he may feel responsible for placing Jolen in danger, it was quite another to see the accusation in the eyes of one Estobán *had* knowingly wronged.

"How did the injury occur? Headmaster Oberon was short on details when he contacted me." Theodyne fell into step beside Estobán. He clutched a heavy leather satchel in his right hand, not unlike the one carried by Havero.

"I will tell you, but not out in the open like this." Estobán stalled in the hallway and glanced around to ensure they were alone. "We may be called upon to decide the direction of Dominicál sooner rather than later."

Estobán continued walking. For now, that was all he'd say on the matter. He might pay his staff well, but chances remained someone else might pay them better to spy.

They entered Jolen's room. Once again the alchemist thrashed on the bed, trying to crawl out of his skin. Wendro had both the wide windows open, inviting in the breeze.

The child glanced up with guilty eyes. "This just started, Your Grace. I swear."

He capped Wendro's head with a benevolent hand. "I believe you."

"At least you had enough forethought to open the windows. The elements will heal him faster than any elixir or remedy." Theodyne moved the huge mirror on a stand to reflect the sunlight onto the bed. "It might be filtered, but it's better than no sun."

Estobán watched as Theodyne crossed the room and washed his hands in a basin. "I'm curious as to why Headmaster Oberon sent you to heal Jolen when the school is closer to Gusan than the Valencia villa in Lancor."

"My time in prison saw me become a rather accomplished if an unconventional healer. I've also had experience with Jolen's fevers before. Once they grab hold of him, it takes a divine miracle and vigorous applications of the correct herbs to heal him." Theodyne glanced over as he dried his hands. "Do not look so stark. I did not mention my time in prison to inflict pain on you, Estobán. I've long since forgiven you for your part in my incarceration."

Only now realizing Wendro witnessed the conversation did Estobán turn to the small servant. "Thank you for sitting with Master Jolen while I cared for running Sadonia. You may go now."

Wendro, with eyes large and mouth closed tightly, doffed his cap and hurried from the room as if his shoes had suddenly ignited. He'd have to speak with the boy later to ensure he spread no gossip he'd heard in the room.

Estobán crossed his arms as much to protect his soul as he did his heart. "I want you to know that I live with the regrets of my actions every day of my life. Viola tried to warn me, but I failed to listen to her wise counsel."

Theodyne lifted an elegant shoulder. "I've learned a lot during my time with the alchemists. One of those things is that regrets fester and leave lesions on the soul. If I hadn't experienced prison, I'd not be standing here now ready to offer help to Jolen."

It was far from an absolution, but it was at least a point well taken.

Estobán moved to the bed where Jolen continued to murmur those odd words he occasionally spoke. Out of context and form their meanings were lost to fever and delirium. Even Wendro had given up translating them.

More concerned for Jolen's health than he cared to admit aloud, Estobán busied himself by dipping a towel into cool water to begin the process of mopping Jolen's body again. He'd continued the practice in the days since they'd returned from the basilica—one he did not leave to the servants.

He felt Theodyne's gaze on him and cared not to turn and look into the face of his former lover, where he knew he'd find accusation.

"Estobán?"

He continued to work. "If you need something, I can call for a servant to assist you."

He heard the shuffle of soft shoes over marble as Theodyne came around the end of the bed. "Look at me."

Estobán ran the cloth over Jolen's fevered brow. He hated the fact he still felt shame for his actions so long ago. Married with the disaster he and Jolen found inside the basilica, and he had much for which to make amends.

"Please."

Estobán flicked his gaze to Theodyne before turning his attention back to Jolen. "He doesn't seem to be getting any better. If anything, I think he's gotten worse over the past day."

It didn't help that an unbearable heat scorched the city, making it almost impossible to keep Jolen cool when the ambient temperature worked against them. Even the alcohol baths had stopped having any effect.

"I have a few more cures I'd like to try, but first I want to bleed the wound."

"What do you need?"

Theodyne waved his hand to dismiss the question. "I've brought all I need with me. What I want is your permission."

Estobán frowned. He had no idea why Theodyne asked, but he'd not deny something so simple. "You have it. Anything you need to do to heal him."

With a decisive nod, Theodyne set about taking instruments from his pack. He pulled out bottles, jars, and long metal blades that gleamed with deadly light. Until this moment, Estobán had second-guessed Theodyne's assistance as a cruel joke played by the universe. Now it seemed Theodyne had learned more than a thing or two about healing while in prison.

"Do you need me to do anything?"

"Pull the sheet down so I can see the area. And you might want to hold his arms down once I start. I know from experience he fights like a demon spawn when he's injured." It was said matter-of-factly, but a slight smile of admiration hid in the corner of Theodyne's mouth.

The dressings were freshly changed that morning before Theodyne's arrival. Estobán took down the bandages to green leaves sticking from the site.

"What in all the blazing hells are those?"

"Leaves. My physician, Havero, said they would cleanse the wound."

Theodyne rolled his eyes. "Chances are they are fulminating the infection and keeping the damn wound from closing on its own." He picked up a pair of forceps from his bag and began carefully pulling out the leaves. "How many did he put inside here? Did anyone count them out?"

"Five."

"By the elements." Theodyne worked the leaves out until he got to the last one. He tugged harder. "Hmm, that's odd. This last one doesn't want to come out."

Theodyne reached into his pack and pulled out a rather odd instrument with two metal plates, a cogwheel, and crank handle. "I need to spread the sides so I can see inside. This one might be caught on a rib or adhered to an organ."

The thought alone was enough to make Estobán sick. He watched in silence as Theodyne slid the plates in between the opening of the wound and began to turn the handle. The opening widened, held apart by the force of the hinges.

Jolen tried to buck up off the bed. Pained cries filled the room. Estobán placed his body across Jolen's to keep him still.

Putrid pus, green and vile, flowed from the opening. Theodyne made a face and backed up some. "It's a wonder he isn't dead."

"Pure elementals watch over him at night while I sleep. They haven't been able to help him, but they have done their best to keep him alive."

This news was met with an astonished glance from Theodyne. "Thank the Grand Matter for that small favor."

With the protractor situated where he wanted it, Theodyne picked up the forceps again and reached into the wound. "Ah, I see the problem now." He gave a tug, his face and hand showing the strain of his work. A moist, sucking sound came from the area, and Theodyne pulled the culprit free. He held up the forceps for inspection. Caught between the thin tongs was a long piece of what looked like bone.

"Is it Jolen's?" Estobán came closer to the object, studying it from different angles.

"My guess is no. It's part of the blade itself." Theodyne pointed to the smooth edge. "See how this is filed down like a blade and this side is jagged? I think when he was stabbed, this piece broke off and lodged in the muscle."

"Dearest Gods! No wonder he didn't heal." Feeling he'd failed Jolen, Estobán sat on the edge of the bed and held the injured man's hand. "That must have been what he tried to tell me. I thought they were fevered ramblings."

"Don't make yourself uneasy over it. How were you to know? I wouldn't have found it had that leaf not gotten stuck on it." Theodyne placed the bone fragment into a small jar and sealed it. He then set about preparing a solution with salt, herbs, and water. "The thing you must remember is that now it is gone, Jolen will heal quickly."

Estobán watched Jolen's face as healthy color returned, his breathing evened out, and he rested comfortably for the first time since the injury.

"I'll need you to hold him down again. While the salt in this solution is neutral to the body, it might still cause some discomfort."

"What are you going to do?"

"Lavage the wound so I know all the pus is out. When I finish cleaning it, I'm going to cauterize it closed." Theodyne nodded at Jolen. "Hold him tight."

Estobán assumed his earlier position, but Jolen no longer fought. Theodyne cleansed the gash, waiting until the green exudates ran clear before calling it finished.

Estobán hated like all the hells to witness what came next. "Do you have to cauterize? Can you not simply suture it closed?"

Theodyne appeared to weigh the matter before giving his consent. "All right, but if I don't see improvement of the site by morning, if it does not start to close on its own, I will remove the sutures and cauterize even over your objections."

"Fair enough." At least it gave Jolen a whole day to recover. "Do you think it's likely the infection will return now the foreign body has been removed?"

"There is always the possibility."

For his part, Estobán was going to remain optimistic.

# Chapter Twelve

JOLEN THOUGHT the pain had ended. He had been mistaken. The agony did not come from the site of the wound but from within. The pain was worse than any intrusion by the necromancers. His soul oozed, festering from the infection caused by the bone blade. Strange images danced before his closed lids. He had no notion if they were caused by the fever or induced by some latent necromanical influence. Either way they disturbed him on a visceral level.

Nausea rolled his belly as if he rode on the high seas during the height of a storm. Fear that he'd gag and not be able to roll to his side in time to prevent choking on his own vomit spread through him. He tried to get the attention of anyone near, but he had been alone for hours, days, months… maybe years.

How long had he spent in this horrible darkness, searching for a way out? Sweat poured from his forehead and soaked the pillow. His skin was sensitive, feeling as though a fire elemental danced on his flesh. With all the flames, he'd think the sheets would either dry or ignite. At the moment he rather wished it was the latter—then he might be put out of his misery.

A cool hand moved over his brow. So he was not left to die alone. He longed to say thank you for the kindness of the human touch, but he couldn't move, let alone speak. A scent, familiar and masculine, filled his head. He knew that smell, had dreamed about it since coming to Gusan.

Whispers murmured around him, but he could not make out the words. He'd have an easier time trying to hear through the depths of the ocean.

More hands came to join the first. He was jostled and turned, and when he lay back, it was against cool, dry sheets. The relief was sublime.

Arms lifted him away from the pillows as fingers pried his mouth open. A strong liquid was poured down his throat.

No! They had no idea it was unlikely to stay where put.

The tisane barely made it down his gullet before it sprayed back up in a violent shower. He coughed and sputtered as his stomach continued to spasm.

Another presence grew closer. This one he knew from another time, a separate illness. Surely he just imagined Theodyne at his bedside, administering to his ills. Would he even be able to diagnose and treat the problem? And why bring him all the way from Lancor when that area had problems that needed attention? Surely his life was not worth so much.

However, his body had other thoughts and was too weak to overcome the need for sleep.

When he woke next, it was dark out, and shadow images danced across the surface of the walls. The elementals.

Finally his head felt clear for the first time in what seemed forever. He tried to change positions to get a better look around the room, but his body was too weak to move.

"Don't try to move," a voice came, rough and low, from across the room. Boots against marble made a soft *tap, tap, tap* as the person neared the bed.

Estobán leaned over and placed his hand on Jolen's forehead. "Thank the Gods. I believe your fever is finally gone."

Worry etched lines in Estobán's face. Without conscious thought to the implications, Jolen reached out and stroked his thumb along the bracket beside Estobán's lips. "And I'm very humbled and ashamed to have been such a burden in my illness."

Estobán grew still. His hungry gaze devoured Jolen before he moved back and took a seat in a chair next to the bed. "Would you not have done the same for me if I had been struck with fever in your home?"

"Of course I would."

Estobán's smiled gently. "Then you have nothing to feel ashamed for. You were not at fault for your injury. You saved me."

The memories from the basilica flooded back in a tidal wave. The confrontation in the corridor with the guards. Estobán lifted off his feet by his neck.

Jolen lowered his gaze to Estobán's throat. Fading edges of bruises were visible above his open collar. "Would *you* not have done the same for me?"

When Estobán started to open his mouth, Jolen touched his hand. "And *did* do."

The door opened, and Theodyne entered, carrying a marble bowl. His robes were rumpled and hair stuck up at odd angles.

"Rough night, Master Theodyne?" Jolen tried to choke down the lump in his throat. No, surely the suspicions that bled into his heart were only that and nothing more. He knew Theodyne's devotion to Master Nico well enough not to question it. But seeing Estobán's former lover at the villa—a man the *prolate* had confessed to having loved—was at least a bit of a shock.

Theodyne's expression brightened. He smiled. "I'm glad to see you are awake." He lifted the bowl in offering. "I suppose my quest to find and mix this special healing balm was wasted."

"Oh, I don't know about that. Keep it around just in case I relapse."

Theodyne stood at the end of the bed. "Your color is much improved this morning. Once I pulled out the piece of bone lodged in your side, it was only a matter of time before your elemental powers took over to heal your body."

Jolen placed a hand protectively over the wound. No wonder he'd felt the necromancers seeping into his bloodstream again, though this time not through magical means but physical. "That wasn't an ordinary blade or filed-down bone. It came from a necromancer."

Estobán glanced away. Red crept up his neck to paint flags across his cheeks. "Another apology I owe you."

Jolen tried to rise. He didn't want to face Estobán flat on his back. "Why?"

"Because you tried to tell me, and you were so out of your head I had no idea what you meant. By not insisting that Havero search the wound, I allowed that necromancer's bone to fester." When he turned back to Jolen, his eyes were bleak. "If not for Theodyne's most competent care, I'm afraid you may have succumbed."

"Listen to yourself—*may have*. But I didn't. You wouldn't have allowed that."

"No. I wouldn't have." It was said as solemn as any vow ever spoken.

Theodyne broke the quiet that followed by clearing his throat. "If I may inspect the wound?"

Jolen rolled down the linens to reveal his injured side. His energy was such that was all the activity he could manage. The fever might have been gone, but his body was still ravaged with weakness.

Theodyne's face told nothing as he inspected the area. "You'll have a scar."

That was an odd concern coming from a man who wore one on his face for the entire world to see—a memento of a life no longer his.

Jolen contented himself by saying, "I'll consider it a mark well earned in the war against the necromancers. It also illustrates how deeply into their cause the basilica guards fall."

Theodyne frowned. He stepped back from the bed after returning the bed linens to cover Jolen. "I warn caution in condemning them all before you realize the extent of their involvement. It might only be a few of the *cardgrans'* personal staff are infected."

Estobán looked first to Theodyne, then Jolen. "For my part, I'd rather consider them all guilty and let them prove their innocence in the matter through deed."

Theodyne shook his head. "For all you know, they might be under the same influence we all were—not operating under their own steam."

Jolen had to agree with Theodyne. "It would be very easy to control a common soldier or guard. All they have to do is implant the suggestion that no matter how implausible or morally wrong their orders, they are for the greater good."

Estobán narrowed his eyes. "Isn't that what most governments do now? They decide to invade their neighbors to take land and resources? Telling their people it is for the might of their countrymen? Isn't that how the Great Purge started?"

A dagger thrust to the heart couldn't have pierced as deeply just then. And Estobán was right. The Great Purge had seen the ousting of the necromancers from Dominicál along with the genocide of thousands of elementals. The period was considered the darkest time in the collective history of the city-states.

Jolen had worried since he first realized he'd been under the spell of the necromancers that another purge had begun, but this time with the alchemists as the central focus. The death dancers would have their revenge.

Theodyne crossed his arms over his chest and leaned against a low table. It finally occurred to Jolen he did not recognize his surroundings. Where had they taken him in his illness? This was not his room along the breezeway.

He'd find out later; for now he wanted to hear Theodyne's thoughts on what Estobán had said, and judging from the expression on the *terrathant*'s face it was quite a bit.

"If you have something to say, Master Theodyne, I'd very much like to hear it." Jolen pointed to the pillows. "If one of you would care to help me sit up first."

Theodyne appeared as immovable as a stone wall. "No. You lie still until morning, and if you still feel clearheaded then, we'll talk about getting you up to sit by the window in the sun."

"This is not a dignified position to have a conversation."

"Then perhaps you shouldn't talk so much." The words were a reprimand; the look in Theodyne's eyes was not. The man was damn pleased with his part in the healing.

"You don't understand, Theodyne. There is more at stake here now than my health."

"Yes. All of which can be discussed in the morning. Besides, I'd like to bring Headmaster Oberon and Master Nico in on the conversation. Anything discovered inside the basilica we will discuss in their presence." Theodyne was not about to be countermanded.

Estobán laid a hand on Jolen's arm. Warmth seeped through his skin and lodged under his heart. The touch soothed as much as excited. He tried to swallow down the lump in his throat. Fear he may fast be falling in love with the *prolate* threatened to choke him.

"Don't make yourself uneasy, Jolen. The other *prolates* are already plotting and scheming to keep control of their territories. They'll not give up control without a fight."

Jolen closed his eyes and turned his face away. "Don't you see? The necromancers have the entire governmental and religious structure of Dominicál poised on the brink of implosion. They've infiltrated the *prolatial* seats, the basilica guards, and even the *cardgrans'* staffs. We have no idea who in any of those groups is for or against us."

"I agree that dark times are ahead, Jolen. But I also feel optimistic that we can fight this." Estobán moved his hand down Jolen's arm until he took Jolen's fingers in a firm grip. "We can make plans, build alliances, and gather defenses."

Jolen turned back to Estobán. He spread his hand to link their fingers. "Yes."

Theodyne allowed them to stay that way for a few moments in silence before he interrupted. He clapped his hands together once to get their attention. "If that is all for now, I would appreciate you allowing my patient to get some rest. We will convene this miniature council in the morning."

Estobán glanced up from his seat on the bed. "I might agree to move to the next room, but I am not leaving this suite."

An odd light shone in Theodyne's eyes, one that was as hard to read as it was to describe. "It is your home, Estobán. I'd not think of telling you where you can and can't sleep. I'll only ask that you allow Jolen his rest. There will be plenty of time for... talk when he is fully recovered."

Jolen released Estobán's hand. "Can you give me and Master Theodyne a moment?"

"Of course." Estobán rose, giving Theodyne a warning glance as he walked by on the way to another room. The door closed with a decided click.

Jolen wasted no time letting his feelings out. "Why are you here? Did you come to judge and ridicule or to help?"

Theodyne turned to the closed door, then moved closer to the bed. "Amazing how you can still act so arrogant while lying flat on your back after getting stabbed by a minion."

Jolen gave Theodyne a reluctant smile. "I admire you, Theodyne. You know I do, but if you think to protect me from Estobán, you're wasting your time."

Theodyne said nothing.

"I'm afraid it might be too late." The confession was met with still more silence. "Was I wrong? Was the pointed reference to talking meant to imply you believe something more going on between me and the Medovin?"

Finally Theodyne ran his hand through his hair and took a seat in the chair beside the bed. "I have no excuse for my actions, other than I've never seen that look on Estobán's face before. You must know he's already in love with you."

Jolen let out a ragged breath. His heart thundered. "I feel a connection to him. There are no adequate words for what is in my heart."

"No need. I can see it in your eyes." Theodyne rubbed his chin. "A word of caution where Estobán is concerned. He is a man of great passion and loves with his entire heart. Do not enter into an affair with him unless you are willing to give the same."

Jolen stared at the scar on Theodyne's face. He knew the regrets Estobán carried—and the guilt. He was positive Estobán was no longer the same man he had been back then. "There is too much unsettled business in the world to worry about such matters. If we do enter into an affair, you can be sure I'll do so with the knowledge that he's a man, infused with the same failings as the rest of us."

"As long as you are informed, I'll say no more on the matter."

Jolen closed his eyes. "Good, because I believe I will take that rest you ordered."

# Chapter Thirteen

WARM SUN filtered down through the trees, sending dappled light across Jolen's blanket-covered legs. The weather had turned too hot to wear such a drape, but Estobán had insisted. The alternative was for him to leave the paradise of the balcony and go inside.

He'd rather not be trapped inside the villa when it felt so good to be out in the sunshine. Already he felt the healing rays of the fire elementals working to restore him to prime physical condition. Mental faculties seemed a bit slower to respond.

The nightmares experienced while he was in his fevered state were as disquieting as being led through all the levels of the hells without eyelids—unable to block out the horrific sights. And yet, a small part of his brain worried over the images as one would a sore tooth. No matter how bad the pain, the need to keep sticking a meddlesome tongue against the area arose. Instead of his tongue, though, he kept going back to the one theme that bothered him the most: fragmented pieces of the *Elementica* in the hands of the necromancers.

A chill swept over him from head to foot. Jolen rearranged the blanket on his legs, now thankful for the warmth it provided. Who was to say why he dreamed of such things during the height of his delirium. Perhaps it only represented random thoughts plucked from his mind, solely unconnected to significant meaning.

His gut, however, told him a different story.

The necromancers had made a move to control the *Eye of Truth* three years before—it didn't take a long stretch of the imagination to believe they might have searched for the scattered pieces of the *Elementica*. Hell they had a thousand years since the Great Purge to attempt such a feat.

A door opened and closed behind him. Small, hurried steps crossed the floor to the balcony. "Master Jolen?"

A smile tugged at Jolen's face, and he held up a hand to let Wendro know he was not being disturbed. "Good afternoon. What brings you to visit?"

Wendro took off his cap, held it in his hands, and spun it in a circle. "I wanted to know if you were up for a game of Oxen and Mules."

"Oxen and Mules? I haven't played that since I was a small boy. You'll have to refresh my memory of the rules."

The boy nodded vigorously. "I will."

"All right. Set up the board."

"I have to go get it first. I didn't want to bring it here if you didn't want to play."

Jolen gave him a gentle smile. "I'm not doing anything else at the moment, nor is it likely between the Medovin and Master Theodyne I'm likely to get much more in the way of entertainment. I think it sounds like a fine idea."

Wendro shot off out of the room, banging the door on the way out. A shout to be quiet and slow down came from someone in the hallway. While he waited for Wendro to return, Jolen gazed into the depths of the watered wine on the table. It might not possess the black ink most alchemists used to scry, but at least the deep red afforded enough of a reflection to see the images clearly.

It took him only a few seconds to connect to the Gold School. The communication room was usually attended by one of the students at all times, in case an urgent message came in from one of the practitioners living in the outlying areas of the city-states.

"This is Master Jolen. I need to speak with Master Oberon or Fellini."

The student, Apprentice Oswald if Jolen wasn't mistaken, nodded and left the bowl to contact one of the masters.

A few moments lapsed before Headmaster Oberon gazed at Jolen from the depths of the scry bowl. "You look a funny color. Is that from your illness?"

Jolen touched his face. "Perhaps, or it might be the wine I'm speaking to you through."

Master Oberon nodded. "Oh. Yes. That would do it. I am glad to see you are able to communicate. I feared when I got word from the Villa de Medovin that you were not long for this world."

"If the necromancers had their way, I would have already stood in the great chamber with masters of old." Jolen did not want to get off the topic, not when he had questions he wanted answered. "The reason I've contacted you is I need to know everything we have in the archives on the *Elementica*. How it was destroyed. Where the pieces were scattered. Any expeditions mounted to find the fragments."

"Why this sudden interest? I realize the Medovin owns a piece of that most sacred tablet, but do you fear the others have been found?" Headmaster Oberon narrowed his eyes in concern.

"Nothing substantial enough to make me risk my life on the answer, but enough to warrant a closer look." Jolen shrugged into the small bowl. "I have nothing more than a hunch and fevered dreams to fuel my search."

"And do you feel this hunch is perpetrated by the necromancers? Are you in danger again?" It was a valid question and one that Jolen heartily wished he could answer with assuredness.

"For the moment, I will yield to Master Theodyne's assessment and say that I operate under my own will, but I will not guarantee the claim." What else was Jolen to say? He knew of no other assurances he could give—not at this time. He would not lie to Headmaster Oberon.

Bells began to peal from the direction of the basilica. The echoes vibrated the bricks beneath Jolen's feet and along the slats of his chair. Doves rose over the rooftops, released from their cages. A new *demigoge* had been elected.

Headmaster Oberon's expression changed as the ringing bells reached through the scrying waters. "It is done then, and we no closer to finding the conspirators."

Jolen refrained from slamming his hand on the table in frustration. He'd failed. One bone-blade to the side and he'd been laid low for days, unable to complete his mission. Anger surged to the surface, held in check by the thinnest of threads. He did not wish to have Headmaster Oberon see him out of sorts.

He tried for calm and logic. "That is only the official vote. There are still a few more days of activities here in Gusan. The *demigoge* must be sworn to the holy oath and take the throne. Then the feasts and banquets. It is going to be at least a week before anyone leaves the city." The more he thought about it, the more he liked the idea of the vote being over.

Jolen held up a hand and pointed upward. "This might actually work to our advantage. The problem has been a lack of access to the *cardgrans* and their staffs due to the sequestration. Now the vote is over, they will be allowed to move freely around the city and visit the *prolates*."

Headmaster Oberon grinned wickedly. "I see where you're going with this, and I approve."

"Now I only hope that the Medovin does."

"How can he refuse?"

Jolen cared not to elaborate on the growing connection between him and Estobán Medovin. Let that play out in private for now. "I do have one other thing to ask. Do you know of any of the elemental gifts that would allow a person to hear the sun's rays as musical notes?"

It was hard to tell through the color of the wine, but it appeared as if Headmaster Oberon's face paled. "W... where have you made contact with such a person?"

"It's a lad here, a servant living and working for the Medovin."

"It's a very rare and precious gift. Any chance he might want to come to the Gold School and be educated in the ways of alchemy?"

Jolen let out a relieved sigh. "I hoped you'd extend the invitation. I will have to clear the move with the Medovin, as the boy has no parents to speak on his behalf."

"A foundling?"

"No, his mother worked here when she died. The boy says he never knew his father."

Headmaster Oberon lifted a shoulder. "If the boy's father is a full spirit elemental as I suspect, then she probably never saw his sire again."

Jolen thought on it a moment. No doubt that was why she'd never discussed his father with Wendro. How do you tell your son that he sprang from her union with a being of the ethereal plane? You didn't.

ESTOBÁN SAT in his own secret conclave as the bells began to toll the announcement that a new *demigoge* had emerged. His contemporaries glanced at one another. Worry filled the room like a hungry demon starving for a taste of flesh.

They rose as a unit and began to filter out from the meeting place and walked to the main square where the official proclamation would be read to the assembled masses. *Prolate* Juan-Carlo DiCarni from the city-state of Nequan, a tiny island off the southern shores, fell in step with Estobán as they made their solemn way to the balcony.

Juan-Carlo was a tall, strapping man with piercing green eyes and square jaw. He looked more like a statue than a man. Some said he had a heart to match.

Estobán had known Juan-Carlo from their days at university, and while he found him a rather proud, arrogant sort of man, he'd never call him heartless.

Juan-Carlo turned his jewel-like gaze to Estobán. "There are a few of us who wish to return to the ways of our ancestors and employ alchemists in our courts, to make them official members of our houses. Since you are well connected to their order, what do you think about this proposal? Will it be palatable to the Adepts' Council?"

Estobán sensed no trap but considered his words carefully. "That is a matter you must take up with them. I do not speak for their order, nor would I even venture to guess at how an overture might be taken. I will caution you, they are an independent body and will allow no man to govern them above the laws of their own sect. Understand that, and you may have a chance of convincing them. If I may inquire as to what advantage you wish to gain by employing the alchemists into your houses?"

Juan-Carlo gave a throaty laugh. "You ask that when it is common knowledge you entertain one in your villa? That the entire order is indebted to you for saving the life of an adept?"

Estobán grabbed Juan-Carlo's sleeve and stopped him. The tide of people moved around them like water around a rock lodged in the river. "I repaid a debt. Nothing more."

Juan-Carlo raised an eyebrow. "Come, we are men of the world. It is all over the city he is your lover and that your former lover, the infamous thief Theodyne, is at your villa and now wears the robes of the Gold School."

"To put an end to the rumors, I will answer these charges. Yes, Theodyne is at my villa, but he is not there as an emissary from the Gold School. He came to heal his brother of the robe." Estobán tightened his grip. "As to the fact if Master Jolen is my lover or not—that is no one's business and certainly not gripping enough for speculation. I'd think people more interested in the advance of the necromancers into our society or if the clerics decide to push their agenda for unification."

Juan-Carlo pulled his arm from Estobán's grip. "Rest easy, Medovin. I'm sure there is more jealousy than true malice in the rumor. Though I prefer women in my bed, I am secure enough in my own flesh to appreciate a handsome face in either sex. Beauty is beauty no matter where it is found. Add the power given Master Jolen by his alchemy, and he is a very desirable conquest."

They started walking again. "I'm positive he'd be offended if he heard you call him a conquest."

"Are you telling me you did not bring him here as your lover?"

"I requested Master Nico send me an alchemist well versed in discovering those infected by the necromancers. I had not met Master Jolen until he arrived at my villa." It was the truth, and the sooner others realized that the better. If the other *prolates* kept to the idea that the alchemists remained a single, organized body rather than to be used as the tools of the governors, then the order retained its value. If the *prolates* thought otherwise, it undermined the very reasons for the alchemists' strength. Estobán owed the Gold School too much to take that power away from them.

Juan-Carlo did not look convinced. "Then how do you explain the scene at the opening ceremony?"

Surprised by the comment, Estobán turned his shock to a laugh. "I have no idea what you mean by that statement. We were there to observe the ritual as were the rest of the audience."

"You looked like a couple of love-struck fools whenever you gazed at each other."

Estobán made a *hurmph* in the back of his throat. "I have no idea what went through Master Jolen's mind, but for my part, I will admit that he is handsome. But who among us doesn't like to be in the company of beautiful people."

"Who indeed?"

They continued to walk in silence. The sun beat down hot and unyielding. No clouds marred the sky to give respite from the rays. Thoughts baked and burned in Estobán's head like a loaf of bread left too long in the oven.

The only person in the room that day who could have started such a rumor and spread the word of Jolen's associations with the alchemists was the Agia. Damn the bloody fucking bastard. The man was cock deep in it with the necromancers. Of course he'd make Master Jolen's identity known. If not for Jolen three years before, the return of the necromancers might not have been discovered.

And they had attacked those with elemental blood.

Before his mind took the path that led to the painting hidden in his bedchamber, the balcony doors opened and Cardgran Pontefiore Silvanus stepped out with a rolled scroll in his hand, surrounded by the rest of the council.

Cheers went up through the crowd. Energy rose on the waves of excitement, carried on the breeze by air elementals. Estobán felt them all around. They had as much stake in this announcement as the humans.

Cardgran Pontefiore raised his arm in the air for silence. The noise quieted immediately. He unrolled the scroll with great drama.

Estobán fought hard not to roll his eyes at the pageantry. The *cardgran* knew the name of the new *demigoge,* it wasn't as if he'd been in another part of the basilica or even the identity was someone unknown to him. The ritual was all for spectacle. The name of the successor to the Heavenly Throne was probably burned on his mind.

"It is with great yet solemn occasion, I give you the next Supreme Ruler of the Holy Church. Cardgran Phillipe deRosa of Bonsuret."

DeRosa was on none of the short lists for possible contenders. As a matter of fact, he was probably the last man who should hold so high an office when the country was on the brink of war.

Juan-Carlo glanced down at Estobán with a brow raised in speculation. He clapped along with the rest of the crowd. The Nequan *prolate* had to be thinking the same as Estobán: DeRosa was a good man—too good to sit on the Heavenly Throne. He was gentle and pure of soul, easily corruptible by those who would surround him.

It would be a miracle if the man was not already heavily under the influence of necromancers.

"Oh gentle and lost soul," Estobán whispered.

Juan-Carlo nodded in solemn commiseration.

The crowd dispersed. Cardgran Phillipe deRosa's installation, as protocol dictated, would be held the following day at sunrise. A new day, a new *demigoge*.

This night the Villa of the Bonsuret *prolate*, Claudio Rinni, would host the first of many celebrations to fill the gardens of *prolatial* row. As was custom, the city-state where the newly elected *demigoge* hailed led the feasts and festivities as the sharing of their bounty was believed to bring luck and prosperity to the new *demigoge*'s reign.

From the corner of his eyes, Estobán thought he saw the familiar face of Cesare as he skulked through the crowd. Estobán turned, moving this way and that to see if he could locate him again, but he saw nothing of his cousin.

"Will you bring your alchemists to the Rinni villa?"

Estobán's heart thundered. Blood pumped loudly in his ears. Why should the fact Cesare might be in the holy city raise a panic in him?

He cleared his throat, pretending as if nothing was the matter. "If the alchemists wish to attend the festivities. However, Master Jolen may not yet feel up to such a grand adventure as a *prolatial* celebration."

"Will you attend?"

"Try to stop me."

# Chapter Fourteen

ESTOBÁN ENTERED Jolen's suite to the accusations of cheating and the childish laughter of one unable to defend himself against the charge. He followed the sound out to the balcony where Jolen and Wendro were embroiled in a bitter game of Oxen and Mules.

Mules dominated the board. Oxen littered the table at Wendro's elbows. It appeared Master Jolen was a poor loser. Thunder rode Jolen's brow while annoyance flared his nostrils.

"Hey. Hey. I'm almost sure that was an illegal move." Jolen pointed to the mule in harness standing on a square recently occupied by an ox in collar.

"No. Harnessed mules move up two over one in any direction. I promise." Wendro turned to Estobán. "Ask His Grace. He won't lie to you."

Estobán put his hands up in the air. "Do not involve me in your disputes. I haven't played that game since I was your age."

Jolen waved a splayed hand at his pint-sized opponent. "Might as well finish me off, but I warn you, I'll show no mercy on the rematch."

Wendro giggled. "And you'll lose again."

"We'll see about that."

The game finished quickly after that. Estobán stood in the balcony doorway watching. As Wendro cleared Jolen's last game piece from the board, Estobán indicated the set. "Could you give Master Jolen and me a moment? I need to speak with him."

"Yes, Your Grace."

Wendro hurriedly put the board and pieces away, then dashed from the room.

"That child does everything at full gallop," Estobán remarked as the door slammed behind Wendro's retreating form.

"I mean to take him with me when I return to the Gold School. He needs training in the arts of alchemy."

"As you wish, and if he wants to accompany you." Estobán took the vacated seat across the table from Jolen. "Are you up for a bit of amusement this evening?"

"I would probably maim and kill for the pleasure."

"You don't have to go that far."

"What did you have in mind?"

"The feasts to celebrate the new *demigoge* begin tonight."

"Ah, yes. The Bonsuret *cardgran*."

Estobán frowned. "How did you learn the identity so quickly?"

"Elementals work in mysterious ways, my dear *prolate*." It was said with a twinkle in his eyes and smile curling the corner of that sensuous mouth. "You want me to scan the crowd at the party and the new *demigoge*'s attendants."

"Despite your protests, you are a mind reader."

"No. It's what I would have suggested." Jolen stared off the balcony to the other side of the gardens. "The elementals fear the selection made. They warn of great turmoil to come."

"I knew that without their prognostications." Estobán leaned forward. "I'll admit to an acute disquiet about the elevation of DeRosa. Not for the man, but for the quality of his soul."

"What have you heard?"

Estobán felt ridiculous describing a man of virtue and generosity in a negative light. "It's not so much what I've heard or the reputation as what that means."

"And if that comes to pass, we will be ready." Jolen leaned forward and rested his hand on Estobán's knee. The touch was one of comfort, not passion. "Things will move quickly from here. We must be prepared to go where they take us."

Estobán took a deep breath. Indecisive about how much to tell Jolen about the paintings, and fear over the reaction made him choose his next words carefully. "When we were in the catacombs, you asked if I had seen the symbols painted on the walls before."

"Go on."

"Ever since Theodyne broke the hold of the necromancers over me, I have had… residual effects." Estobán chanced a glance at Jolen, but only saw compassion on his face. "I can't say where the images come from, but I seem to get them from my sleep."

Jolen let out a breath and leaned back in his chair. "Dreams are funny things. They may be prophetic or refuse. Who is to say? However, if you saw the sigils in your dreams, I'd tend to believe there are more to them than mere flotsam."

"I never said they were dreams." With that Estobán rose. "Care to take a little walk with me?"

Surprise rounded Jolen's eyes. "Are you going to let me leave the room?"

"How do you feel?"

"As if I'm going to jump off the balcony if I am not allowed to move about soon." Jolen threw the blanket off his lap. "Not that it isn't a lovely suite."

Estobán helped Jolen to his feet. Jolen vibrated with strength and vitality. Perhaps he'd been wrong to hold him in convalescence for so long. But the man had been just too weak and out of his head to do anything less.

"Thank you, Your Grace. I can manage from here."

"Not if you insist on using my honorific." He released his hold on Jolen. Hearing that particular form of address hurt more than he cared to show. "I thought we'd moved past that?"

Jolen raised a brow. "Yes, but I suspect I should remember to use it when we are seen together at the celebrations."

"I wouldn't worry about that if I were you. It seems you and I have been the subject of gossip since your arrival." Estobán led Jolen from the suite and up to the *prolate*'s private apartments.

Once inside, Estobán led him to the bedchamber. "I must ask you to make a solemn vow that what you see here will not be mentioned by you to another living soul. It must remain our secret, or I fear I may lose my right to hold my office. I cannot allow that to happen until Viola's ascension to the *prolate*'s seat is secure."

"Your Grace… Estobán… I'll hold the secret as close to my heart as if it were my own. Please have no fear on that score."

Estobán nodded and opened the door.

The easel sat off to the far left of the bed. Midday sunshine filled the room, highlighting the painting as if on display by the Gods.

Jolen smiled briefly. "You paint?"

"Not until the necromancers."

Estobán allowed Jolen to make his way over to the easel. His brow furrowed as he gazed at the images of the broken ruby tiles.

"Images from your sleep but not your dreams," Jolen whispered.

"Yes." Estobán gazed at the painting, trying to see it through Jolen's eyes but came up way short. "I started this one the first night of your illness. I fell asleep in the chair next to your bed and woke here, covered in paint, without memory of walking the halls."

Jolen nodded. "I questioned whether you had powers of some sort— and it appears you do. Though I will not profess to knowing the nature of such ability."

"I don't rightly care about the nature of it, only if we can use it to our advantage in some way."

Jolen closed his eyes and held out his hand so his fingertips were only a mere hair's breadth away from the canvas. Air shifted in the room. The curtains billowed out on a strong gust of wind. Flames exploded in the candles along the wall.

"This is not of necromantic origin. It came from the elementals trying to speak through you. Their only way of communicating with someone not of the blood, but given other, more unusual gifts, sometimes comes through unexpected mediums."

Shocked, Estobán sat down on the bed awash in relief. "Then why choose me? They could have more easily spoken to you as they do now."

Jolen shook his head. "Full elementals have their own reasons for doing things the way they do. It is best to take the message they give and say thank you."

"For making me believe that I was still infected by the necromancers? If I didn't feel as if I owe them a debt for keeping you alive until Master Theodyne arrived, I'd be extremely cross at the moment."

Jolen bent down onto his haunches and took Estobán's hands in his. Jolen gazed at him with those sky-blue eyes that tore through him like a wind shear. "The message to you is quite clear. You hold the last piece of the *Elementica*. The necromancers have claimed the others. We are one fragment away from the death dancers gaining control of the elementals."

"I didn't know."

"How could you?" Jolen squeezed Estobán's hands, then stood. "I am so glad you decided to confide in me."

So was Estobán. He should have come clean on his nocturnal artistry sooner. They could have taken precautions.

Jolen's expression turned worried. He rested his hand over his injured side.

Estobán started to rise, but Jolen waved him back down. "Are you in pain?"

"Tender, but no real pain."

"Then what is it?"

"I'm only thinking of a way to inform my brothers of the robe about this turn without spilling your secret or how I came by the knowledge. They will need to know. This is too big to leave alone."

Estobán understood the reasons and agreed in theory. He just didn't want too many questions asked. "Are they likely to want to know the details? Can you tell Master Nico and Headmaster Oberon that the information came to you from the elementals during your healing? It would not be an outright lie."

"Nor would it be the complete truth." Jolen sat down on the bed next to Estobán. "However, there is no rule that says alchemists must at all times be one hundred percent truthful with each other. You swore me to secrecy, and I will abide by my promise. My brethren need only know that the story is verified through the air and fire elementals. That is all the proof they will need."

"Thank you."

Jolen smiled, and it went straight to Estobán's groin. "We're in this together. We must do what we can for each other."

"Jolen—"

He got no further before Jolen put his hand over Estobán's mouth. "Please do not say anything you might regret or wish to call back later. I don't think I could take it. Not from you."

Estobán's breath caught and held. He let his eyes fall shut and kissed Jolen's palm. Jolen took his hand away. His chest rose and fell quickly with each breath.

"I'm not a moral man, Estobán. I've already crossed a line with you once. I would not wish to do so again."

So he hadn't dreamed or imagined that night. They had made love several rooms and floors apart. "Not even if it's what I wanted as well?"

"Can you be sure it's me you want and not a substitute for Theodyne?"

"It was not Theodyne who risked his life to save me from a basilica guard." Estobán brushed a thumb down the side of Jolen's face. "It was not Theodyne's bed I sat next to for days, praying for a miracle and fearing I'd no right to ask for one."

"Bán…." The nickname was sweet, short and full of passion as Jolen leaned forward and took Estobán's mouth.

He'd not expected Jolen to become the seducer, but the kiss they shared proved to Estobán beyond any doubt that their feelings were mutual. He pulled Jolen into a gentle embrace, afraid that to hold him too tight might injure him.

Jolen chuckled against Estobán's lips, his breath tickling as it puffed out. "I won't break."

"You've been so ill."

"Yes. And now I'm better." Jolen leaned his forehead against Estobán's. "I need this. You don't know how much."

It was enough to make Estobán moan. He swept his lips over Jolen's cheeks, chin, and then moved back to his mouth, claiming Jolen with tender intent. For now he contented himself with modest kisses and caresses, nothing more than learning the contour of Jolen's body, over his clothes. Nothing had ever felt so erotic and right.

A knock sounded on the outer door of the suite. Estobán reluctantly pulled away. "Come into the salon with me. We'll see what our ill-timed guest needs."

Jolen brushed his mouth one last time over Estobán's. "Afraid for someone to catch us in bed together."

Estobán lifted Jolen's hand and pressed his lips to the tender palm—one that had performed thousands of spells in his magical lifetime. He marveled at the warmth there, as if the very essence of alchemy lived within his flesh. "I have not worried over what others think of my sexuality in a very long time. Nor would I ever be embarrassed having the world know you are my lover."

Jolen gave him a sly smile and slid from the bed to stand. He moved to the window and spread his arms. Wind moved through the opening, sending a cool breeze to swirl in the interior. It ruffled Jolen's hair and fluttered the arms of his shirt. "It is your man Silas at the door."

"Ah, then I have no need to hide at all. He knows most of my secrets." Estobán rose and headed to the salon. Soft footsteps behind him, and he knew Jolen followed at a distance.

The knock sounded again.

"Enter."

Silas came fully into the room and bowed. "Your Grace, Master Theodyne inquires the whereabouts of Master Jolen. He is quite worried."

"You may send him in, and please have a slight repast for three ordered. We'll dine in here for midday meal."

"Yes, Your Grace." Silas bowed again and exited the suite.

Jolen took up a place by the window, looking out over the gardens. "It must be odd having him in residence."

Estobán poured a glass of wine and took a sip. "It is uncomfortable but necessary."

"You can't change the past. You can only reconcile to live with it." Jolen picked up a small piece of brass twisted into the shape of a sea serpent. The piece was hollow, only the outline of one, a mere suggestion as to the creature in question.

"It was the hardest lesson I've ever learned." He watched as Jolen rubbed his thumb over the brass, making it glow slightly until the brass burned away leaving shiny gold in its wake.

"Every lesson builds our character. Strengthens us. Makes us more than we were before." Jolen set the golden serpent back on the shelf and turned to face Estobán. "The gift of those lessons is how we use what we've learned for the betterment of ourselves and others."

The door opened again, and Theodyne entered the room. Relief washed over his features. The T-shaped scar branded into his cheek was stark white against his tan face. "I thought something had happened to you."

Jolen shook his head. "After going stark-raving mad from boredom, I was soundly thrashed in a game of Oxen and Mules by a miniature hustler who I suspect cheated on every move. His Grace rescued me before I had a chance to call best two out of three."

"Wendro." The name was met with a dramatic roll of Theodyne's eyes heavenward. "He beat me in six straight games last night. He is indeed a hustler."

Jolen laughed. "Headmaster Oberon will have his hands full with that one."

This news met with some surprise from Theodyne. He glanced over at Estobán who nodded. "I have given my consent as his employer on the condition that it is what the boy wishes."

Theodyne walked over to the sitting area and took a place on one of the chairs. "I sensed something in him but not the nature of the talent."

"And I don't know what it is either, but Headmaster Oberon believes the child is the direct result of the union between Wendro's mother and a full spirit elemental," Jolen confessed. "He can hear energy as musical notes. Read the elementals as a conductor reads a symphony. It is quite extraordinary."

"Yes, but there are other more imperative matters that must be discussed." Theodyne was rather autocratic in his manner. "Like for instance how to ferret out the necromancer's plans."

Jolen looked to Estobán before turning back to Theodyne.

"I'm sure Master Nico has told you about the piece of the *Elementica* that resides at this villa."

"Yes. Of course. After all this time, a fact even a piece survived is amazing." Theodyne raised a brow and looked to Estobán and then to

Jolen. "Why do I get the feeling this is only a small part of a very big puzzle?"

"More like the last piece." Jolen moved away from the window and came to sit on the lounger across from Theodyne. "I have it on very good authority that the other pieces have been found and are in the possession of the necromancers."

"What is being done to secure the last section?"

"It is safe." Jolen placed his hands in front of him, linking his fingers between his legs. "We need to find the location of the ones acquired by the necromancers. The *Elementica* cannot be put back together under their direction."

"No," Theodyne agreed. "Do you suppose that is what they wanted all along? Control over the *Eye of Truth* would enslave the alchemists; the *Elementica* would do so to the elementals and to a lesser degree the hybrids."

"I believe it is part of a greater plan." Jolen rubbed his side again.

Estobán didn't care for the fact the *aerothant* had started to look a bit pale again. Perhaps he'd done too much too soon. He pressed his lips together to keep from expressing such a sentiment in front of Theodyne. "What plan is that?"

"Think about it. If they can control the elementals through the tablet and the clerics through the *demigoge*, there is not much standing between them and total control of Dominicál and from there, where else?" Jolen leaned against the lounger back. "I'm sorry. I may need to lie down for a bit before we make our way to the Bonsuret villa this evening."

"Yes, of course." Estobán gave Jolen a hand up. "You can sleep in here if you like."

Jolen gave him a weak smile and winked. "Perhaps you can join me after Theodyne leaves," he whispered.

Heat curled low in Estobán's belly. "Let's just worry about getting you in there without cracking your head open on the floor."

# Chapter Fifteen

HUNDREDS OF candles lit Villa de Rinni. It glowed like the lights of heaven. White silk festooned the walls and billowed on a gentle breeze in otherworldly splendor. Guests were dressed in their finest clothing. Wine and food was of the highest quality and skill in preparation. Rare blooms from distant lands scented the garden in a heady fragrance.

Jolen took in his surroundings as if the scene had been drenched in a filthy patina. The others might not sense the evil lurking beneath the surface, but he did. Glancing to his companions, Theodyne and Estobán, he knew they felt the disturbing presence of the necromancers as well.

A tall, devastatingly handsome man approached Estobán. His wicked smile hid nothing of his intentions, nor did it pretend to. "Estobán. I see you've brought your retinue. Have you spoken with them on the matter we discussed earlier?"

"No. I have not." Estobán's manner was clipped and a bit unfriendly. He turned. "Masters Jolen and Theodyne, I would like to introduce you to His Grace, Juan-Carlo DiCarni of Nequan."

Jolen and Theodyne both bowed at the introduction. So this was the legendary DiCarni. His looks had not been exaggerated by the stories told of his exploits. Rumor had it he'd fathered more children around the various city-states of Dominicál than was humanly possible. Yet those same rumors held that his wife was barren.

"Keeping your fingers clean, Theo?" DiCarni asked in a familiar manner.

"On the contrary, Your Grace, I find they are often stained with soot."

DiCarni tilted his head back and gave a throaty laugh. "You have not lost your sense of humor."

"That was the one thing prison did not strip from me." Theodyne looked around the room. "I see your sweet Angelique is not with you."

DiCarni looked into his wineglass in disgust. "She said it was too hot this time of year for travel to a city the size of Gusan. She preferred to stay at our villa."

"Ah. Yes. This time of year is particularly lovely on the island."

Jolen had no idea what game Theodyne played, but he did know for a fact the man had never been to anywhere of note before he met Nico. Perhaps it was to get under the DiCarni's skin. If so, he appeared to be doing a fine job.

"Indeed it is." DiCarni gave a smile in accordance with a man who owned the keys to paradise. "But come, let us not speak of these matters when we are here to celebrate the continuation of the divine seat and the elevation of one so true and noble of heart as Cardgran DeRosa."

"Of course." Theodyne took a glass of wine off a tray as a servant walked by. "A toast to our new *demigoge*."

DiCarni raised his glass. "Salute."

Jolen shifted his gaze from the men in his party and scanned the crowd. He shifted through the energy of those assembled, even the oily touch of the necromancer, but failed to pinpoint the location among the guests. Giving a formal bow, he excused himself from their company and weaved through the revelers.

Splitting up was the only way to cover all the ground in a short time. The necromancer could be anywhere—even gazing down from one of the many balconies that overlooked the courtyard.

Jolen scanned the rooms above, but no one lurked behind draperies or windows. At least not that he could see or sense. Still, the essence felt closer, so he felt no real need to wander around the Rinni's living quarters. That would be more of a job for Theodyne. He knew how to get in and around places without being seen.

A pain grew in Jolen's side. It radiated outward, a compass trying to find magnetic north. Theodyne had assured him the poison was gone.

Why, then, did it feel as if his side was going to split open and something heinous crawl out?

He rested his hand over the wound and continued on through the crowd. Perhaps he should return to the Medovin villa. No. That would only make Estobán want to leave the party early, and, the Gods knew, they needed this opportunity. Maybe he should find a quiet corner and take a rest there—just until the pain passed. Get a second wind.

There, on the other side of the garden was an unoccupied bench set off from the heavily trafficked areas. It appeared as good a place as any to sit and gather his thoughts and commune with the elements while observing the other guests.

He wended his way back through the chatting celebrants, trying to be as unobtrusive as possible. Snippets of conversations flowed over him, a waterfall of emotions rushing from every direction. It became harder to move, to swim against the current, as if the words alone had the power to slow his course.

An essence brushed by him. Thick, oozing, putrid. *Necromancer.* Jolen turned to find his prey but saw no one physically walking by. They had blended into the crowd. Acute pain seared his side. He winced and doubled over.

Hands gripped his shoulders. Heat penetrated his back at the same time a calming scent invaded his head. "Jolen?"

He tried to straighten, but the pain intensified. "I don't know what's wrong? It just started hurting like I've been stabbed afresh." He pulled his hand away, sticky and warm with blood.

Estobán glanced down at Jolen's hand. "You've pulled your sutures loose."

"I've not done anything to cause such a thing to happen." Jolen heard the defensiveness in his voice and didn't care for it. Estobán hadn't chastised him, only meant to explain what happened.

"Let's get you back to the villa and have Theodyne tend to you."

"You can't leave." Jolen grabbed a handful of Estobán's shirt and pulled him close enough he could whisper what he'd discovered. "A necromancer just brushed passed me. I lost him in the crowd. Please find him before something awful happens. There is evil intent ripe on the air.

So much so I can fairly taste it coating my tongue. This night will not end well for anyone."

Applause started at the far end of the garden. Jolen and Estobán turned to see the procession of the newly elected *demigoge* and the Council of *Cardgrans* as they entered the garden. Servants refilled glasses, and the Rinni met his former *cardgran* with a bow and proud smile.

A man moved into view on the Rinni's left. A ripple of awareness shot through Jolen's body as their gazes connected. A sly smile lifted the corner of the unknown man's mouth.

"Who is that standing next to the Rinni *prolate*?"

Estobán moved to get a better look over the crowd. "That's his magus. Recently appointed to the position. His former one died under mysterious circumstances."

Just like that, the pieces fit together.

Servants continued to move through the crowd to refill glasses for the formal toast and benediction to DeRosa.

Jolen started forward to stop the toast. Certainty ran through his blood. They were headed straight into a trap set by the necromancers.

Words fell from the Rinni's lips, and the crowd hushed, but Jolen heard none of it. Only the echo of his heartbeat and thunder of the breath in his lungs filled his awareness.

He watched in horror as Cardgran DeRosa placed his glass to his lips and drank. The holy man made a face and grabbed his throat. His glass fell to the bricks and shattered. Slowly his face went from healthy pink to red, then purple. He clutched at his heart, the ring of his office stark against his blanched fingers.

Shouts erupted as he fell back into the arms of one of the other *cardgrans*.

"Murder!" The accusation came as swiftly as DeRosa's death.

The Rinni's magus leaned into his master and whispered. Rage-filled eyes turned to Jolen. "You there. Alchemist. You caused this."

All movement in the garden ceased. Jolen kept moving forward, Estobán at his back.

Estobán glared at his counterpart. "You ignorant man. He was trying to stop an assassination."

One of the *cardgrans* looked up from clutching his fallen brethren. "He isn't even cold yet, and you're bickering over the culprit? Can we exhibit a bit more compassion and respect?"

Estobán glanced down at the gathered clerics. "You have my sympathies and condolences, but I will not allow anyone to accuse the alchemists of this act. What have they to gain by it?"

Theodyne bent down over the body of the fallen *cardgran*. He felt for a pulse, something none of the others thought to do. "He lives, but barely. Move him into the villa. *Now.*"

The Rinni's magus leaned in to whisper to his master again. Jolen reached out with his senses, trying to pull the words from the air. They were shielded.

Suddenly the garden filled with elementals. Glass globes burst with flames, fountains sprayed water into the air, and a gust of wind roared.

"The elementals are not pleased." Jolen held his side. Blood leaked through his fingers. The injury throbbed with every beat of his heart. Pain jolted him with every step. He pointed to Theodyne. "See to Cardgran DeRosa."

The Rinni's magus stepped around his master and started to raise his hand. The odd sigils from the catacombs were tattooed on his palm. White lacy scars adorned his wrists and forearms.

"Necromancer!" Jolen shouted and tried to lunge for the man, but the pain in his side knocked him to the ground. Blood ran freely through his fingers now.

"He's injured!" Someone shouted.

Another picked up the cry. "He's been stabbed."

The wound had not opened on its own. Jolen had not done anything to precipitate the event. No, the necromancer had controlled the action from across the room. Every manipulation had been orchestrated to maximum effect.

However, the necromancer had not counted on the fact two alchemists were stronger than one, and Theodyne was a strong healer. If he couldn't save the life of DeRosa, no human could.

The Rinni's eyes were glazed. His personal guards had filled the courtyard, stationed around the perimeter. "Seize and arrest this man."

Estobán rose from where he squatted beside Jolen. "What are you about? This man is under my protection. Arrest him, and it becomes open war with the House of Medovin. Is that what you want?"

Jolen grabbed Estobán's hand. "Not him. He's under control. It's the magus."

Estobán's eyes narrowed in hatred. His nostrils flared. "Damn you, Rinni."

Jolen rolled to his side and tried to lever himself up against the pain. "No… Est… Medovin. I'll go with the guards."

Estobán gave him a horrified look. "You can't be serious."

"Yes, I can." Jolen allowed the guards who now surrounded them to take him into custody. They wrenched his arms back painfully and manacled him in iron. "Tell Theodyne when he is finished seeing to DeRosa to surrender himself as well."

"You cannot expect me to ask that of him. *Me* of all people."

"You can and you must."

The Rinni looked around as if pleased with the outcome. "See he admits his guilt."

"I admit nothing. I will, however, sacrifice myself to prevent a war." Jolen's side ached like a demon. Blood continued to trickle from the opening. His shirt was saturated and stuck to his side.

"Take him away."

Jolen looked back once as he was led away. The necromancer had slithered from the crowd, a snake in the grass.

ESTOBÁN HURRIED to find Theodyne. He and the *cardgrans* were not far from the doorway leading to the garden. DeRosa lay on a bench, his skin stretched taut over his cheekbones, face pale, lips blanched. Sweat rolled from Theodyne's brow, and his hair around his face was damp.

A thick stench of vomit filled the space.

Theodyne stepped back and wiped at his forehead with his sleeve. "What is going on in the courtyard?"

"Jolen allowed himself to be arrested by the Rinni's guards."

"What?" Theodyne started to the garden. Fury trailed him like a comet.

Estobán grabbed both of Theodyne's arms and held him back. "He requests you to turn yourself over as well. He has something planned, but I do not know what it is."

"He's gone mad."

Cardgran Jarens from the city-state of Auflaven near the border of Kraukeur stepped forward. He was a slight man with a shock of white hair and a wizened face. "Master Theodyne has saved the life of our most beloved *demigoge*. We will not let him fall."

Estobán bowed to the *cardgran*. "And I would not ask it if I did not believe Master Jolen has a plan, and also didn't fear for his life."

"You think they'll try to kill him now he's in custody?" Theodyne's expression softened. Worry pulled his brow into a *v*.

"There is that, but I think it's already begun. He's losing a lot of blood for a wound that was on the mend."

Estobán hardly had the words out before Theodyne was in motion again, leaving the safety of the villa for the chaos of the garden. With a heavy heart, he watched as Theodyne walked up to the guard captain with his hands out.

Cardgran Jarens placed a comforting hand on Estobán's shoulder. "Fear not, my son. We will not turn from you in this hour of uncertainty."

"I thank you, Your Eminence." He continued to watch the scene unfold as Theodyne was led away to the horrified guests looking on.

Estobán turned back to Cardgran Jarens. "Do you happen to know the name of the Rinni's magus?"

Cardgran Jarens's mouth turned down at the corners. He sniffed as if he smelled something foul. "Hazrael."

At least now he had a name to take to Master Nico and the Gold School. With the support of the *cardgrans*, Jolen and Theodyne would be released soon, but it was going to come at a price. Estobán only wondered if Master Nico would pay it.

# Chapter Sixteen

JOLEN LAY against the cold stone wall of the dirty cell. He'd become lightheaded in the last few minutes. A terrible buzzing filled his ears. Blood made a pool under his backside, soaking his pants.

It was the necromancer's doing. He'd reached into the part of the wound once kissed by the bone of a brother and ripped the healing flesh apart. Mind, body it was all the same to a necromancer. Much as the Grand Matter was the same to alchemists.

At the master level, an alchemist should by rights be able to heal his own injuries, to knit the flesh back together by the simple act of calling upon the higher powers. Not Jolen. He had the ability to help restore others, but not his own body. Sometimes he marveled he'd ever advanced to the master level given that flaw.

Boots struck stone in a march of angry feet. The *stamp, stamp, stamp* grew closer. Guards. What manner of torment were they going to inflict on him? He'd not done anything wrong. He'd only tried to prevent Cardgran DeRosa from drinking from a poison well. The Rinni was so infected by necromanical influence that he'd failed to see the logic in his accusation. Why would Jolen try to stop an assassination if he—or the alchemists— were the culprits?

The guards stopped in front of a cell across from where Jolen was held. Theodyne stood with his back straight and rage filling the air around him.

"I don't think you'd better put him in there, Tomkin," one of the guards addressed the one with the keys. "If that one over there bleeds to death, they'll send vengeance down on our heads."

"If we don't follow orders, the Rinni will sic his magus on us. Which do you think is the most immediate threat?" Tomkin started to unlock the cell across from Jolen. A jangle of metal on metal echoed in the empty corridor.

Theodyne glanced over at Jolen, then back to the guard Tomkin. "I am a master level alchemist. These bars will not hold me nor stop me from going to my injured brother. It is best if you put me in the cell with him where I can heal him instead of having to explain to your *prolate*'s magus why there are no longer doors on either cell."

"He has a point, Tomkin."

"How can we be sure you'll stay put if I let you in with him?"

"You can't, but I will give you my word that we will not stray."

Tomkin let out a heavy sigh and shuffled over to the cell where Jolen lay. "Don't make me regret this."

A smile kicked up the corner of Jolen's mouth. Did the man not realize the futileness of that threat? Neither Jolen nor Theodyne mentioned it to him. That way was best. Make no waves and stay as polite and nonconfrontational as possible. Give the guards no reason to think ill of them or spread unfavorable stories of the alchemists to their *prolate*.

Another jangle of keys in the lock, and the door swung open. Theodyne held up his hands for the guards to remove his cuffs. They did so without question. He remained where he was until they left the cell and locked the door behind him.

Their retreating footsteps broke the spell on Theodyne, and he hurried to Jolen. The puddle of blood had spread out, saturating the straw on the cell floor. "My Gods, how much blood can one man lose and still be alive?"

"I don't know, but I may be fast on the point of discovering the answer to that question."

"Lift your shirt and let me assess the damage." Theodyne tugged at the fabric, not waiting for Jolen to do the honors.

The movement caused a jolt of pain to lance through Jolen's side. He sucked in a hissing breath.

Theodyne's face pulled into a frown. "It doesn't look too bad. The blood worries me, but the site itself looks clean."

"I can't tell if that was supposed to be encouraging or not."

Theodyne glanced up and smiled. "No. It's good. I expected to find it festered again or at the very least gangrenous."

"Thank the heavens for small favors."

"This has nothing to do with the heavens. This is from the very darkest depths of the hells. Fucking death dancers. Why attack you a second time?" Theodyne laid his hands over the wound and recited an incantation. Sigils both familiar and comforting painted the air, as if they fell from his lips like confetti on a parade route.

Odd how Jolen not only felt their healing power but also saw them as vividly as the ones painted on the walls of the catacombs. He reached up and touched the symbols, bringing them down to him.

They burst across his cold skin like bubbles from a bath and lay there tickling. He wiped a hand across his face to try and remove the residue, but it was tenacious.

Theodyne glanced up in concern. "What are you doing?"

"You manifested the incantation. I can see the words."

Theodyne smiled briefly. "You are supposed to see them. It creates a protective shield around you so the necromancers will have a harder time getting to you."

"Why didn't you do this before? It would have saved me a lot of pain and agony." Not to mention keep the necromancers at bay. He'd not have to feel as if he were at risk every time one of them brushed by him.

"It's not as sturdy as armor. It can be penetrated. The best it can do is slow them down and give them pause. By then you have a chance to mount a defense." Theodyne moved his hands away. "There. I stopped the bleeding and closed the wound again. This does not have sutures. I knit it together with a spell. It should hold much better."

"Why didn't you do this the first time?"

"Actually I wanted to cauterize it last time but was countermanded. However, there was logic to do it the way I did before. You may have still had infection the last time. I see no evidence of it this time. And besides, Estobán requested I use sutures." Theodyne lowered the tail of Jolen's shirt back over the site. "Other than to heal your injury, why did you want me to turn myself over to the Rinni's men?"

"His magus is a necromancer. We need to break the hold he has on the Rinni, and I can't do that alone. Not from this distance and not when I'm so weak." Jolen rubbed a hand over the injury. It tingled as the skin continued to knit back together. "It was safer to let them believe acquiescence than stand there and fight in the middle of a crowd filled with those who may be under the direct influence of the magus."

Theodyne rubbed his chin. "I see your point. Good thinking. If we're in here, we are somewhat protected from the mob."

"And the magus."

"What about Estobán? He's in the middle of the crowd alone." Theodyne took a seat by the wall and rested his head against the stones.

"I believe his place as a *prolate* will protect him in this instance. The suggestion of a house war has already been made, and the reaction was not favored by the crowd." Jolen closed his eyes, hoping he was right. "I don't believe the Rinni will risk it. Not now."

"Who do you think poisoned DeRosa?"

"Oh, I believe it was the magus, though he did so knowing two things." Jolen raised a finger ticking off the first point. "That there were going to be alchemists at the gathering on whom to place the blame. Two, that you in particular would appear to save his life."

"Appear? That's quite the gamble."

Jolen gave a knowing laugh. "You don't think for one moment DeRosa hasn't been specifically elevated for what he will do for the necromancers? Because I am not so convinced. Whether the rest of those gathered are conscious of the fact or not, the magus controlled that poison the entire time. He never intended to let DeRosa go to the grave, but he had to make it look as real as possible."

"That's quite convoluted, even for a necromancer."

Jolen gave a shrug. "I can't explain how I know I'm right. Maybe it was the reaction of the elementals or the fact they've surrounded me ever since I came to Gusan, but I know I'm right about this."

"I bow to your conviction that you are." Theodyne pulled his knees up and rested his arms on them. "How do you want to go about this?"

"We need to connect—you and I—then call on the forces of the elementals. They should be able to give us the augmentation we need to reach through the necromancer's hold and break the Rinni free."

"All right." Theodyne nodded. As a descendant of an earth elemental he had the power to call them to his cause as did Jolen as an *aerothant*. "Do you feel strong enough? You lost a lot of blood."

"It doesn't matter. We have to do this."

"Agreed, but can it wait for an hour or so? I want to see some of your strength return before we attempt to oust a necromancer from the mind of a *prolate*. It's not such an easy task to accomplish even when at your best."

To prove he meant no delay, Jolen pushed himself up along the wall until he stood. His legs shook from the effort. Black spots filled his vision, and his hearing muffled.

Theodyne reached out to steady him. "Perhaps you'd better remain seated for this."

Jolen took a few deep breaths, blowing them out between pursed lips. Slowly he lowered himself back to the floor with Theodyne's assistance. In this instance he'd be best served to listen to reason.

He brought his legs up and rested his forehead against his knees. The action pulled at the newly knitted skin along his side. It felt tight, immovable.

Theodyne sat down beside him once again. "I will help you with this, but I strongly advise against it in your condition."

Jolen looked up over his arm. He gave his brother of the robe a slight smile. "All the more reason to go ahead. The bastard probably thought to slow me down by reopening the wound. He won't expect an attack, especially while we're locked away down here."

Now Theodyne smiled. "You are positively political in your thinking."

Jolen didn't know whether to take that as compliment or insult. "I remember very little of when Masters Nico and Oberon were in my mind ousting the necromancers. It's all a series of vague flashes without substance."

"Me either. I think it's best we don't." Theodyne brushed his hand along the floor, picking up bits of dirt. He turned his palm over and began to swirl the debris into a globe. "We'll trap the essence in here as Nico and Oberon did before."

"Will that be large enough?"

"Size doesn't matter in situations like these."

The tiny sphere was no bigger in diameter than Jolen's thumbnail. The finished product was murky brown, not a favorable color for such a delicate instrument. Though Master Nico had developed the spheres, Theodyne had perfected the art.

"Are you ready, Jolen?"

"I am." He lowered his head and closed his eyes, concentrating on the signature of the necromancer who had brushed against him at the celebration.

All entities contained a unique feel—the necromancers were no different. The taint of their vileness could not be mistaken for anything else. It tasted foul on the palate. Filled the nose and lungs with the stink of rot. Images of unfilled graves came to mind and stayed there, burying themselves deep in the consciousness.

Jolen took a deep breath and rode the waves of the astral, following the path laid down by the death dancer. Next he searched for the essence of the Rinni—thick and robust with a hearty appetite for life. The nexus where the two essences combined was where Jolen and Theodyne needed to strike.

His companion in this most important endeavor shone as a bright green light, earthy and lush. The elementals, who followed beside, though they had not as yet been summoned, were dots of blinding white.

They always knew when he was in need. Had they always been there and he'd not noted it until now when he needed them the most?

Jolen, Theodyne, and the elementals reached the nexus. Stray energy pulses crackled like lightning around them. The Rinni's essence tried to break free from its captive, but the suppression was too complete, too consuming to do more than send out the random spikes that only someone traveling on the ether might see.

The necromancer's presence rose up before them, large and black as the moon hiding the sun. Shadows grew long, casting the astral into eclipse.

Undeterred, Jolen attacked.

ESTOBÁN SEARCHED the crowd for Magus Hazrael before coming back around to where the Rinni lorded over the crumbling festivities as some fallen god might preside over a banquet of the damned. The Bonsuret *prolate* continued to pontificate over the dangers of the alchemists and how no one in the Dominicál city-states should hold them to their bosom.

Guests shuffled nervously, raising glasses to their mouths to hide their embarrassment over the Rinni's harangue. They had come to celebrate the elevation of DeRosa to the highest religious authority in the whole of the city-states, not listen to the host call down the heavens to rid the world of the alchemists.

If he knew anything about the discipline, he'd realize it was as much about the elevation of the soul as it was the practice of the esoteric and scientific. Estobán came around the edge of a small circle of the Rinni's family. His younger brother, Edgari, had waved his hand in a motion for him to lower his voice. Edgari glanced over at Estobán as if silently asking for help.

How could he let the poor man stand against his house head without aid? It was not a generous thing to do.

"Why don't you sit down and take a rest, Brother?" Edgari pulled a chair over to a table for the Rinni to sit. "The alchemists are both in our cells below the villa. They are of no danger to you now."

Rinni shook his head as if trying to get water from his ear. He didn't seem to hear his brother. His eyes were glassy and unfocused. The glass slipped from his hand and crashed on the marble paving stones. He doubled over, grabbed both sides of his head. A terrible keening wail issued from his throat.

Edgari wrapped his arms around the Rinni and eased him to the ground. "Someone help him."

Estobán knelt down over the fallen *prolate*. "He's being purged."

"What does that mean?"

Estobán grabbed Edgari's arm and squeezed. "I suspect he's been under the influence of the necromancers. It takes a moment once the purge begins to see the healing effects."

Edgari looked down at his brother with wide, uncertain eyes. "And you think this because he dared to question your beloved alchemists?"

"No. I say that because I know the effects in the most personal of ways. It's not an experience I'd ever wish on any man." Estobán watched as the Rinni stirred and his eyes opened.

"What happened?" The *prolate* glanced around, confused at his surroundings. "Why are we at the villa?"

Edgari helped his brother to sit upright. "You don't remember?"

Rinni shook his head, then put it into his hands with a moan. "It feels as if I've been bludgeoned."

"Let me take you to your suite. You need a tisane for the pain and to rest."

Rinni waved his brother away. "No. Not yet. Let me sit here and gain my bearings." He turned over onto his side and laid his head on the grassy area.

Estobán motioned to Edgari and leaned forward, lowering his voice. "Send someone into the linen stores for heavy blankets. We'll make a sling to carry him into his suite. You cannot allow him to remain here in front of the guests."

Edgari looked around him. People had not left the party; instead it looked as if more had arrived to witness the spectacle. "Agreed."

"While you tend to your brother, I'm going to look for his magus. For someone who was adhered to the Rinni's side earlier, he is conspicuously absent now."

Edgari narrowed his gaze and glanced around. "I never trusted him from the first day he presented himself to our home."

Estobán did not bother to tell Edgari the damage had been done. The Rinni family might have been targeted by the necromancers from the start. Any and all footholds the death dancers managed to gain inside the *prolatial* families were exploited. The necromancers orchestrated their plans that way. It had to be. Why else would Hazrael insinuate himself into the lives and service of the Rinni if not to gain some kind of knowledge or power over them?

Estobán left Edgari and the rest of the family to help their leader. He took the path out the back of the villa and hurried along the lighted streets teeming with people celebrating the election of a *demigoge*, and headed back to his own villa. He needed his guards to help find the necromancer. This was not an endeavor to undertake alone.

If he found Hazrael, he did not care to face him without even the benefit of a weapon. What he really needed was the presence of Jolen and Theodyne, but he dared not ask for their release now. Not when keeping them in the Rinni's cell might improve Jolen's chance of survival. If he did anything more to endanger Jolen's life, it was not going to be done intentionally.

Estobán entered the guard barracks. "Where is Captain Fessen?"

One of the guards, a young man not long out of training, stood straight as the wall behind him. Terror filled his eyes. "I have no idea. He and some of the others took to the streets to find drink and women."

Then the captain was probably well into his cups by now or between the thighs of a willing bed partner.

"Who besides yourself is available to accompany me on a special mission?"

"There were some of the guards in the garden."

Estobán raised a brow. "Is that a fact?"

"They didn't mean anything by it."

"Didn't mean what?" Estobán was afraid he did not want to know. Granted, he had given most of the guards a few hours leave to enjoy a conservative celebration—nothing that would make it hard for them to perform their duties should the house come under attack.

The young guard fingered the brass grommets on his uniform. "Tests of strength."

"Accompany me." Estobán turned on his heel and started for the door. Even from across the main space, he heard cheers and shouts of encouragement coming from the garden. He stopped and turned back to face the young man.

The guard started forward with only his person as protection.

"With weapons, if you please." Estobán wondered how this particular soldier had been recruited into the household guard.

The man was lean, awkward, and had the look of someone chronically terrified. When he went for his short sword and dagger, his hands visibly shook. "I have one more item, and then I'll be ready."

Estobán waited patiently, watching as the guard opened a small cubby and pulled out an exquisitely made pistol. The guard strapped it onto his side with a leather belt, intricately tooled in a pictorial design.

"Where did you come by such an interesting weapon?"

The guard glanced up from the belt buckle as he fastened it. "It's the family business, Your Grace."

Estobán motioned for the young man to hurry. "We need to step lively before my friends the alchemists are released from the Rinni's prison."

A frown creased the youthful face. The guard could not be a day over seventeen. "Why are they imprisoned?"

"It is a long and fantastic story, but suffice it to say, the root cause is the necromancers."

The guard glanced down at his weapons. In a flash of an instant, the fear vanished, replaced by anger. "I don't believe my weapons are sufficient to kill one who can cheat death."

"We'll worry about that when and if we find him."

"If you don't mind me saying so, Your Grace, but that may be too late."

Estobán led the way to the garden. Cheers and sounds of revelry reached him before he ever made it to the hall leading to the garden proper. He picked up speed, walking at an angry pace until he breeched the entrance with the young guard at his back and stood on the stairs looking down at his men.

They were a sight to behold. Dirty, unkempt, and looking as if they'd already been through a battle, they were as ragged a bunch as he'd ever seen. However, they didn't have to be pristine to hunt a necromancer.

Estobán cupped his hands around his mouth and shouted into the melee. "Attend me!"

The bellow had the desired effect, freezing the men stationed in the yard. The two grappling in a wrestling match on the ground were slower to realize their potential peril. One of the other guards broke them apart and nodded to where Estobán stood on the stairs.

"Grab your weapons and follow me. Tonight we hunt a necromancer."

A ripple of shock moved through the guards a second before they erupted into more cheers. Anticipation of the battle to come lay thick in the air. It rose to Estobán's nostrils in the scent of sweat and male. His guards showed no fear as they dressed and gathered their weapons.

One by one they came to stand near the steps. A voice from the back of the assembled heckled the guard who stood beside him. "If you want the necromancer brought to ground, you'd better leave the lad behind."

Standing so close to the young guard, Estobán felt him stiffen at the insult. He lowered his voice so only the one next to him could hear. "Raise your gun and point it at the man who offended you."

Shock came from the lad. "You can't mean that."

"But I do."

Slowly the guard took his gun from the hip belt and raised it in the direction from which the voice had come.

"The next person to make a comment about this man, he has my permission to shoot. Is that clear?"

Silence.

Estobán raised his voice and gave it an edge. "I *asked* if that is clear?"

Ascents rose all over the garden.

"Then follow me." He turned away and started walking to the villa's main gate.

The young guard kept behind him. Estobán called over his shoulder. "What is your name?"

"Renvic, Your Grace."

"You are now in charge of guarding my person. I intend to come out of this hunt alive."

"I understand, Your Grace." Renvic glanced behind him at the other guards who were hurrying to keep pace. "But wouldn't you wish to have someone more experienced guard you?"

"No. I want a man who knows and honors loyalties."

A look of confusion clouded Renvic's eyes. He seemed at a loss for how to explain this singular honor. Estobán decided not to tell him. Let him discover the reason for the assignment. One day perhaps it would become clear, but confidence was only gained through experience. If the others were unwilling to give Renvic the chance to find his fortitude, then as his *prolate*, it was up to Estobán to provide. Besides, Renvic possessed a hatred of the necromancers that was deep enough to overcome his fear. Estobán trusted that emotion more than he did the training Renvic had to undergo to become a member of the guard.

If he had not passed all the skills required, he'd have never been issued a uniform. That was the bottom line. The House of Medovin only employed the best into her fold. The guard captain did not suffer fools lightly either. The situation suggested a deeper story here, one that Estobán intended to uncover in time.

They left the gate and took to the street. Estobán led them to the opening of the catacombs where he'd taken Jolen. Underground was the only logical place Estobán felt positive the necromancer would flee. With the sigils of his discipline painting the walls to ward off intruders, it was as likely a place as any.

They struck fire to torches and fell into the darkness.

# *Chapter Seventeen*

JOLEN SHIVERED.

Gods and devils it had gotten so cold in the cell. Doubt grew that he'd ever be warm again. He raised his head to see if Theodyne was affected by the drop in ambient temperature. His brother of the robe lay on his side, legs drawn up, and wracked with shivers. His golden eyes were staring forward, unfocused, void.

"Theodyne? Theodyne?"

Jolen reached out a hand to shake his friend. Theodyne's body was hard as stone, immovable. Despite the incapacitation, Jolen crawled over to Theodyne and began to chafe heat back into his arms, legs, and torso. This was no ordinary cold. The cause not rooted in the temperature of the cell as he'd first thought. His breath did not fan around his head in a cloud. No, this frigid air was much more insidious. It came from within and spread outward, freezing every fiber of a man's soul.

"Theodyne. You have to wake up. Fight the cold. It's not real. It's an attack from the necromancers." Jolen shook Theodyne again, this time with a great deal more vigor. "Listen to me."

Theodyne mumbled. The words were too low to hear.

Jolen's teeth chattered uncontrollably. "It's not real. You are in a warm place. There is no cold breeze."

He had a hard time convincing himself that his blue fingertips and numb lips weren't caused by a temperature change in the cell, and that it was indeed an external force that had insinuated itself in his soul.

He took a deep breath through his nose. The air didn't feel cold as it hit his nostrils, nor did it burn his lungs, more clues that the chill was a product of physical manipulation.

Jolen looked around for the source of light that dimly illuminated the cell. From the way it looked, a series of torches hung along the walls in the corridor that led to the cells. He closed his eyes and called to the beings that inhabited the flames.

A trio of fire elementals entered through the bars and spread their fiery wings out to hover over Theodyne.

Pain and pressure filled Jolen's head. It felt as if his brain might push out through his nose. Slowly the cold began to recede. Sweat beaded his forehead and upper lip and ran down his back into the tops of his breeches. He kept a close watch on Theodyne to see if the elementals had any effect on the *terrathant*.

Theodyne curled up into a ball. He grabbed the sides of his head and let out a wail. Jolen leaned over him, rubbing his back in an awkward show of comfort.

"Take a deep breath and try to relax, Theodyne. Don't fight it. It's the necromancer's grip loosening."

"Fucking bastards," Theodyne managed to puff out on heaving breaths.

The sound of running feet filled the corridor. "Fire!"

Jolen glanced over his shoulder as the guards reached the door. Keys jangled in the lock, and the door swung open. When the house guards started forward, Jolen threw up his hand to stop them. "Leave him be. The fire elementals are driving back an attack by a necromancer. Unless you want caught up in the web, I suggest you stay where you are."

The lead guard spread his arms out to keep his men in place. "Do as he says. The fire isn't touching anything. It's hovering."

Slowly the tension left Theodyne. He lowered his hands from his head and looked up at Jolen. "That was in some ways worse than the initial attack."

Jolen thanked the fire elementals and watched as they receded back to the torches where they'd originated. He laid his hand on Theodyne's shoulder. "We aren't alone."

Theodyne glanced at the guards. "You have news from above stairs?"

The guard leader approached and knelt down on one knee. "The Rinni is resting after the evening's… ordeal. Half my men have gone to join the Medovin's to find Magus Hazrael."

Panic clawed at Jolen's insides. "Did the Medovin accompany them?"

"I believe so, but I cannot say for sure. He left to return to his villa to gather his forces. I did not see him after that."

Jolen held his side and pushed to his feet. "Of course he did. It's the only way they'd know where to look."

Theodyne rolled to his bottom. He continued to hold his head in his hands, but not as tightly. "What do you want to do, Jolen?"

"A contingent of guards and a *prolate* are no match for a necromancer. And who knows if this Hazrael is alone or not. He might have been merely an agent sent to infiltrate the Rinni's service. He may have other brethren dispersed throughout the city." Jolen reached down to give Theodyne a hand up.

Theodyne raised a brow. "Let one of the guards help me. You're still holding your side."

Jolen brushed the observation away. "It's nothing."

"It *is*, or you wouldn't be holding it." Theodyne lifted his arm. "If you please."

The guard leader obliged. "I take it you are going after the Medovin."

"Yes." No way under the heavens was he going to let Estobán walk into a trap. "Follow me if you want, but I'm going."

Theodyne placed his hand on Jolen's neck. "Of course I'll go with you. As you said, it's very likely this Hazrael was not alone."

The guards turned and led them from the cell. Jolen had no idea if the Rinni's men meant to accompany them to the catacombs—and since he had yet to tell them where they were headed, it seemed unlikely. As he'd observed before, they were no match for a full necromancer, but they might be more than adequate protection from some of the basilica guards who were under the death dancers' influence.

They exited the Rinni's villa through the garden and right into the middle of the revelry that filled the streets. Getting hit by a flood tide had less impact than swimming in the middle of the current of celebrants. Energy swirled and eddied around them as they pressed forward to the entrance of the catacombs. It would be best to try and enter from another point and head off Estobán and his men before they got into trouble.

Jolen threaded through the crowd to catch up with the guard leader. "Do you know of a back way into the catacombs from here?"

"There are hundreds of entrances to them if you know where to look." The guard held his torch higher. "This way."

The column of guards, accompanied by Jolen and Theodyne, slipped between two walls that separated the villas of St. Marins and LaCana. At the end of the alley stood an altar, a leftover remnant from the old religion. A single godhead stood above a reflecting pool with arms outstretched calling true believers home. The structure had been used as a place where the faithful came to cleanse their skin before heading into the sanctuary for devotional.

Jolen knew this and felt a shudder go down his back as they skirted around the awesome display of a fifteen-hundred-year-old carving. He'd studied the old religion at length and depth. His maternal grandfather had practiced it in secret to his dying day, though to do so was considered a punishable offense by the *prolate* local to his village.

The guard leader turned the carving on the pedestal, and a hole opened behind the pool. Stone stairs were barely visible in the torchlight.

"We have to descend down a level, traverse a short corridor, and then we'll come out into the catacombs." The guard leader gave Jolen a questioning look. "Still interested in going in?"

"Yes. The Medovin and some of your brothers-in-arms might be going into a trap. I refuse to leave them to their death." Jolen took the torch from the leader and with a few whispered words split it in two before handing it back. "If you want, I will lead by reading their presence."

The guard leader shook his head. "You're too important to go first. Allow me to lead, and you can tell me which direction. If it is as you say and impossible for a mere soldier to kill a necromancer, I'd rather keep you alchemists safe until we need you."

More of the guards began to cluster around the opening, volunteering to breach the darkness first. Soon they were going down into the hollow earth, disappearing into the void. Jolen fell into the middle of the line, pulling Theodyne behind him.

Jolen opened his mind, searching as much for Estobán as he did the necromancer. As long as the two he searched for stayed far from each other, a chance remained that their line of defense might arrive in time to help. The thought haunted him as they pushed onward.

The ether was filled with the energy signatures of hundreds of people deep in the throes of jubilation. Still others clung to fear of a world on the verge of dramatic and cataclysmic change. The task of separating out one essence from thousands, especially when emotions registered across his senses as areas of extreme heat, became very difficult. However, the heat was a welcome change after the frigid feel of the necromancers.

Knowing Estobán on the ethereal plane, Jolen had an easier time locating him than if he'd never touched that essential part of the *prolate*. He searched for what seemed hours as their small party continued to press on through the dank, fetid tunnels of the catacombs. Finally as they neared the center of the labyrinth, he brushed up against Estobán's troubled mind. Worse, Jolen detected the presence of necromancers closing in on Estobán's location.

"We need to hurry." Jolen held his side and picked up speed. The torch flickered in the wake of the wind.

"Did you find something?" Theodyne caught up, close on Jolen's heels. "Feel them on the ether?"

The notion that Theodyne could not pulled Jolen up short. "You mean you can't?"

Guards stalled behind them, anxious to be stopped in the tunnels with death dancers on the loose.

"We need to keep moving, Master Alchemist."

"Yes, of course." Jolen jogged to catch up with the point group. He kept the flame of Estobán's presence in the front of his mind.

It became necessary for him to push to the front of the column, or at least behind the leaders, directing them on their quest. "To the right at this passage."

They turned as a unit and kept moving.

Shock and horror vibrated down the tether that linked Jolen and Estobán. "To the left. Hurry!"

Sounds of battle echoed down the corridor. Not armor and metal, but more like the hollow sounds of wooden practice swords connecting in a tiltyard. The unlikely percussion sent a chill through him. Their party rounded a corner and came upon a scene so unreal as to make Jolen doubt his very eyes.

The dead *demigoges* had risen and battled Estobán's forces with brittle bones of their fellows who had been beyond the reach of resurrection. Armed with only femurs and ulnas, with the occasional tibia thrown in, the skeletal remains fought as hard as any warrior against the forces wielding more conventional weapons.

Jolen spotted Estobán with sword in hand, slashing his way through a line of advancing dead men. Estobán leveled his blade and in one glorious arc, sliced the skulls from the bony necks. Decapitated, the dead *demigoges* fell to the dirt, sending up puffs of dust into the air.

A steady scrape of dragging feet came from the adjacent corridor. Jolen raised his hand and let a stream of power shoot from his fingertips. Tiny tornados filled the space, zeroing in on the threat of more necromantic puppets as they entered the chamber.

Wind howled, sending the space into chaos. Bones flew like twigs. Jolen ducked as semicircular bones from a spinal column came within inches of hitting his head.

With his back to Theodyne, Jolen couldn't see what Theodyne did but noticed a tiny shift in the atmosphere of the catacombs. Dust cleared, bones fell useless on the floor. Reanimation ceased. Energy from the necromancer faded as the last ragged robe floated down.

Jolen turned around, looking down all the tunnels, waiting for something evil to spring from the darkness. Nothing came. Any and all residue from the ether that contained traces of the necromancer were now piled on the ground like so much rubbish.

Jolen hated to inform the men who had fought so valiantly, but it had to be done. They had to realize the breadth and scope of the necromancers' reach. "The Bonsuret's magus was never here. He controlled the remains from a remote location."

Estobán pushed his way through the stunned guards, sheathing his short sword as he did. "Are you sure?"

Jolen's mouth compressed into a tight line of displeasure. Anger at Estobán soared in his blood, making it hard to even answer the question with anything resembling civility. "Positive."

Theodyne approached, brushing dust from his sleeves. "No telling where he fled after leaving the villa. This guess was as good as any, but Jolen's right. The only energy in here laced with the necromancers' is the poor remains of the *demigoges*."

Estobán's gaze sunk into Jolen's, an unexpected descent into quicksand that threatened to suffocate. The *prolate* started forward, hands out, but Jolen stepped back before contact was made. Hurt and confusion filled Estobán's dark eyes. "Jolen?"

"We need to get out of here and return to our respective lodgings. Just because the necromancers aren't here now doesn't mean they won't return or with the intention of sealing us in. This is, after all, a tomb." Jolen turned and started the way his party had come. If Estobán had brought his group in the same way he'd shown Jolen, then the entrance by the statuary was a good deal shorter distance to their current location.

Theodyne caught up and leaned into Jolen. "I thought you'd be glad to see Estobán unharmed? You should at least pretend you're happy to see him."

Jolen cut Theodyne a glance meant to shut him up. It didn't.

"No one knows the man better than me. I'll be the first to say he's stubborn, pigheaded, and on occasion makes horrible decisions. He's human. Let him see you are too."

The words struck a chord but didn't smooth all the anger away. "I appreciate what you're trying to do, but I will deal with this in my own way." They marched in silence for a few moments before Jolen lowered his voice. "He's had more than enough proof of my humanity. What I want to see is his."

Theodyne rested his hand on Jolen's shoulder. "Then tell him that. Don't act as if you feel he betrayed you by running off to try and purge the necromancers from Gusan."

As they neared the place where they'd entered, Jolen glanced up and noticed for the first time the shiny gold leaf on the walls. It glowed in an eerie inner fire as if lit from within. The elementals incased inside the metal or fire did not exude a joyous existence. Wendro's words came back on a rush. The elementals did not always get along as the alchemists believed. Power struggles were inherent in their associations. Fire could melt gold, but it did not burn it out completely.

Surely the necromancers wanted to control the elementals, not pitch them in a war with each other? The destruction of such a pass would have far-reaching effects. Not only the people and political systems would undergo a change but the very landscape. Altering the elementals was not conducive to life for any being.

Gods, he hoped he was wrong.

Jolen caught Estobán's gaze as the guards began to file from the depths of the catacombs and up the stairs. Worry had his mouth pulled down at the corners. Heat speared Jolen through. Yes, the *prolate* was human with all the frailties and faults of man. His limited ability to communicate with the elementals was no protection against necromancers, not when he'd been used by them in the past.

"These weren't here when we came down this passage earlier." Jolen started up the steps. "He's toying with us."

"A diversion?"

"Perhaps." Jolen hurried to the top and didn't stop to wait for Estobán once they entered the alley. He hurried back to the Medovin villa.

If this was indeed a diversion, was it used to gain entrance to the villa and find the hiding place of the last fragment of the *Elementica*? There could be no chances taken in its safety. That must take precedence over everything else at the moment.

He raced through the halls to his former room and opened the closet. He dropped down to his knees and pulled back the loose brick he'd found under the floor. The tiny package remained there. The fragment untouched. A sigh of relief came hard. He sunk back against the door.

"What are you doing, Master Jolen?" Wendro stood behind him with his cap in hand.

"Nothing. Thought I left something in here when my things were taken to the new room." Jolen positioned his body in such a way as to block what he did. "It's not here. Perhaps I misplaced it in my packs. I'll have to check again."

He stood and closed the door. "Have you enjoyed the evening?"

Wendro scrunched his cap into a roll. "No. The elementals are unsettled. They're so noisy it's making my head hurt."

Jolen squatted on his haunches to be closer on a level with the boy. "Have you asked for a remedy?"

Wendro shook his head. "Can you make them go away?"

"What? The sounds? I wish I could." Jolen pushed to his feet and took Wendro gently by the shoulder and guided him from the room. "Let's go find Master Theodyne and see if he has something to help your poor head."

"Do you think he has something?"

"I don't see why not. When he came to heal me, he came prepared for anything."

ESTOBÁN PACED his suite, a tiger caged in a humidor. The walls closed in without enough room to move or air to breathe. Savagely he tore his shirt away from his throat, opening it a bit so it didn't decide to strangle him.

The entire evening had been a disaster from start to finish.

What had he done wrong? Why was Jolen angry with him? If anything, the damn alchemist should have been proud of the steps Estobán had taken to attempt to recover the necromancer.

But no. He'd been sulky, cross, and put out that Estobán had given chase. Well, that was fine. As a *prolate*, Estobán owed no man neither apology nor explanation for his actions. He was the law and the judgment.

A knock sounded on the outer door. "Go away. I wish to remain undisturbed."

"Very well, Estobán. But we will discuss your actions in the morning. I am far from pleased at tonight's events." Jolen's voice held more than a trace of annoyance.

The emotions were so strong that Estobán swore he felt them through the walls. Though he'd told him to go away, Jolen was the only person in the entire villa who he wanted to see. Estobán hurried to open the door. Jolen had not moved, but he had his hand braced high on the jamb, leaning into the archway. He held his side over the injury.

Jolen had a brow arched and turbulent eyes. "Do you still wish for me to go away?"

"No. You, I want very much to see." Estobán stepped aside to allow Jolen to enter. "Where did you go when you ran so far ahead?"

"I wanted to see if the diversion created tonight was used to locate the last piece of the *Elementica*."

Light dawned, and Estobán immediately felt the damned fool for thinking it had been simply to get as far and as fast away from him as possible. He lowered his head and shook it in self-recrimination. "I thought you were angry with me."

"I am. As I said, we will discuss your actions, but I thought it more important to ensure the fragment was safe." Jolen crossed the room to the drinks cart and poured a large goblet of wine. He shot back a mouthful and swallowed before turning back around. "Then when I ensured the piece was safe, I turned to find Wendro behind me. He said the elementals are unsettled and creating so much noise his head hurts from it. I took him to Theodyne for a remedy."

"And now you've come to say your peace with me."

"It won't be peaceful. I am damned angry with you, Estobán." Jolen set the drink on the table with a decided click and advanced on Estobán. "Don't you understand what we're up against here? That your guards, though trained well, are no match for necromancers? Do you not know the danger you were in? That you could have been killed?"

Estobán did not flinch from the verbal assault. For with each question came a greater dawning that Jolen was not furious for perhaps losing the chance to halt the necromancer himself, but because of Estobán's level of risk. It had quite the opposite effect than offense. On the contrary, it made hope, love, and happiness well inside him until he thought he'd either fly or burst.

Very calmly, Estobán sat. "Come, Jolen. Sit by me."

"Oh!" Jolen swirled away, his fury not yet spent. "This is no game."

"Nor am I claiming it as such." Estobán leaned back and rested his arm against the back of the lounger in a casual pose. "I left the Bonsuret's because I knew you were safely ensconced in the cells. Your wound had opened again, and I wasn't about to take a chance in your weakened state that you'd succumb to your injuries or place yourself in greater danger. In other words, I didn't want you to come."

Jolen turned slowly around. "Why not? You know Theodyne and I are the best chance we have of defeating the death dancers?"

Estobán gave him a knowing smile. "Do you have to ask that? I wanted to protect you."

All the fight seemed to leave Jolen then. His tense body physically eased. His shoulders lowered and his fists unclenched. "I am a full-grown man with the arts of an adept and blood of the elementals. I do not need your protection."

"Even so, you got it anyways."

"But at the risk of your own skin. That is too high a price to pay to keep me safe." As Jolen spoke he neared the lounger, until he gazed down at Estobán with those sky-blue eyes that never failed to stir emotion. "If anything happened to you and I wasn't there to stave off an attack, I'd never be able to forgive myself."

"Do you believe my guilt would have been any less if you had fallen?" Estobán stood on the ledge between confession and desolation. A stumble either way, and he'd slip beyond the reach of amendment; however, at the moment, he hadn't the ability to care. "I may very well be falling in love with you, Jolen. I'd like you to survive long enough for me to discover if that's true."

"Bán...." The endearment stretched out on a breathless sigh. Jolen all but crumpled onto the cushion beside Estobán. His gaze stayed fixed ahead, not meeting Estobán's.

When Jolen remained quiet, Estobán reached out and covered Jolen's hand with his own. "I don't expect you to declare the same for me, but I wanted you to know my decisions tonight were not based on arrogance or entitlement but on deep respect and affection. I care about what happens to you not only in your role as an alchemist but as a man."

Jolen turned, running his hand down the side of Estobán's face. His gaze lowered to Estobán's mouth a moment before he leaned forward and kissed him.

Estobán wanted to be the one to make the first move, but was glad Jolen had taken the initiative. Any anger Jolen had felt toward Estobán no longer lingered on his lips. Far from it. Jolen's lips tasted of passion, lust, and an unbelievable tenderness.

"Let me make love to you," Jolen breathed against Estobán's mouth.

Heat spiraled outward, sending tongues of flame throughout Estobán's body, lodging in his groin. He rested his forehead against Jolen's. "After your illness and relapse, I'd think you need your rest more than loving."

Jolen pulled away, his gaze never leaving Estobán's lips. "There are ways to make love that do not require vigorous exercise."

"So you've shown me." Estobán ran his mouth along Jolen's jaw, tasting the salt on his skin.

"And so I have." Jolen moved his hands from Estobán's shoulders, tracing a line down the front of his doublet. "I wish to show you more."

Estobán moved his hand deeper in the thick, silken strands of Jolen's hair. The Gods had never made a man so beautiful, both inside and out. Every good intention and kind thought he had was etched lovingly in the angles of his face and arch of his brow. Surely he'd only grow more handsome when age and experience placed lines of their own. Estobán only wished to be around to see the change. To know he was still in Jolen's life years in the future.

However, he had no scrying bowl or way to commune with the elementals in which to ask. All he had was this moment, this time to express how he felt and hope that in time, Jolen felt more than lust or attraction for him in return.

An uncertain smile lifted the corner of Jolen's mouth. "Do you not wish to know?"

"More than anything in the world."

The smile morphed, became so bright it rivaled the sun. "Then come with me to bed. Let me show you all I feel but am lacking in words to tell you."

It was enough to make Estobán laugh. "You? Lacking words? Is that even possible?"

Jolen looked off to the side as if considering the prospect. "It may surprise you how often I hold my tongue."

Estobán pressed his lips to Jolen's forehead. "Feel free to tell me anything."

As if Jolen could no longer hold back his emotions, he took Estobán's mouth in a savage kiss. Estobán matched him, then took control, slowing the kiss, setting a more leisurely pace.

Nothing in all the heavens above could make him hurry this. He wanted to remember every touch, every stroke, and every kiss. He wanted it to feel like forever.

Perhaps it was too much to demand of Jolen, since he'd not admitted to feeling anything for Estobán outside of passion. Love and passion were not the same emotion, though often confused.

Jolen began to unbuckle Estobán's doublet. The sounds of their harsh breathing and the metal clasps opening filled the space between them.

"You've seen me without my clothes plenty of times over the past week. It's only fair I have proper time to study you now." Jolen let the last buckle loose and slid his hands up inside the fabric, then pushed it back to reveal the lightweight homespun shirt beneath.

It might have been made from a whisper for all the protection it gave against the heat raging inside him. Jolen skimmed his hands over the crest of Estobán's chest. He tugged on the shirt. "Take this off."

Estobán grabbed the back yoke of the garment and pulled it over his head, bending forward. He let the shirt fall from his fingers at the look of admiration in Jolen's eyes. If a gaze could devour living flesh, Jolen's would have eaten Estobán alive. Every place his gaze touched, his hand followed. First he moved down the muscled wall of Estobán's chest, then down the hollow to the segments of his abdomen.

Estobán tried not to move, wanting to give Jolen the opportunity to explore at will. The more Jolen caressed, the looser Estobán's grip on control. His cock throbbed with each heartbeat. He closed his eyes and put a hand up to cup Jolen's cheek. Jolen began to tug on the tie of Estobán's hose.

"Lift your hips, Bán."

Estobán's pelvis moved upward as if of its own volition, as if Jolen commanded not only elements, but his lover's body.

He opened his eyes to watch the slow progression of his breeches down his hips and upper thighs as Jolen worked them down. Estobán's cock stood erect, nestled in the patch of dark hair.

Estobán held his breath. Jolen pulled the hose the rest of the way off Estobán's feet then tossed them aside. He ran his hands, hard and calloused, up Estobán's thighs as he leaned forward. Then he was there, taking Estobán into his mouth.

Estobán was lost, completely and utterly lost in the tender ministrations of Jolen's lovemaking. This was not the heated passion he was used to from any of his other lovers. This was slow, gentle, and kind. A complete melding of hearts and temperaments. An absolute communion of souls.

Estobán lifted his hips in time with the movement of Jolen's mouth, offering, sharing all he had and all he'd ever be. Each pass of Jolen's lips and tongue felt an acute torture, rife with sublime pleasure. He knew it would be this way between them. That the heavens and earth would sing and stars would collide, then reconfigure.

Breathing became a challenge as Jolen moved lower, tracing the tip of his tongue along the seam of Estobán's balls. Involuntarily his body arched upward, showing Jolen how much he enjoyed the sensation.

Jolen pulled away and stood, holding out his hand for Estobán. "Come, let us go where we have more room to explore one another."

Truthfully, Estobán had no idea if his legs would even hold him at the moment. His knees might have turned to magma under the molten heat of Jolen's ministrations. "I don't know if I can move."

A sly, knowing smile tilted Jolen's mouth up at the corner. "Then you need to build your stamina, my love. I plan to work you much harder in the future."

Heat shot off inside him like a powder keg blowing. Sparks ignited along every fiber of his being. He moaned. "I must have died in the catacombs and landed in paradise."

Jolen gave a throaty, self-satisfied laugh. "No death will come to you while I breathe. I will cherish and protect you all my days."

It was hard to swallow around the lump rising in Estobán's throat. Not even Theodyne had made such a heartfelt and limitless vow. Forever danced in Jolen's eyes. He might not have come out and said the exact words Estobán longed to hear, but he'd come close. For now it was enough.

Estobán placed his hand and trust into Jolen's and followed him to the bedroom with heart pounding and desire scorching his veins.

JOLEN HAD never been more captivated by a lover. He'd like to believe he wasn't so shallow as to think physical appearance meant more than the soul wrapped in a decorative package, but it would be a lie. He'd been fascinated by Estobán from the first moment he'd looked into his dark, fathomless eyes. Jolen likened it to staring into a starry night sky where one can see the vastness of the heavens and feel insignificant and lost in the grandeur. That, however, was only the surface beauty. Underneath the handsome face, perfectly muscled body, and powerful countenance dwelled so much more. Estobán Medovin was so much more than the crimson robes of the *prolate*'s office.

Estobán lay across the bed staring up at Jolen in invitation. Jolen would not leave him alone for long. Slowly Jolen began to remove his clothes as he gazed at Estobán, feeling the hunger pulse between them like a living entity.

Where Jolen had always considered his own body to possess a lean, graceful strength, Estobán's was composed of thick, hard muscles and interesting planes. His cock lay against his belly, long and fat.

Jolen's breath caught in his throat. This remarkable and powerful man laid out on the bed waiting for his lover had confessed to falling for Jolen. He'd never expected to hear such a declaration from Estobán. The emotions were so strong and took up so much space in his chest he didn't think his corporeal form able to contain them all.

With his doublet and shirt on the floor at his feet, Jolen slid the knot free on his hose and let them fall to puddle around his ankles. He stepped out of them and crawled across the bed as he did.

Jolen kept moving forward, up and up until he hovered over Estobán. Body heat rose from Estobán's flesh. A strong scent of wood, spice, and man filled Jolen's head. He'd forever link the scent with Estobán. The sensation more potent than any alchemical experiment he'd ever conducted. It had the power to hypnotize and control a man—even a stronger one than Jolen.

He lowered his body down to press against Estobán's entire length. He drew his tongue across Estobán's mouth. Estobán moaned and opened for him. The kiss was slow and languid. This wasn't a time to show supremacy but a mating of souls—a calling of like minds and hearts.

The pain in Jolen's side began to throb with every beat of his heart. He'd not let Estobán know the surge of agony making itself known, fanning out from the site. Estobán would call a halt to the lovemaking, and Jolen, for his part, had no intention of stopping. Not even if he fell into a fevered delirium where only desire and need drove him.

Estobán captured the back of Jolen's head, pulling away. "You're in pain."

Jolen should have known he'd not be able to keep that from Estobán for long. "A bit. It's of no consequence."

"Of no consequence!" Estobán scoffed, then gently rolled them so they lay side by side. "Your pain matters to me. How can you think it doesn't?"

Jolen ran his hand down the side of Estobán's face. "I never thought that for one moment. However, I do know you enough to realize you'll want to take this slower if you recognized my pain. I am selfish enough to want this to last all night and to know you completely when morning comes."

"And I am selfish enough to wait until you're well." Estobán rolled away and laid his arm over his eyes.

Resting up on his elbow, Jolen faced Estobán. "And if tomorrow comes and the necromancers win? Will you use that as an excuse to wait? You can't tell me you're falling in love with me in one breath and tell me you want to wait to love me in the next. I won't allow it."

Slowly Estobán lowered his arm. His eyes were dark and accusing. "And if I'm tempting you to fill my baser needs when you are ill, what kind of man does that make me?"

Jolen had the good sense to feel heat rise to his cheeks. Estobán spoke the truth. If he tried to coerce or force Jolen to make love when the injury flared like a fire elemental bent on revenge, he'd think the *prolate* a heartless, self-serving man. "Not one I could love," Jolen admitted.

"Just so. And I do want you to love me, Jolen."

An arc of lightning raced through Jolen's blood. He opened his mouth to declare how he felt but held back. With the world in flux and outcome uncertain, he was almost afraid to grab hold of the emotion. What if he unburdened his heart only for tragedy to strike? How would he ever survive?

A voice, breathy and light, whispered in his ear. *"Take the chance. A love like this comes but once in a lifetime. This is yours."*

Jolen turned to see the shadowy essence of a spirit elemental shifting patterns at the foot of the bed. It appeared as a prism, deflecting multicolored shards of light to the walls.

Estobán sat up. His gaze, too, fixed at the foot of the bed.

"Did you hear that?"

Jolen nodded. "What did it say to you?"

"Love heals. Use mine to cast the remains of the necromancer from your soul." Estobán turned to Jolen with a perplexed expression. "Is that even possible? Can I rid you of the final dregs of that monster? Has my holding back caused you more pain when I meant to help?"

Jolen searched his memory for incantations and rites gleaned in recent times from the old texts. One incantation he vaguely remembered reading spoke of such things. At the time it meant nothing to him because he'd had no lover or relationship close enough in which to practice the unbinding. He wished he recalled the steps of the rite at the moment, but all he had was a sense of intent. In this case that might be enough to heal. He and Estobán were connected on a higher plane. The question was if Estobán possessed the skills to see inside the ether, to go beyond flesh and blood, to find the corruption that continued to plague Jolen?

"Outside of the times you've painted clues in your sleep, have you ever meditated or gone into a trance state?"

Estobán scratched his flat stomach. "I can't claim to be a very religious person. When Desan Karis calls for deep meditation during holy rites, I have to confess, I am usually engaged in solving governmental problems. It's one of the few times I'm granted a moment of peace."

Jolen rose from the bed and lit candles about the room. He then blew out the main lamp, plunging the space into a seductive ambiance. "Do you have any incense?"

Estobán frowned. "There might be some in the wooden box near the wardrobe. I generally don't use it."

Jolen opened the box in question and rifled through various odds and ends until he found a sachet tied with a ribbon. He lifted the small bundle to his nose and sniffed. Myrrh, sandalwood, a hint of jasmine. It would do. Deeper in the box he found a small charcoal disk.

He set the items on the table and picked up a glass bowl. "May I use this to burn the charcoal?"

"Yes. Of course."

Jolen smiled. For a wealthy man who was surrounded by every luxury, Estobán thought nothing of letting priceless items be used for potentially damaging tasks. The bowl, Jolen was sure, was worth a couple hundred silver *damsks*.

He placed the disk in the center of the bowl, then took flame from one of the candles and started charcoal to burn. When it glowed, he threw the loose contents from the sachet onto the coals. Scent, heady and sexual, ripped through Jolen's body. He turned and started for the bed.

"Take in slow, deep breaths, Bán. Let the herbs work their magic."

Jolen watched closely as Estobán closed his eyes and drew in a deep breath. His sensual lips parted on a moan the moment the scent hit him. His thick cock jerked as it once again grew to full erectness.

Jolen watched the erotic scene as Estobán moved a hand down his belly and gripped his cock in his fist. "Yes, that's it. Follow the feeling. Let it take you where it will. Hold nothing back."

"Jolen."

"I'm here." He lay down next to Estobán, his own erection brushing against Estobán's thigh. The heat of the *prolate*'s skin was nearly his undoing. "Touch me, Bán."

Estobán rolled over to face Jolen. When he opened his eyes, they were heavy-lidded in passion. He took Jolen into his arms, kissing him deeply.

Heartbeats skipped, touched, then tripped before picking up again in perfect synchrony. Jolen placed his hand over Estobán's heart, feeling it as it pulsed in time with his own. "Do you feel that? We are as one."

Estobán made no response but moved lower on Jolen's body, licking, caressing, and flicking until he took Jolen into his mouth.

What exquisite torture. What perfect bliss.

Jolen flexed his hips, offering himself up to Estobán. He lowered his hand to the back of Estobán's head, sifting his fingers through the thick dark mane. "Yes, Bán. Just like that."

He sent a tendril of his mind out, gently searching for Estobán on the ethereal plane. Colors shifted, changed. Jolen's consciousness looked down on the bed and watched two lovers from above, and it was beautiful.

Estobán glowed like a beacon of love. His body surrounded completely by a golden light.

Estobán moved away, letting Jolen's cock fall from his lips. He rose, kissing a path up Jolen's side to the injury that burned with the coldness of thousand lonely crypts. Estobán ran his tongue over the seam where Theodyne had knitted the skin back together. Sensation exploded along his flesh. The flat coin of his nipples became erect. His cock jerked in reaction.

Oh, by the Gods in Heaven he was going to have a most powerful release before they'd done much of anything—before the healing had barely begun.

Jolen returned to his body stared up at the ceiling, counting backward from a hundred. Having Estobán's mouth working that sensitive bit of flesh was more erotic than anything Jolen had ever experienced. He closed his eyes and tried to focus on the feeling, of the transferring of love into a spot that had known nothing but illness and disease of late.

He tried once again to focus on the couple on the bed but now saw only a vista of clouds and swirls of elementals as they danced about, triumphant in their rites.

Estobán sucked and licked the skin there until Jolen begged him to stop.

Estobán pulled his mouth away and looked up. "Are you in pain?"

"No. It feels exquisite. I just…." He held his cock away from his body. Fluid at the tip glistened in the candlelight. "I'm going to come."

Estobán's eyes glittered like stars. "You are the one who said not to hold back. Perhaps you might take your own advice."

Estobán shifted on the bed. He placed his hand under Jolen's rear and delved into the cleft of his buttocks. He lowered his head again, taking Jolen's cock back into his mouth as he rubbed a thumb over Jolen's anus.

It was more than a mortal man could take—surely more than his elemental ancestors would allow. Jolen's release came with a fury he'd never expected. He felt a pop in his side and the sensation of a dark liquid oozing from the wound. He ran his hand along the area, but nothing was there, save a slight sheen of sweat.

As his orgasm pumped into Estobán's mouth, Jolen felt lighter and more alive than he had since before being stabbed with the bone blade.

The rite, though not performed according to any text, had worked.

Jolen lifted his arms out to the sides, stretching out as the last spasm rocked through him. After he quieted he brought his arms around Estobán and held him close. "You did it, my love. You banished the necromancer for good."

Estobán smiled. "Is the pain gone?"

Jolen felt his side again. He pressed on the area. The only thing that remained was a slight tenderness that would be considered normal for an injury of such magnitude. "Yes."

"Good." Estobán loomed over him, a seductive god with lust in his eyes. "Roll over for me."

Jolen's breath hitched, but he did as instructed. He heard more than saw Estobán moving around behind him. Shadows danced along the walls, huge in scope. A scent hit Jolen. It smelled of Estobán.

Then Estobán was there again, rubbing scented oil over Jolen's anus, preparing him for the consummation of their affair.

Not an affair—a joining.

It was supposed to be this way. He'd never let another soul ever tell him differently. They were fated mates. This communion of souls was the reason Estobán and Theodyne had not lasted. The Gods had already deemed Estobán belonged to another—to Jolen.

Jolen spread his legs, giving Estobán better access. He felt the warm tip of Estobán's cock, teasing, ringing his anus. Jolen's heart pounded so hard he thought Estobán might hear it. His breathing became labored, and his blood turned to warm syrup.

Jolen moaned as Estobán pushed inside, claiming him. "Bán. Bán."

But Estobán did not answer as he continued a slow, steady thrust. His balls slapped against Jolen's bottom.

Words failed him. Thoughts skittered out of control, and he was lost on a sea of pure indulgence. He became nothing more than a vessel that felt and needed and wanted. Cravings both erotic and transcendent rose in his chest. He wiggled his hand under his lifted hips and wrapped it around his cock. Gods of mercy, he was hard as stone again.

The lovemaking was more than Jolen could bear. Tears leaked from the corners of his eyes, landing on his lips salty and warm. He'd been raised to believe he was a part of something bigger, something grander than the lot of mere mortals. He had always assumed his father spoke of his place as an *aerothant* and inclusion in the Gold School. He'd been wrong.

This love he shared with Estobán was everything. The beginning and the end.

With each thrust of Estobán's cock, deeper into Jolen's body, he stroked his cock, as if he were on top, riding the *prolate* to fulfillment.

Estobán leaned forward, his breath warm on Jolen's cheek. He slid his hand over Jolen's and stroked with him.

Jolen had a vague feeling of being watched by others. He turned his head, and there standing beside the bed were the ancient ones. The elementals who had stood as guardians for eternity. They nodded as one—confirmation and approval.

Couldn't they choose a less inopportune time to visit? He'd never been one for displaying his affection in so public a manner. Not to mention they were ensconced in Estobán's bedroom where they should have been confident in the expectation of privacy.

Slowly, one by one, the guardians faded into nothing.

Estobán tightened his grip on Jolen's cock. His thrusts quickened. "Come with me, Jolen."

Jolen linked their fingers, joining together with Estobán at every point along their bodies. Their hearts beat in time. Their breath rose and fell as one. Intense pleasure peaked.

When they fell, it was as one.

# Chapter Eighteen

SUN SLIPPED through the windows, liquid in its warmth. Jolen rode the crest of the energy, extending his senses for miles over the Holy City before coming back into his body to open his eyes. He looked over to the pillow beside him and the empty impression left by Estobán's head and smiled.

It was no surprise that he'd left the bed earlier in the morning. Jolen had felt him get up, lean over the bed, and kiss Jolen before making his way to the bathing chamber. The loving had been so exquisitely exhausting, Jolen hadn't been able to move but fell back into peaceful slumber.

Perhaps it was wrong to indulge in such lazy pursuits when the survival of the entire Dominicál city-states hung in the balance, but when the body needed sleep, it was a signal. Mistakes were made, and people were killed when sleep deprived—or maybe that's what he told himself to justify the fact he still lay abed when the rest of the household was awake and partaking of the day's activities.

He threw the covers off and crossed the room naked to retrieve his clothes as they were scattered on the floor. The easel and paints were no longer in sight. Estobán must have moved those when he woke.

Jolen made quick use of the bathing chamber, then headed to his rooms for a fresh change of clothes before going to find a meal. He was on his way down the hallway to his door when Theodyne found him.

"Did you manage to cure Wendro's head?"

"Yes, but the poor boy has terrible nightmares. The tonic I gave him made him sleep almost immediately. He curled up in the chair in my room, so I left him. He woke me up as dawn broke, shouting as if someone had torn off his arm and beat him with it." Theodyne shook his head. "I had a terrible time waking him up enough to get control."

"He told me his mother died. Said she went to the late market and never returned. I wonder if perhaps he knows more than he lets on."

"Wouldn't be the first time a lad witnessed something horrific and chose to deal with the events by remembering an alternate history. It actually happens more than you'd believe." Theodyne glanced off in the distance as if reliving a particularly nasty memory. "I came looking for you because Headmaster Oberon contacted me this morning. He wishes to speak with you."

"Oh, yes." Jolen felt the heat rise in his cheeks. His relationship with Estobán was too new to share it with anyone, especially Theodyne. "I asked Headmaster Oberon to research something for me in the archives."

"Like what?" Theodyne raised a brow. "I have been into the secret annex."

"True, but you seemed as baffled as I am about Wendro's abilities. I thought perhaps one of the older texts might have some mention of a sound-energy conversion as musical notes."

The alchemists turned in tandem and headed to Jolen's room. Strange air hit him a moment before he put his hand on the door. He moved back and put his hand up to stop Theodyne from going forward.

"There's been an invasion here."

"How long have you been out of your room?"

The earlier blush returned full force. "Since yesterday evening before we left for the Bonsuret's villa."

Theodyne gave him a worried but resigned look. He rested his hands on his hips and studied the door. "I have a feeling we're going to have to risk it and go inside to see what happened in there."

"I know what happened without opening the door. The room has been ransacked. All my clothes and belongings will be strung about, and they will have upset furniture and cut stuffing from pillows and cushions all to find something that was never there in the first place." Confident he was right, Jolen put his hand to the door latch and opened.

As if the scene he described materialized from the depths of a crucible, the devastation became apparent the wider the door swung.

"I wondered if the diversion in the catacombs was meant to cover someone going through the villa searching for the fragment. It appeared I was correct." Not that he wanted to be in this instance. He'd never wanted to be more wrong.

"Are you sure it's still safe?"

"It was when I checked it last night." Right before he'd been walked in on by Wendro. But it couldn't have happened like that—the shield of protection had given off no indication of being breached.

Sick to his stomach, Jolen rubbed his gut. "Where is Wendro?"

"I left him in my room. He was still sleeping." Theodyne frowned. "I didn't have the heart to wake him after the rough night he had."

"Come on." Jolen turned and hurried down the twisting corridors to find Theodyne's chamber.

They burst open. The chair was empty. Wendro gone.

Jolen turned to hurry from the room. Theodyne stalled him. "He is a servant; perhaps he woke and realized the time and did not want to get punished for neglecting his duties."

"No. There's something more here. I can feel it."

"All right. Let's go retrieve the piece and see if it remains where you found it last night. If it's not there, then we know who is responsible."

"No!" Jolen surprised himself with the vehemence of his denial. "Not responsible. Manipulated."

"Jolen, I felt no necromanical influence on the boy last night. I scanned him when I gave him the tonic."

"Why did you think to scan him at all if you didn't think he was involved?"

"You aren't being rational. Listen to what I'm saying, not just the words." Theodyne cupped Jolen's shoulders in his hands. "I scanned him because of the headache. You and I know only too well what happens after a specific mental manipulation takes place. That was all the suspicion I needed."

"If you didn't find anything, then he's not going to be the one responsible. Right?" Angry, Jolen marched from the room and hurried back to his former room.

The stone in the ledge had been changed, indicating the room was occupied once more. Without thought to propriety or manners, Jolen burst through the door, startling a young couple in the throes of connubial bliss. The woman shrieked and held the covers up to cover her breasts as the man jumped off the bed with his cock still hard.

"Get the fuck…." His words died off when his gaze landed on Theodyne. He bowed. "Master Theodyne."

Theodyne held up his hand. "We will only be a moment and then will be on our way. My apologies for disturbing your activities."

The young man grabbed his hose from the floor and stepped into them, bouncing as he tried to get them on without tripping. "What's going on?"

Jolen opened the closet door and ripped the brick away. The fragment was gone. His heart sunk, and he hung his head. He should have grabbed it and relocated it the night before when he had the chance.

Why hadn't the protective shield alerted him it had been penetrated? He shifted his hand through the air where the shield had been and found only faded traces of the energy. Whoever had stolen the fragment had been adept at unweaving the spell without tripping the mechanism.

Greasy tendrils floated along, stuck to the lingering threads. Necromancer influences—no mistake.

He swung on the young couple. Accusations painted the air in bright colors before he ever uttered the words. "Where is it?"

The young man began to shake at the brilliant manifestation of an angered alchemist. The girl on the bed pulled the covers over her head.

Jolen advanced. "I said *where is it*?"

The young man shook his head. "I d… don't know what you're talking about. We just arrived this morning. We were hired to perform at the Medovin's party."

Theodyne placed his hand on Jolen's chest, preventing him from getting any closer to the couple. "I can vouch for them. They aren't responsible for this."

"Even so, they will be watched." Jolen turned to leave the room. His only thought was to find Wendro and discover what had happened to the fragment. Knowing the child, he'd probably thought he was helping. He might have come back to check the closet, found the piece of ruby, and thought Jolen had missed it while looking for it the night before. That's all that happened.

It did not, however, explain the manipulated shield.

Jolen tried to keep calm, but panic continued to rise. "I'll go to the kitchen and ask Linka if she's seen Wendro this morning."

Theodyne nodded slowly. "Good. Do that, and I'll search the rest of the house."

Jolen left, he heard Theodyne apologize again to the couple. He was good to do so since Jolen still wasn't positive the couple hadn't found the piece while settling into their room. Besides, he wasn't sure he believed their story. Estobán hadn't mentioned a party.

Estobán. Damn. He needed to inform the *prolate* a potentially fatal problem had arisen. He'd do that after he ascertained if Wendro had discovered the piece and thought he saved it for Jolen.

Activity in the kitchen had reached fever pitch. Linka stood in the center waving a spoon and shouting orders loud enough to make a battlefield general proud.

"Linka, have you seen Wendro this morning?"

Her dark eyes cut to Jolen, her mouth about to issue a reprimand when she realized who spoke. "Master Jolen." She gave him a bow. "No, I have not seen that wretch this morning. Try the laundry. He has duties there first thing."

"Thank you." Jolen took off at a run, though he had no idea where he headed.

He stopped and closed his eyes, taking in a deep breath and concentrated on Wendro. Jolen had spent so much time with the boy since coming to the villa he'd know Wendro's essence on the wind during a hurricane.

Jolen entered the astral to complete chaos. The elementals were in a rage, unable to hold form even in the ether. He reached out a hand as a spirit elemental moved by. The being turned on him and hissed.

*"Wendro. Where is the child who reads the notes of your souls as song?"*

*"Gone. You failed to protect him. He's taken the last fragment with him. The* Elementica *is about to be reunited in whole."*

Guilt almost took Jolen to his knees. He fought off the oppression of despair. *"Which direction?"*

*"The covered tomb. Hurry."*

Jolen threw back his head and shouted both mentally and physically. The house shook with power. Frightened servants ran for cover. Guards hurried into the corridor to see what had happened.

Estobán ran from the end of the hallway. "Jolen!"

Jolen met him halfway, grabbing the *prolate*'s arm. "The necromancers have Wendro and the final piece of the *Elementica*. They've headed to the tomb of Akabar Kolhen."

"Guards. Attend us," Estobán commanded.

As they had the night before, the guards fell into line to protect their *prolate*.

Theodyne met them near the front gate. "The elementals aren't responding. They're trapped in the astral."

Overhead the sun cast its shadow, eclipsed by a fast moving moon. Soon darkness would blanket the land. Without the elementals, life would cease. The world would turn cold and dark as a crypt, the perfect place for the necromancers to hold sway. The entire realm from sea to sea forever dark and corrupted by power that was never meant to be wielded by death dancers.

They headed to the catacombs once again. Without the ability to use the elementals to augment their abilities, Jolen and Theodyne were as any other alchemist, any other man. The experience was humbling and fear inducing. Jolen felt as if he'd been plunged naked into an icy river and being told to react normally. What was normal when your entire life was spent hearing the voices of the elementals and living by their bounty? Then to suddenly have nothing but silence where they'd once been?

Every time the guards tried to light their torches, the fire dampened and went out. No wind blew through the trees. No rain poured from the heavens. All was still.

"How are we going to find our way through the catacombs?" Estobán looked to Jolen for guidance.

"Theodyne and I will have to lead by energy signatures left by human passage. Once we know where the necromancer is, we'll be able to guide everyone through." Jolen untied the belt from his waist and placed one end around his wrist, the other he handed to Estobán. "This might be a crude way of staying together, but it's all I have at the moment."

"How are we going to fight the necromancers once we find them if we can't even see them?" The guard captain's eyes were large dark gullies in the shadows of the eclipse. "We can't protect you from what we can't see."

"A valid point, but I guarantee that no matter how much darkness they try to veil us in, they'll not do the same to themselves. The Medovin and I found torches all along the path to the tomb. I think it's safe to say they'll use some light. If they control the elementals, they control the power to light the torches." Jolen addressed the rest of the men. "You'll need to fashion some sort of tether to each other so as not to become separated."

The captain gave a decisive nod and set about getting his men prepared to enter the dark of the catacombs.

Theodyne grabbed Jolen's hand. "We have to be very precise in our direction. There are too many guards walking into death's den."

"I know. Don't think for one moment that I'm not filled with regrets where that's concerned, but we already have proof that the necromancers have made their final move." Jolen started for the entrance. "As of that moment the entire world became shadowed by death."

Jolen opened his mind, flooding it with memories of having come down this way before—letting those visuals guide him as he navigated his way into the bowels below the city. No thoughts of bugs, animated corpses, or intricate gold leaf with an evil message kept him from his mission. The necromancers might have polluted the sacred space and turned it for their own heinous purposes, but that was of no great consequence in the grander scheme. Only the flight to find where they hid mattered.

Jolen led the group around a corner, his essence brushed up against the strong, solid mind of Theodyne. Jolen grabbed hold and allowed their energies to combine in joint purpose. On the horizon of the astral came the sick, infested energy of the necromancer. A plane opened in Jolen's consciousness, as if he looked down on a model of the catacombs from above.

Shocked, he sucked in a sharp breath. He'd never seen anything so amazing.

"Are you seeing this, Theodyne?"

"I believe so. It's dim, though, hard to hold onto enough to concentrate."

Theodyne must have gotten the residual from where his mind linked with Jolen's. The picture Jolen saw was as vivid as if it were directly in front of him. More confident now that they were headed in the right direction, he picked up the pace.

Voices whispered down the twisting passages. A small glow of distant fire pierced the darkness. They were getting closer to their destination.

Suddenly Jolen walked into a curtain of tenacious vines. Where had those come from? He batted them away, but the more he tried to free himself the more tangled he became. Tentacles wound around his arms and torso, squeezing the breath from him.

Theodyne gave a grunt of pain. He thrashed beside Jolen. The unmistakable sound of swords being drawn filled the corridor. Each hack and slash of the guards' blades elicited a scream from the fleshy tendrils.

Jolen worked an arm out, the one tied to Estobán. "Untie us. Now."

Estobán worked frantically. "I can't. The knot won't come loose."

More vines swung down, capturing the party.

Jolen had no idea if the entities were vegetable or animal, perhaps a perverted combination of the two. No matter they had to have fluid of some sort inside. Nature tended to use similar configuration for all life forms no matter the vast differences in appearance. He concentrated on that fact and called to the Grand Matter. The tentacles around his waist began to shudder. A steady drip started falling from the ceiling until it moved from trickle to downpour. A foul stench reached his nose, gagging him.

Jolen tried not to breathe it in, but it was hard. He dared not open his mouth for fear he'd swallow some of the liquid decay.

Finally the tentacle holding him in place melted enough he slid free and fell to the mess on the floor with a splash.

Estobán helped Jolen to stand. "I think it's safe to say they've made some modifications down here."

Jolen only nodded. He felt bruised and sore but shook it off and started forward again, careful not to trip over the fallen limbs.

They forged ahead. Light from the torches up ahead began to fill the corridor. Able to see without using his inner sight, Jolen picked up the pace. Time was of the essence, and they were going to lose it all if they didn't hurry.

The passage hooked around in a U shape. This was not the way he and Estobán had come—this way bypassed the crushing corridor. Thank the Gods for that small grace.

Firelight flooded the area, bright and blinding, as if a thousand suns had been released. Jolen turned away, covering his eyes. Tears rolled down his cheeks, burning. When the flash of white subsided, he turned to see the necromancer, Hazrael, leaned over Wendro's unconscious form surrounded by a host of others he did not recognize, all except for Cesare Medovin.

"No!" Jolen yelled and started into the chamber.

Estobán pulled him back as his foot hit air. Jolen looked down, only then noticing they stood on the rim of a great chasm.

Jolen stared at the necromancer. The man's eyes were as dead as his soul. There was nothing good or salvageable in his nature. He'd been corrupted in the worst possible way.

Jolen started working on the tie around his wrist. When the knot refused to come lose, he held up his arm. "Cut me free."

The guard captain glanced at Estobán before complying with the request. The blade came down and sliced the belt in half. Estobán lifted his hand and pointed at his cousin. "You are dead to us, Cousin! You will no longer enjoy the rights and privileges of the Medovin family."

Cesare had the bad sense to laugh. "You are the most ridiculous little man to ever hold the title of *prolate*. Don't you understand that I don't need you or your blessings? I will take the family one way or another."

"Not if you're dead," Estobán spat.

"Death is one thing I no longer have to fear." Cesare turned in a swirl of a long red cloak and walked back to the tomb of Akabar Kolhen. "Come Hazrael, we have work to do before your master arrives."

Hazrael raised his face to Cesare and narrowed his eyes. "You do not give the orders, mortal."

Jolen watched as the argument escalated. A power struggle between Cesare Medovin and the necromancer was just the opening he needed. He turned and waved for the others to back up a bit. He might not have the elementals on his side, but he had always been physically fit. The chasm was wide, but with enough of a run, he might make it over.

It was the only chance he had. Going around the other way would take too long. Wendro's life hung in the balance—if the bastards hadn't killed him yet.

Jolen walked back a ways, then turned. Estobán blocked his path. Horror filled his dark eyes.

"Don't even think of doing it, Jolen."

"I have no other choice. Now get out of my way, or I will run you down."

Estobán closed his eyes and stepped aside.

Jolen ran as he never had before. The ground was uneven, causing him to stumble a step or two as he neared the rim. He righted himself and gained speed. Air rushed under him as he left the ground. He windmilled his arms, trying to gain forward momentum. The action spurred him enough to see him over the gorge and into the tomb chamber.

Hazrael drew back. His dead eyes widened, as if not sure he believed what they showed him. A scuttling on dirt sounded behind Jolen. Cesare Medovin made a sound of victory. Jolen tried not to turn and watch the spectacle he knew unfolded behind him.

"*Prolate!*"

"Medovin!"

Shouts and protests echoed in the chamber followed by a dull thud and a grunt. Shadows on the walls grew large, dark, and dangerous. Estobán drew his sword and hunted his cousin across the room.

Necromancers converged on the *prolate*, arms raised and chant dripping from their lips in the most poisonous venom. Jolen threw a hand up, calling on the metals in the body. Slowly the advancing necromancers began to diminish, returning to the elements from which life began. Such a fitting end to ones who thought to cheat the grave. But if he thought to reduce them so easily, he was woefully mistaken.

Jolen kept his attention focused on Hazrael. The youngest of the necromancers might not be the leader, but he had the run of this particular route. All decisions went through him and, therefore, made him the one most responsible for the recent outrage—the one holding Wendro's life in his hands.

# Chapter Nineteen

ESTOBÁN CIRCLED the sword above his head. Cesare backed up, coming hard against the tomb. Cesare lifted his arm to block the blow. Reflections in his eyes showed Estobán his own frightening visage.

If any man deserved to die it was this wretched creature before him—a man who had no loyalty to blood ties or family, but paved a separate agenda. When it came to family, it was high offense to take arms against the *prolate*—the sovereign of the city-state.

Cesare braced his other arm over his belly. The shiny edge of a dagger glinted in the firelight. Estobán backed up a step. The point missed his gut by a hair's breadth. Cesare had never been a skilled opponent when it came to blade work. His proficiencies lay in subterfuge and betrayals.

As the *prolate*, it was within Estobán's purview to hold trial, sentence, and execute as he saw fit. With Cesare guilty of so much, it was a pleasure to end the perfidy now.

Estobán brought the sword down, striking Cesare's head from his body. Blood sprayed out in a crimson arc, bathing him in hot liquid. How little it took to feed his soul until it lifted in a cry for more.

Without thought to his safety, Estobán turned, leveling the blade to bring down those in his path. Men fell as trees under a woodsman's ax. Odd how the necromancers bore no blood but a similar substance as came from the living vines. Were these once men, or had they been other, constructed from the bits and pieces of several species?

It mattered not. They were unholy abominations before the Gods. They served the death dancers without thought to the consequences of their actions, and for that they had to die.

A body flew at him, slamming him against the tomb. A hideous face, contorted with decay and rage opened its cavernous maw and screamed. Estobán held his breath, not wanting to take in the foul air it emitted. He reached up and pulled on its exposed spinal column, visible through the being's open neck. Cervical vertebrae snapped with the crack of a broken twig. The head fell back, swinging on the lacy, decomposing skin that kept it attached to the rest of the body by only a few thin strands. Estobán finished the job with a quick sweep of his sword.

More men poured over the gorge. Theodyne had managed a makeshift bridge fashioned from the remains of the vines. At that point, Estobán and Jolen were in desperate need of reinforcements. Wave after wave of creatures rose from the catacomb floor, fashioned from earth, bugs, and any other matter of debris. They were created with the same speed as Estobán attacked. At that rate his rage and energy might fail before he cleared the room.

Estobán dared not look down to see the remains of those he'd thought dead knit themselves together to form bastard versions of their former selves. He knew it happened, saw it in the movement on his periphery. Behind him, the sounds of earnest battle escalated.

A rumble began under his feet. Vibrations started in the tomb and rippled outward. Quake? Had the necromancers turned the elementals against them to use as Jolen had done in the basilica? A crack of rock splitting forced his heart to drop and breath to hitch. If the tunnels collapsed they'd never survive.

Estobán glanced to Jolen for confirmation of his fears but caught a felling blow to the back of his neck. He hit his knees on the stonelike floor, the jar so violent he bit his tongue. Blood filled his mouth, but he swallowed it down, unwilling to give the necromancers more material to build their heinous subjects.

"Bán!"

Estobán heard Jolen's shout but had no notion of the direction it came. It seemed to be everywhere and nowhere at once. His head throbbed in time with his heartbeats, but the cracking of stone continued as an ominous counter beat in the dim light.

Pops and sparks of light rained down on the combatants. Spirals of glowing embers shot outward, racing to their targets. Tiny rods of power pierced through the hearts of the necromancer's servants, burrowing deep before exploding.

Estobán rubbed his neck. Pain lanced outward from the impact site. A large lump started to form there, and it became ever harder to hold his head upright.

But he had to. He had no choice. Pain or no pain he had to press on and fight. Their very lives and those of the entire world were in serious jeopardy. This was no time to let a sudden, blinding injury stop him from defending the whole of Dominicál. Estobán gritted his teeth and pulled himself up, using the crust-covered tomb for leverage.

It was when he reached down for his sword, when his head quit spinning that he noticed the cracks along the protective casing Jolen had erected over the tomb. With each new vibration, the split expanded showing more of the glass casket inside. A flutter of movement proved Jolen's concerns had been justified.

"Jolen!" Estobán motioned for his lover. "The tomb, it's opening."

Jolen's eyes widened. He fought his way from the other side of the chamber to stand beside Estobán. Much of the top half of the crust crumbled, falling useless onto the coffin lid.

"I don't have time to rebuild it. Not with this fight. It's taking most of my energies to—" Jolen frowned and rose up on his toes, looking into the crack on top of the tomb. "Great Gods!"

"What?" Estobán squinted against another stab of pain and moved some of the dirt out of his way for an unobstructed view. There, nestled in the folds of Akabar Kolhen's shifting robes were the horded pieces of the *Elementica*. The vibrations had to have revealed what was not noticeable the last time they were here.

Estobán turned his sword around, holding it hilt down. "Please, Gods, forgive me for what I'm about to do." He smashed the hilt through the glass, shattering the ancient coffin into millions of tiny pieces. The body of Akabar Kolhen lay inert in death. Luckily the necromancers had not as yet resurrected him. Careful not to cut himself, Estobán reached in and scooped out the fragments of the sacred tablet. He shoved them down into his shirt, knowing his belt created a pouch with the fabric to keep them safe. Glass fragments nipped and bit at his skin, but he ignored the irritations. After the pain in his head, a few scratches were easily overlooked.

Jolen did likewise, only since he no longer wore a belt, he too threw the pieces he collected down Estobán's shirt.

"Do you think that's all of them?"

"We don't have to have possession of all of them to thwart their plans." Jolen lifted his head and his expression was sublime. "I can already feel the elementals set free from the ether. They are not happy."

Air filled the chamber, a hiss of hot, angry breath from the mouth of an elemental dragon. Fire and air no longer fought but worked in concert to eradicate their former captors. They were not hidden, not looming as shadows along the walls any longer, but made their presences known to all inside the chamber.

Estobán did little more than stare gape-mouthed at the awesome spectacle. The necromantic servants created from the dirt and parts of felled soldiers disintegrated and returned to the dust from which they sprang.

Guards stepped back from their opponents in astonishment. Others continued to hack and slash to ensure the monstrosities were truly dead. An injured Hazrael shuffled away, dragging Wendro with him through the maze of bodies sprawled down in a garden of the dead and damned. When he turned zigzag lines of blood covered his back, making his clothes stick to his body. Whip marks?

Jolen took off after the necromancer and his prisoner, jumping the desecrated tomb. "You give him back. He's done nothing to you."

"It's not what he's done to me; it's what he'll do for your cause. There's not been one like him since… me."

A great roar came from Jolen. He glowed in maniacal fire. The elements lit him from inside. They burst from his mouth, eyes, ears, head, fingertips and feet. For an *aerothant*, Jolen sure as all the hells looked as if he'd just caught fire.

Jolen lunged for Hazrael, who flung the boy away from him. The small body hit the wall and fell to the dirt floor. Wendro's neck lay at an impossible angle. Knowing it was futile, Estobán scrambled for the limp child. Theodyne hunkered down by his side, feeling the neck for a pulse. He shook his head, tears filling his eyes.

They had not managed to save the boy.

A brilliant, vibrant life snuffed out way too young, the victim of a necromancer agenda. This crime would be answered for—the guilty punished.

It had to be. Anything less would not do.


JOLEN WAS aware of a powerful presence inside him—a collection of elementals out for blood. Vengeance tasted dark and metallic on his tongue. It burned with an almighty fire born from the center of the planet—lava hot only quenched with the death of the necromancer.

Jolen reached for Hazrael, fitting his curled hands around the bastard's neck. And squeezed.

The spark of life had fled Hazrael's eyes a long time ago. Ancient knowledge swam in their depths, telling Jolen that the necromancer had trained as long and hard at his craft as any alchemist. Something else lurked there, elusive as smoke on the wind. Familiar, yet altered, molested from its original purpose.

All this Jolen read as he put more force onto Hazrael's throat. Even as the necromancer turned purple from lack of air, he smiled.

No! This was not the way!

The elementals might want retribution for what the necromancers had done, and Jolen might seek it for what the man had done to Wendro, but they'd gain more by keeping him alive and a prisoner of the alchemists. Bind him in mental chains the way his kind had done Jolen, Theodyne, and Estobán. Unlock the man's soul, and the secrets of the death dancers' plans would be revealed.

It was their last, best hope to gain intelligence.

Jolen threw his head back and yelled. Pain, frustration, and rage filled the chamber. He let the elementals channel through his body, using him to subdue the necromancer but stopping them before they ended his existence. Whatever manner of being this Hazrael had become, he was not of the same makeup as those who were known to frequent the Agia. More human than corpse remained of him. Indistinguishable from any other man, save his long pale hair and magic-washed eyes, and yet he was as fully a necromancer as any Jolen had ever seen.

The energy feeding through Jolen intensified. Fear widened Hazrael's eyes. Blinding light exploded around Jolen. He closed his eyes against the flash that emitted from him. If he ever stood within the center of a fire or the surface of the sun, it could not have hurt more.

A pained cry reached his ears. It wasn't until he felt arms around him and took in Estobán's unique scent that he realized the scream came from him.

"Jolen?" Estobán whispered in Jolen's ear and ran his lips over his cheeks. "Jolen, wake up."

Wake up? He was awake. His mind was filled with thoughts and images he wished to forget. Jolen curled his fingers around Estobán's to show he heard and understood every word.

"Oh, thank the Gods."

Jolen tried to open his eyes, but his lids snapped shut in an involuntary protective motion. "My eyes."

Estobán lifted him up, his arm around Jolen's waist. "I'll guide you from the chamber."

Jolen turned in the direction he believed Wendro had fallen. "Don't leave Wendro."

"It's all right. Theodyne carries him."

Jolen relaxed a bit against Estobán. "And the necromancer? Who has him? He will try and get away."

Estobán gave a snuff of sound that might have been a laugh. "Not after what you've done to him. He'll need a month of rest before he ever wakes—if he wakes."

"I wanted him alive. We need him alive."

Estobán grew silent. Palpable tension came from him. "I'd rather execute him and stick his head on a pike outside my villa as a trophy."

"That will have to wait until after we've gotten hold of his plans. These attacks will only escalate if we don't uncover the plot."

"Believe me when I tell you, Jolen, how much I wish that weren't true."

# Chapter Twenty

AN ASSEMBLAGE of people gathered in the garden behind the villa's back entrance. A small hole had been dug in the shade of an *uta* tree. The casket was carved of the finest wood. Symbols of the five elements were crudely engraved across the lid by Jolen's own hand.

Jolen had never claimed to have any artistic ability. But what the symbols lacked in composition they more than made up for in emotion. He'd poured every ounce of his grief, sadness, and affection for the child into the endeavor, trying to purge them from his heart. It hadn't worked.

His eyes burned with unshed tears.

What had been the point of killing Wendro? Did Hazrael not want the alchemists to claim the boy as one of their own? Had it been a fit of greed or spite that senselessly saw to the boy's demise? Or had he simply not wanted a power to rival his? Did the reason even matter? It was done.

Soft sobs peppered the mourners. Linka dabbed at her eyes with a handkerchief that had seen better days. Guard Captain Fessen worked his jaw back and forth as if trying to hold his emotions at bay.

Jolen stood, stiff and cold, between Estobán and Theodyne. He tried all the tricks in his arsenal to not show how deeply the pain etched scars on his heart. Estobán reached over and touched his hand, somehow sensing Jolen's struggle.

The cleric finished saying the prayers, and the casket was lowered into the ground. Estobán had given Wendro a place of honor in the gardens. The spot was beautiful, filled with singing sunshine and dancing wind, so fitting for a lad who had possessed the powers to read such things.

He held tightly to Estobán's hand. They had all risen to the challenge of fighting off the threat of the necromancers—all of them by choice. Wendro had not been given a say in the matter. He'd been taken and used as a puppet, a lure. Oh, the death dancers would pay for this outrage. Pay until the streets filled with the scent of their burnt robes and ashes floated down on the land like dirty snow.

Slowly those present to witness the rites filed by the casket being lowered into the ground and threw handfuls of dirt across the top, sending up a hollow sound to echo through the garden. Each thump of earth against wood resonated in Jolen's blood like an ax strike.

Failure to save the boy put a sour taste in his mouth and turned his stomach. He had to find some way to avenge Wendro while preserving Hazrael's life—if only long enough to learn the necromancers' plans.

And structure.

Damn, he'd all but forgotten they needed to know the actual structure of the organization. Were they segmented from lower to upper tiers as the alchemists? Or was there one supreme head that spawned evil minions to do his bidding?

Jolen bent down and grabbed a handful of dirt. The rich aroma rose to his nose, clean and innocent. He took a deep breath, pulling the fragrance into his lungs, gaining strength and sustenance from the earthy perfume.

He lifted his fist to his mouth and said a few words, a benediction to protect and preserve Wendro's remains. Then he blew a breath over the handful, infusing it with his power and sent it falling into the hole.

"Come, Jolen." Estobán steered him around to return to the villa proper, but all Jolen wanted to do was to stay in the garden and watch as the servants filled in the grave. A final act of friendship that cost nothing.

Jolen shook his head and released himself from Estobán's gentle embrace. "I want to stay. He shouldn't be alone now." He felt more than saw Estobán and Theodyne exchange looks. "What?"

Theodyne slid his arm around Jolen's shoulder. "There is nothing more we can do as practitioners or mourners. He is in the arms of the elementals now. They watch over him."

Jolen searched for the truth in that statement, but the elementals did nothing more than weep in their own grief. "I don't believe that's the case. Not this time."

He only allowed Theodyne to move him as far as a small bench beside the herb garden. He sat down. "I'll stay here for now. I have much thinking to do."

Theodyne frowned down at him. "All right. But if you get it into your head to go after the necromancers behind Hazrael's outrage, I'll caution you to not go alone."

Jolen's gaze landed on Estobán who stood only a few steps away from Theodyne. "Oh, I know only so well to take protections with me into a battle."

Theodyne glanced back at Estobán before giving a stiff nod and heading into the villa.

Estobán took a place next to Jolen on the bench. "That comment was entirely uncalled for, Jolen. I have no intention of going after them alone again."

Jolen leaned his head against the bench's wooden back. "I know. I'm sorry. I'm just soul weary and heartsore. It's my fault they made Wendro a target."

"You can't know that. They may have had their eyes on him since he came here. You said yourself he had powers you didn't understand. If you felt his potential, I'm sure the necromancers did as well." Estobán leaned over, resting his arms on his thighs. He linked his hands between his knees. "I wish with all my heart we were faster, stronger, better prepared for what we confronted in the catacombs, but the fact of the matter is we had no time and had to act when we were called to action."

When Jolen started to protest, Estobán held up his hand to stop him. "No. The blame for this doesn't lie at your feet, Jolen. It lies at mine. Wendro worked and lived in a villa that bears my family name and crest. He was under my protections, and I am the one who failed him. Well, no more. I will see these bastards run from the city-states if I have to take them all on single-handedly. I will see Wendro avenged. You can count on that. My word as the Medovin and *prolate*."

Love and gratitude filled Jolen to overfill. It did nothing to stop his self-recriminations, but it did help to know his lover shared in his pain. He leaned over and pressed his lips to Estobán's. "I think I may very soon find myself in love with you as well."



*PROLATES* FROM the four corners of Dominicál sat in the large banquet hall of Juan-Carlo DiCarni. Conspicuously absent was one Ignatius Agia.

Estobán glanced down the length of the table at Juan-Carlo. He presided over the gathering as an ancient king might have over his courtiers, and yet, Estobán could find no fault in the arrogance. An odd comfort arose that another had taken the reins and spearheaded the conference while he tended to household matters.

The death and burial of a child was a sad event. He had a hard time shaking it from his mind. Images of the small coffin being lowered into the ground were burned onto his mind. As was Jolen's grief.

"Medovin? Are you with us?" Juan-Carlo gazed at him from down the length of the table.

"I'm sorry. We buried the servant child Wendro this morning."

Condolences were whispered from around the table. Estobán gave his thanks for their sentiments.

Juan-Carlo frowned. Rage filled his green eyes. "I for one would take this outrage directly to the man most responsible for it. Ignatius Agia. If not for bringing the filth of the necromancers into the city-states, young Wendro would be alive. We cannot let this go unanswered."

Estobán leaned back in his chair. "I have taken care of the problem in my own house."

The Rinni shifted uneasily in his seat. "I am heartily ashamed of my actions during the feast. I accused your friends of acts I now know they were in no way guilty."

"You have no reason to apologize," Estobán assured the Bonsuret *prolate*. "The effects of a necromancer are so subtle as not to be noticed until they are firmly engrained in your mind. However, my cousin allowed them to infect his soul to the point he needed excised like a tumor. Redemption, in his case, was not possible."

True, they had only tried once, but he'd known Cesare all his life, and more was at work than a mere necromancer's influence. Cesare had been a bad seed since birth.

Juan-Carlo raised a brow. "Are you suggesting we kill the Agia?"

"I'll leave that to a vote. Once it is done, it is forever. We can have no qualms or dissent. It will need to be a unanimous decision." It was the only way to undertake such an irrevocable measure. "Also, if we decide on that—what scope are we prepared to engage? The Agia and his heirs, all his wives and concubines? Any one of those might be named heir, and the House of Agia will stand. We don't yet know how far the infection runs."

Discussions broke out around the table. The noise grew to a level loud enough to promise a headache. Estobán let the debate continue around him, adding nothing to the conversation. He knew what side of the argument he stood.

The Jezdel combed his thin hair with old, wrinkled fingers. "Will the alchemists come to our aid before we decide? Is there a way they can extricate the influence from the House of Agia before we make the decision to... remove them... from the *prolatial* palace?"

Estobán nodded. "Masters Jolen and Theodyne assure me they can find if the influence is present, but they have to be in relatively close proximity to discover the precise victim."

"Are they the only alchemists who can perform this service?" Rinni poured himself a generous goblet of wine.

"Those are questions I'm not prepared to answer. I will need to consult with the alchemists on the matter."

Whispers started around the table again. Speculations rose, taking on lives of their own. He'd let them discuss their fears and worries without hindrance. They had to reach a decision, but it did not have to be this night. Correspondences were possible between the city-states, though that way was dangerous. Any one of the Agia's agents might gain access to missives and realize their peril or turn the necromancers on the whole of Dominicál before the *prolates* had a chance to mount a credible defense.

Estobán tapped the table to gain their attention. "I would like to introduce a subject that I have discussed with the DiCarni."

Heads turned to look at first Juan-Carlo, then Estobán.

Rinni kept his gaze locked on Estobán. "What is that?"

Juan-Carlo answered. "To reinstate the old tradition of appointing an alchemist at the court of every ruling house."

The murmurs turned to all out astonished rumblings.

The Karnacki stirred in his chair. The big bearlike man hadn't stirred since the proceedings began. "But will the alchemists agree?"

"I will speak with Master Nico myself. As I told the DiCarni when we discussed it, the alchemists will never agree to join houses but may allow the assignment of their brothers as separate entities to assist during this crisis." Estobán wanted that point to sink in before he continued. Master Nico would never allow his order to become embroiled in *prolatial* politics. "To decide a course of action, we need a reliable means of communication. The alchemists can provide that service without the fear of missives being confiscated by the Agia's men. It also helps to ensure those living in the *prolatial* villas do not wear the taint of the necromancers. Any infections will be taken care of as they are noted."

Discussions rose again.

Another hour passed before the group reached a consensus.

Estobán rose from his seat. Heart heavy, but he knew it was what must happen. Grim times were ahead for Dominicál.

They filed out of the house and from the villa. Estobán took his time walking the streets back to his abode.

A guard in a dark uniform stepped from the shadows as Estobán neared his address. "Your Grace? I have a message from the *demigoge* elect."

Estobán took the plain folded sheet embossed with Cardgran DeRosa's seal. "Where is he staying at the moment?"

"He remains in the Rinni villa."

"Thank you, I shall go there directly." Estobán turned and started toward the Rinni's villa.

The streets were only moderately traveled for the time of evening. Most of the visitors in town for the conclave had returned to their respective city-states. The only souls who remained in this quarter were the *prolates* and those attached to their houses. Festivities had not lasted long. Most of the great houses along the promenade had canceled celebrations in the wake of the events at the Rinni villa.

It was interesting to note that the newly elected *demigoge* stayed within the confines of the Rinni's hospitality. Why had he not removed to the *demigogal* apartments in the basilica? Tradition stated the head of the church took over his place in the living quarters after appointment and before the installation ceremony.

Guards stood sentry at the front gates. They parted to allow Estobán to pass when they recognized him, opening the heavy portal. Another guard waited on the other side. He bowed deeply.

"If you will come this way, Your Grace."

Estobán fell in line behind the guard. They crossed the expanse of the *plazo* and on to the private galley of rooms situated in the guest wing. The guard showed him to a large sitting room.

"The *demigoge*-elect will be with you momentarily, Your Grace. Can I get you anything while you wait?"

"Thank you. No."

"Very good, Your Grace."

The guard left the room. The door closed behind him with a quiet click.

Estobán stood in the center of the room. Treasures from all over the world decorated the walls and tabletops. The Rinni spared no expense in furnishing his villa. Estobán's was understated by comparison. There didn't seem to be a space on a tabletop, mantle, or wall where some trinket, picture, or statue wasn't perched, hung, or was stashed. The effect looked like some demented collector had taken all his possessions and threw them together without thought to theme or color. Presentation wasn't even a blind afterthought.

"Makes your eyes burn and head ache, doesn't it, Medovin?" The dry, scratchy voice came from behind Estobán.

He turned around and bowed to the *demigoge*-elect. "You look much improved since the last time we met."

DeRosa waved away the compliment and took a seat in a chair covered in green velvet. "If not for your alchemist, I would have died." He tapped his index finger to the side of his nose. "It shows good forethought bringing them into the fold when you traveled here."

Estobán took the chair across from the holy man. "I feared the necromancers might place one of their own on the Heavenly Throne."

"And the alchemists?"

"Agreed."

A small smile curled the corner of DeRosa's mouth. "My papa used to tell me to never underestimate the alchemists. He called them soul magicians because their beliefs are far more spiritual than any cleric's."

Surprise flittered through Estobán. He'd never expected to hear a member of the ecclesiastical set utter such words. It gave Estobán hope that in time perhaps all the different sects that made up the city-states—the clerics, alchemists, and *prolates*—might come together in mutual accord.

DeRosa laughed. "I see I've shocked you, Medovin."

"Yes, but in this instance I can't say I mind. I hope you plan to sanction the important work performed by the alchemists."

To this DeRosa frowned slightly and held up his hand in caution. "I will, but with only as much latitude as canon allows. I am still beholden to my brethren. If I do not appear to tow the ecumenical line, then I will find myself, once again, the victim of poison. You see, we under holy orders are not without our enemies within the fold."

Estobán nodded in understanding. "I doubt this is the reason you summoned me."

A mischievous twinkle sparkled in the depths of DeRosa's eyes. "In a way it is very much what I wished to speak with you about. You see, I have heard the rumors of what happened to Master Jolen within the confines of the basilica." DeRosa held up a hand to stall Estobán's protest. "I do not wish to know why you were skulking around the halls during a closed conclave, but I do want to know if your alchemist can detect the stink of the necromancers on my guards."

"Yes. He and Master Theodyne both."

DeRosa pursed his mouth and turned away. "Good. Good."

"You have need of their services?"

DeRosa fanned his hand in the direction of the drink tray. "Pour us a beverage, if you please."

Estobán did as asked, handing DeRosa a goblet of red wine.

The *demigoge*-elect took a sip and closed his eyes. "I cannot take a chance that the guards who protect me are under any form of necromanical influence." ·

"And you want Masters Jolen and Theodyne to test your guards."

"Yes. If it can be arranged?"

"I'll put the proposition to them and let them contact you when and how the task can be accomplished. As I've told many of my *prolatial* brethren, I cannot speak for the alchemists. I can only relay messages."

"But the head of the order, Master Nico—the Count de Valencia—he is a friend to you, is he not?" Judging from the *demigoge*-elect's expression, DeRosa already knew the answer.

"I will take the cautious road and call him an ally."

"Allies are good in these troubled times. Do not discount them." DeRosa leaned back in his chair and studied Estobán at length. Finally he said, "I wish your alchemists would be amenable to ferreting out corruption in the church as they have within your ranks."

Estobán held DeRosa's gaze. "For that you must apply directly to Master Nico."

"I shall."

# Chapter Twenty-One

JOLEN SILENTLY threaded his way through the throngs of the faithful as they watched the installation rites of the new *demigoge*. He allowed his senses to run open, feeling the air for anyone who may have been touched by the necromancers. Theodyne did the same on the opposite side of the room. They were both dressed in ecclesiastical robes with cowls pulled low over their faces to hide as much of their identities as possible.

The *demigoge* had set them both a tall order. A necessary one, but tall. As with the other times Jolen had attempted to discover necromancers in a crowded room, he had a hard time fixing the exact locations of the disturbances. The corruption seemed to come from everywhere and nowhere. The guards were much better at hiding their allegiances than the *prolates*.

Why was that?

Arrogance? A sense of entitlement. Intelligence?

Guards did not necessarily have to enjoy a keen intellect to allow them to join the holy order, only brawn. Jolen doubted half of the men could even read the scriptures they were sworn to protect. Not to say that illiterate men were more easily influenced than those of higher learning— some of the wisest men he knew lacked formal education—though the men within the ranks of the basilica lived a rather insular existence. Dogma came with the morning meal and stayed with them throughout the day. Doctrine permeated the walls and atmosphere of the building. In that respect it was no different from the Gold School.

Jolen brushed up against one of them as he moved through the crowd. Instant and unimaginable evil rose, grabbing him by the throat. His breath stalled. Heart shuddered. Spirit elementals walked through the proceedings, ethereal wraiths seeking out those who meant them harm. Each tainted soul they passed fell to the ground unconscious.

A horrible keening wail came from the observation gallery. Cardgran Pontefiore lifted his head from reading the holy text, his gaze chill enough to freeze a man.

"Silence!"

Jolen was close enough to the dais to overhear the DeRosa's whispered words. "Pay no attention to them. They work for me, through my instruction."

Cardgran Pontefiore paled and continued the invocation.

Jolen motioned for the Medovin guards to enter the sanctuary and carry the fallen men from the sacred space. The next step he and Theodyne needed to take would be done in the privacy of a smaller chamber on the other side of the complex.

Theodyne joined him as the last man was pulled from the room. The invocation continued.

"Get me out of these robes," Theodyne whispered. "They feel wrong. A betrayal."

Jolen shook his head. "The only betrayal would have been to refuse the *demigoge*'s request."

"As if we had that option. I'd have felt guilty if I hadn't agreed." Theodyne linked his hands together in the large sleeves of the cassock. "I promised myself when I agreed to become an alchemist to regret nothing of my new life."

They entered the chamber set aside for their use. The unconscious guards were laid out on the floor in a haphazard fashion. Jolen studied the configuration. There had to be a better way, one that connected the men both physically as well as mentally.

"Help me to put them in a circle, feet spread and hands out to the side. Make sure they can touch the one next to them." Jolen arranged one of the men in the position he wanted. "Like this."

Theodyne and the Medovin guards followed instructions. Jolen tapped into the ether, trying to find the resonance of the tainted men. A single connective cord shimmered there but weak, their link to Hazrael dampened by the necromancer's injury.

Another string moved from Hazrael outward, rippling on the ethereal breeze to its primogenitor. He had no idea how far it reached or where it ended. From what he could see, it stretched into infinity.

If he could follow it back to the origins, he might be able to find the source of the necromantic infection. Right now, however, he needed to concentrate on driving Hazrael's influence out of the guards.

"Link with me, Theodyne."

The bond was immediate and stronger than steel, a thing of beauty to be cherished and admired. Coursing through the prism of colors were the shades associated with friendship, and if Jolen read the pattern right, fraternal love. Theodyne looked to Jolen as a younger brother. The association much closer than between two alchemists—and Jolen was filled with a sense of belonging he'd not felt in a very long time.

Jolen turned his attention from his connection with Theodyne to the unfortunate guards placed in a circle on the floor. Between each man hovered the specter of a full spirit elemental. They gazed down at the group with condemning faces. If this extrication didn't work, Jolen had every confidence the spirit elementals would exact revenge in their own way—and it would not be pleasant.

Captain Fessen placed an iron cask with lid open in the middle of the circle. The inside was filled with salts to bind the necromancer's influence and neutralize the effects on the men. The alchemists had learned a lot about how best to extricate an entity in the past three years. Volumes of books on the practice were now readily available from the hidden library, no longer guarded by the elementals.

Jolen and Theodyne raised their hands, conductors giving the signal to begin a symphony. In a twisted way, it might be considered a concert of harmonic notes used to tune a consciousness to feel or act in a proscribed manner. Jolen and Theodyne's task was to score the music to a different arrangement—to one more in accord with the acts of righteous men.

Like taking a jump from a high cliff, Jolen plunged into the icy quay of the necromanical tether. Cold suffused his body all the way to his bones, freezing the very marrow. The essence stuck to his ethereal form, sliding down him like congealed blood. He had to concentrate to conceal a shiver. At this stage he could show no fear. These men needed his guidance and strength, to do less was undeserving of him as a master of his craft.

Jolen followed the stands to the source, feeling Theodyne's presence beside him, keeping pace. The infestation glowed sickly green in the distance, a huge, hulking ball of corrupted thought. It sat there like a cosmic giant, devouring all goodness that flew into its orbit. Comets streamed off in all directions. Tails composed of pure evil trailed behind in a ghostly shadow.

How did one go about destroying something that appeared as a planetary body? Only a god could make a world; only a god could destroy one.

No. That was not the way to think. In this world, he *was* a god. And if not *a* god, then he was an agent of the heavens come to cleanse these wretched bodies and souls of evil.

Jolen raised what passed for his hands in the ether and sent a shockwave of vibration along the cord. The corrupt planet shook, but did not break free.

Theodyne's essence moved around the perimeter, gathering the strings of thought leading to each of the infected guards. Jolen watched as Theodyne picked up the cords and held them tightly. When he shook them, the entire planet swayed.

Yes. They needed more momentum, enough to rock the corruption off its axis and make it tumble and blow away on a celestial wind.

Mist leaked from the sphere, an angry corona of vengeance. It rose in a cloud, forming a death mask the likes of which Jolen had never seen save in horrific paintings of damnation. Hellfires erupted along the strands, burning them to ash. Jolen felt the searing pain burn through the ether and leave his hands smoldering. A cry of agony echoed in his ears, bleeding over from the material world.

He lifted his charred palm and struck.

The nightmare visage's head fell back as the shot hit true. This was no ordinary infestation or suggestion, but the soul of a death dancer living inside the confines of a crusty prison.

And it was angry.

The entity came at Jolen as if it woke from a dream and found its home invaded. Perhaps it had, but if a trespasser showed in this story, it was that of the entity who used the collective minds of the guards to hide away until called upon by its maker.

Oddly enough, the cord that tied both the guards and the entity to Hazrael remained inactive. It lay there as if unaffected by the turmoil surrounding it.

Jolen used no finesse but slashed at the thread, breaking it. Moans from several of the guards filled his head, but he pressed on. One connection cut, several more to go.

If Hazrael was not their controller and a second entity stayed housed within the barricade built by the primogenitor, this infestation had more layers than they'd anticipated. The infection was also a very well-planned and executed possession.

Jolen lifted both arms, deflecting the ethereal wind outward. He was born of the wind; it was his to command. He moved in circles, generating higher gusts with each turn. Little by little, in that spinning, twirling world, he saw pieces of the hard shell of the necromancer's home fly away, carried away by the hurricane of Jolen's creation.

A tingle of warning shot up Jolen's spine. All along the outskirts of the circle, death dancers swarmed, called by their angered brother. They enveloped Theodyne so completely the thickness of their shadows cut off his essence from Jolen. Nothing but the haze of their spectral robes remained. Above the din of their growling came an agonized cry from Theodyne. Jolen tried to reach his friend, but more ghouls filled the space between them. He held tightly to their link, afraid if he let go for a moment, Theodyne might be lost.

*"Tap into the elementals, Theodyne. We have to break this hold, or we'll be consumed."* Jolen didn't know if Theodyne heard him over the fear and torture of his own pain, but he had to try—had to let him know that he wasn't alone in the abyss.

*"These fuckers are strong. I've never seen anything like them. Not even at the Medovin court."*

If Jolen had been in his body, he'd have smiled. The comment was so like Theodyne it came as a comfort, even if the news was not promising.

*"Can you tell if they are separate entities or shades of the one housed here?"*

*"It's hard to determine. They keep changing color and form."*

Jolen had noticed that as well. They were like a school of vengeful cephalopods, using their suction cupped tentacles to draw victims to their doom. Each arm lashed out, giving a bright, sick hue to the world, stealing a bit more of the light from the ethereal plane.

An idea came to Jolen then. *"Search for the center, meet me there."*

*"I'll try."*

He'd better more than try. Their survival and that of the guards depended upon it.

Jolen fought his own way through the mass of festering death. The entities tried to hold him back. They bandied him about, throwing him from one to another and back again. He turned, twisted, and stumbled, no longer knowing which way was up or down.

There had to be something he could do to combat them, sweep them out of his way to allow him to pass unhindered. Yet nothing came to him. No defense seemed enough against these particular foes.

If one died they simply sprouted more. With a never-ending supply of combatants, how were they to ever win?

Jolen continued to push his way to the center—or what he thought was the center. Masses of thick limbs and trunks rose to cover his escape. They were not going to let him pass so easily.

In this world, he could be whatever he wanted, and right now seemed a time for more aggressive measures. He fashioned his essence into the shape of a blade, then began to slice and cut his way through the tenacious arms.

Each severed limb grew two in their place. They wrapped around his ethereal body and squeezed his soul.

He lifted what passed for his arm and cut the head from one. Dark matter oozed from the neck, sending millions of black droplets outward. As the liquid spread, the drops grew until they were a rolling wall of pitch.

Again, Jolen pressed up and out with his hand, using the power of air to beat the wall back. The tide changed and buckled in the opposite direction. While the mass of necromancers fought the wave, Jolen went under and around, coming up on the other side. Theodyne came out beside him.

*"Do you see the anchor?"* Theodyne's essence shimmered as he turned to look for the spot where the infestation was grounded to the guards.

*"I arrived only a step ahead of you."* Jolen paid no more attention to the conversation as he searched for anything that might look as if it held the necromancer's influence in place.

The sphere where the entity had risen sat before them, cracked down the center like an egg whose inhabitant had hatched. If they destroyed this domicile, then the entity would have nowhere to hide.

Jolen made his essence big, towering over the structure as if it were nothing more than a small shell washed up on a beach; then he crushed it underfoot.

*"Stop! Jolen, I see the knots now."*

Theodyne grabbed the pieces that were held together by corruption and nightmares. With a turn of his wrist, they fell away fluttering on the celestial breeze, going up like kite tails chasing the wind.

The entity returned, rising higher than Jolen's form. It held its arms out and roared. He held on, quickly diminishing to avoid the blast of sound.

Spirit elementals rushed in to protect, tearing the beastly creation to pieces. Air elementals blew the fragments into the casket, sealing the damn thing in forever.

There had been very little style or ritual here. The destruction not performed by the book or regimented by rote. Both Jolen and Theodyne had flown blind and reacted instead of doing as they were taught.

Now they needed to clean up the mess they made and ensure no more attachments lingered to either Hazrael or the possessing entity. All cords to the primogenitor had to be completely severed and burned away.

It was going to be a very long day.

ESTOBÁN WOKE when he heard the outside door to his suite open and close. He'd spent most of the night tossing and turning, wondering if he'd ever see Jolen again or if the extraction might claim his life.

He rose and pulled on a robe before stepping out into the salon.

Jolen stood at the drink table, his hand on a bottle of amber liqueur.

"That one might be too strong if you haven't eaten today."

At the sound of Estobán's voice, Jolen turned and lifted the glass. "At the moment I just can't seem to care." He kicked the drink back, then set the glass on the table.

"Come sit. I'll have some food brought up to you."

Jolen waved away the offer. "If you don't mind, I only want to fall into bed."

"You can do that as well." Estobán took a few steps, bringing him close enough to touch Jolen's cheek. He turned his lover's face to the light. "You look terrible."

Jolen gave a brittle laugh. "I feel as if I've aged a score of years today. It's amazing that no matter how much training I've had over the years, it all seemed to flee at the sight and scope of the influence thrust upon the basilica guards."

At the news, Estobán guided Jolen into the bedroom. "Was it different than the one inside the Rinni?"

"Yes. I've never seen one like this. Not in all my readings. It only reinforces what we've suspected all along: the necromancers can take many forms and hold a person in thrall in various ways. The worst part is the fact we can't be sure we got it all. Some of the infection might still remain." Jolen shuffled to a halt by the bed and began stripping. When he finished he went face down onto the mattress.

Snores erupted a few breaths later.

Estobán removed his robe and crawled in bed beside Jolen, moving so he held him close. He might not be able to protect him on the astral plane, but he'd damn sure do so in the physical realm.

Estobán woke several hours later to the feel of lips moving over his body and the caress of insistent hands over his thighs. He opened his eyes and watched Jolen move down in erotic pursuit of a very erect goal.

"Did you replenish your strength?" Estobán placed his hand in Jolen's hair, brushing it back from his face.

"Enough for this."

Estobán held onto the world as Jolen took him into his mouth. By rights he should protest and pull away, but it felt too good to resist, and who knew how long they'd have to indulge. The world was in turmoil. Happiness had to be wrested from the arms of those who thought to take it from the world. If Jolen wanted to fill these remaining hours by making love, so be it.

He moved his hand, skimming it through Jolen's hair to cap his skull. "If you turn around, I can reciprocate."

Jolen looked up, taking his mouth from Estobán. "No, let me do this for you. You've given me so much; I only want the opportunity to give back."

Heat raced through Estobán's blood. "You have. In more ways than I can possibly count."

Jolen moved up and took Estobán's mouth in a savage kiss. They rolled over the bed, each trying to claim possession of the other.

Estobán had tried once before to hold a strong man to him, and he'd failed in every way possible. If Jolen left him, he'd be desolate. With Jolen pinned beneath him, Estobán lifted his head and gazed down into those blue eyes that never failed to move him.

"The other *prolates* and I are going to petition Master Nico and the Gold School to begin sending alchemists back to the courts." Estobán searched Jolen's face to see if he understood what seemed so hard to say.

Jolen brushed his thumb tenderly across Estobán's cheek. "And you want me to come to Lancor?"

"If Master Nico approves the proposal and you agree. I don't wish to conscript you into a position you might find uncomfortable or distasteful."

Jolen frowned, then braced his arms on Estobán's and rolled him away, putting some space between them. In doing so, they now lay face-to-face, side by side. Jolen propped his head up on his hand. "Why would I find living in Lancor by your side distasteful?"

Estobán sat up, turned away from Jolen. "Because you may have ideas and dreams of your own you wish to explore. There might be other avenues to defeating the necromancers you wish to take. I don't want to be the one to hold you back from doing as you wish."

"Bán, love?" Jolen rose and touched his hand to Estobán's shoulder. "Look at me."

When fear kept Estobán in place, Jolen slid his arms around Estobán and pulled him close, back to chest. Estobán closed his eyes against the tenderness.

Breath, warm and sensual, bathed his neck. "Placing alchemists in each of the courts is a wonderful idea and quicker, more reliable means of communication between the city-states. I'm sure Master Nico and the

Adepts' Council will agree. I want to be wherever you are, fighting by your side."

Estobán turned halfway so he could see Jolen's handsome face. "You mean that? You won't feel like you're being kept?"

Jolen let out a crack of laughter. "No. It's not as if I'd be living off your sufferance. I am a master-level alchemist and can make my way in the world. As an attaché to the Medovin court I'd be contributing my own skills to keeping Dominicál safe from the necromancers. I hardly think that institutes being kept."

Estobán let out a breath he didn't realize he was holding. He placed his hands over Jolen's. "I want time with you. To know you, understand you, and to enjoy your company and companionship."

Jolen ran his hand lower down Estobán's belly. "I'll give you all that and more. The only thing I ask in return is that you are loyal to me. If you wish to take another lover, you tell me first so I can withdraw. No matter what transpires between us, I will always uphold my commitment to caring for the best interests of Dominicál."

Now Estobán fully turned in the circle of Jolen's arms. "Another lover? Are you mad? Why would I do that when I've finally found my equal?" At Jolen's shocked expression, Estobán smiled. "As you told me once before, you are the *Air*. And don't we all need air to breathe?"

Jolen's smile blinded. He hung his head and started to laugh harder than Estobán had ever heard him. When he looked up again, his eyes sparkled with love and happiness. "Oh, Bán, you are the most sentimental and loving man I have ever met. Even your melodramatic words touch me like no other."

Consternation made Estobán frown. "It was supposed to be heartfelt. Not make you laugh."

Jolen slid his arm around Estobán and pulled him so close their lips touched. "Don't you know laughter in a time of great sorrow is a gift? When someone presents it to you, you are blessed beyond measure." Then he took Estobán's mouth in a tender kiss.

The lovemaking that had threatened to ignite the room earlier had mutated into a slow sharing of hearts and bodies. There was no rush, no urgency, only the need to show one another how much they cared and the mutual joy of being together.

Estobán made it his mission to explore every taut plane of muscle and river of vein on Jolen's graceful body. No one seeing him in his masters' robes would ever guess what sheer beauty and strength lay beneath the fabric. What a shame to ever cover up such perfection.

Estobán skimmed a hand up Jolen's side, enjoying the way his touch brought a moan to Jolen's lips. "I am going to commission an artist to paint your portrait as you are now," he whispered against Jolen's heated skin. "Hot. Aroused. Beautiful."

Jolen turned hooded eyes to Estobán. "I'd rather you paint me."

Estobán kissed a trail over Jolen's body, until he reached his mouth. "I could never do your image justice."

Jolen lifted Estobán's hand to his mouth and kissed his knuckles. "Ah, but the work would be done by someone who knows the subject intimately."

"And can only paint in fits and starts during his sleep."

Jolen ran his free hand down Estobán's back, over his bottom and squeezed his cheek. "I think in this case the elementals might be persuaded to assist you while awake."

A knock on the outer door stalled the lovemaking. Jolen let out an exasperated sigh that mirrored Estobán feelings.

Estobán rose and picked up his robe and put it on, tying the sash around his waist with something close to violence. All he wanted was to make love to Jolen and sleep a peaceful night through.

He moved to the salon and commanded his late-night visitor to enter the apartment. Silas slipped in the door, his expression urgent. "What is it, man?"

"Master Nico has appeared in the large mirror in the upper hallway. He wishes to speak with you and Master Jolen immediately, Your Grace."

Estobán realized the alchemists could speak through water, but mirrors? The idea alone gave him a cold shiver. "I'll alert him. Please tell Master Nico it will be a few moments."

Estobán turned back and headed into the bedroom. "Master Nico is in the mirror waiting for us to arrive. He wishes to speak with us."

Jolen jumped off the bed. "The mirror? Then it is serious. This time of night he probably didn't want to risk someone not seeing him in a bowl of water." He picked up his clothes where he'd discarded them earlier and only made a feeble attempt at putting them on properly.

Estobán threw on some breeches and one of his *prolate*'s robes over them. He'd forgo the shirt for now.

They left the apartment and crossed the upper story to the large mirror in the hallway. Instead of the opposite end of the corridor reflected in the glass, Master Nico sat behind his desk in what appeared a private office. He tapped a quill against the desk as if marking time until their arrival. When he spotted them, he set the quill aside and folded his hands.

"Sorry to pull you from your beds, but I have an urgent mission for you, Master Jolen."

Estobán felt Jolen stiffened beside him. "Yes, of course. What is it?"

Master Nico called him closer and lowered his voice. "I want the pieces of the *Elementica* taken to the Delaneux school immediately. Do not waste time or stop on the way. The sooner it is safe within the walls of a secured structure the better. Also, I want the necromancer agent you caught transported there as well. We will debrief him at length once he's behind fortified walls."

Estobán was hit with an overwhelming urge to defend his house. The walls of the Medovin Gusan villa *were* fortified. No one could breach their defenses. Yet the argument fell apart when he remembered it was within these very walls the last piece had been hidden and from where it had been taken. Master Nico had every reason to doubt his ability to keep something as sacred as the *Elementica* safe from the necromancers, even if he had risked his life to regain it.

Master Nico turned his attention from Jolen to Estobán. "Your Grace." He bowed his head in respect. "Word has reached me that you plan to petition me for the right to include alchemists in the *prolatial* courts. I thank you for cautioning your contemporaries in the matter of how this discipline operates. I will discuss this matter with the Adepts' Council but will give you my provisional blessing. I stand behind my feelings in the past of not becoming a part of the government but acting as a separate but equal entity. As long as the other *prolates* abide by this tenet, I will do my best to ensure the council votes in your favor."

Estobán nodded in thanks. Theodyne must have contacted Master Nico at some point during the day, though how Theodyne knew the bent of the meeting with the other *prolates*, Estobán hadn't a clue. Perhaps he didn't want to know. Master Nico was amenable to the suggestion, and that was all that mattered.

# Chapter Twenty-Two

JOLEN WISHED with all his heart Estobán had accompanied him on this journey. They had not even reached the halfway point, and already he missed his lover so much the pain had become acute.

He glanced over at the small caravan of riders to the trussed up form of Hazrael. At the outset of the trip, Jolen had suggested they drag the prisoner behind the wagon, but his idea was shot down by Estobán's guard captain. Damn the man and his morals. Jolen realized it was his own sense of urgency and need to uncover the necromancers' plot that kept Hazrael alive in the first place, but that didn't mean he had to like his decision. Prudence and want were often bitter enemies.

Theodyne rode beside the cart on a horse. Memories of a similar trip a few years before rose in a mirage of feelings too intense to hide. How he'd hated and resented Theodyne in those first days. Beautiful, strong, confident, intelligent. What was to like about him?

A smile tugged Jolen's mouth. What a true and dear friend he'd become.

Theodyne pulled his horse a little closer to the wagon. "Why are you smiling? The elementals whispering naughty things in your ears?"

Jolen shook his head. "No. Comparing you now to how you were when you first joined our order."

"And this amuses you?" Theodyne raised a brow in mock offense.

"Not in the least. It only means I was very glad you were there for us when we needed you most." The reason for Theodyne's assistance was a sobering thought. A chill moved through Jolen, and he pulled his cloak closer to his body.

At times he feared the infection from the necromancer bone-blade might return. The thought frightened him in no small measure. But he'd had no relapse in the days that followed Estobán's healing lovemaking, no sense of invasion. He had to believe this time the healing had worked or risk going mad with worry.

A noise came from the direction of the necromancer. For the first time in days a shock of gray shone from the slit of the man's eyelids. It didn't appear any intellect dwelled in that gaze. It might very well be the elementals kept the man alive but had rendered him useless for the alchemists' purposes. If that proved the case, then they had no reason to put up the illusion of allowing him to live. Better to put him to death and avenge Wendro.

The scold's bridle kept Hazrael from spitting any spells to hinder their travel, though judging from the vacant look, it might have been unnecessary. The Gods above knew Hazrael's accomplices followed their progress as hungry shadows across the land. For this reason, Jolen had bid the guards to take them the long way to the school and not pass through the streets of Delaneux and the Agia's lands.

The circuit added days more to the journey, but what the party lost in time, they more than made up for in safety. Traveling too close to those areas where the necromancers already had a steady foothold might prove dangerous.

Unintelligible grunts and gurgles issued from the necromancer. Jolen watched Hazrael as the death dancer's panic increased. The straps holding him to the horse cut across his chest. Each wiggle and thrash made the horse sidestep, trying to get away from the active burden on its back.

"Stop, or you'll injure the mount, and Gods help you if you ruin one of the Medovin's horses," Jolen warned.

Another string of sounds accompanied by twists and turns.

"Fight all you want, but you're not going to get out of the shackles. I made sure of it."

A gargle that sounded suspiciously like a curse issued forth.

Jolen lifted his hand, collecting crisp energy from the air into a small lightning bolt. He fired it at Hazrael, striking the necromancer in the center of the chest. A shout rose, then cut off.

The guard captain raised a brow. "What did you do to him?"

"Nothing permanent. Only enough to shut him up for a while."

Captain Fessen gave a wicked grin. "On behalf of my troops, we thank you."

Light began to fade from the sky, the sun sinking below the foothills off to the west. They only had about another hour or so of travel time left before full night fell. With luck they'd make it to the valley proper before having to stop and make camp.

Each moment they lingered between the rises put them at greater defensive disadvantage. Apprehension grew the more they forged a path eastward. Air became heavy, hard to breathe through, as if smoke from a thousand campfires remained on the ground.

Jolen tried to make contact with the elementals living in the area, but they were not speaking to him. The sensation differed from when the necromancers held all the pieces of the *Elementica*. For that short, horrific time, he could not feel their presence at all. At present, Jolen knew they were around, but they chose to ignore the situation.

Was this recompense for having allowed the necromancers to gather and control so many pieces of the sacred stone without the alchemists' knowledge? Or were they simply biding their time? It was hard to tell. Oftentimes full elementals had their own agenda that did not necessarily follow along with the wishes and dreams of man.

"Look!"

Jolen sat up in the wagon, searching for the direction the shout had originated. The point guard motioned to the north.

The sky had grown incredibly dark, much more so than the time of evening might suggest. Great storm clouds had moved in with unbelievable speed and then stalled over the northern rise. The tempest had a menacing quality. It watched and waited, calculating the best time to strike.

Jolen was torn. Was it better to stay and fight the weather or to try and outrun it? Judging from the size, it might be impossible to run far or fast enough to get away from the fury once unleashed.

Theodyne turned his horse in the direction of the storm and stared. The last rays of daylight painted golden across his tense face, his expression just as angry as the clouds above. "They've managed to bring a few *aerothants* and *aquathants* over to their side."

"Corruption is a universal concept, Theodyne." Jolen rose to stand on the front of the wagon to get a better look at the enemy sky. "Why would you believe for one moment that the elementals were immune?"

It was enough to break a heart, but it was not the end-all. The alchemists still retained the greater number of elementals on their side, and having tried to control those beings by force, the necromancers had not made any allies.

"What should we do, Master Jolen?" Captain Fessen shifted in his saddle, trying to keep the horse in place with his knees. "Our route is to take us northeast. We'll run right into the storm."

"Is there no other pass to take that will not lead us either into a squall or through Delaneux?"

Captain Fessen lifted his hand and snapped his fingers twice. One of the men at the rear came forward to answer the summons.

"Aye, Captain."

"Maps."

"Aye, Captain." The man reached behind him and pulled one out of a saddle holder. He eased his horse up close to his captain so they might look at the map together.

Jolen moved to the side of the wagon, closest to where they conversed. Theodyne rode up to them, also looking at the map.

"We will have to make haste, no matter the direction we take. Unfortunately we'll not make shelter before we lose the light." Theodyne's horse stamped and threw its head in a nervous manner.

Captain Fessen moved his finger along a line on the map. "We can take the southeast pass and double back around and swing north at the Barangate Road."

"No. That road hasn't been traveled in years by anyone of repute. I doubt all the passages are still maintained," Jolen protested. "It will prove as dangerous as heading into the storm or riding through Delaneux."

"Then there is but one other road, and that will take us through the hills and into the mountains. It is dark and travel rough. We may have to leave the wagon to negotiate the terrain." Captain Fessen directed the last of his assessment to Jolen.

"Impossible. How will we transport the pieces of the *Elementica*? The iron cask is too heavy for a horse to carry without a wagon." It was a weak argument, but it was all Jolen had at the moment. He'd rather walk the rest of the way than to get on a horse.

"Better to split up the pieces as they once were and carry them separately. They will be easier protected." Theodyne turned his horse in the direction of the road they were to take. "We'll take the wagon as far as we dare. Master Jolen and I can augment the light as much as possible until we make the road south."

"We will have to stop and rest the horses at some point." The guard gave his steed a pat on the neck.

"Not until that storm passes or we clear the thunderhead." Judging from Theodyne's expression, he wasn't going to have his order countermanded.

"Then let's pull out." Jolen made his way back into the wagon and the cask. If they were going to ditch the wagon when they reached the south road, then he'd better make sure they were prepared to move fast when the time came.

A linen sheet lay in the corner, a piece of bedding that Estobán had insisted Jolen bring on the journey. The Medovin family crest was embroidered at the top along with the motto.

"Sorry about this, love, but the *Elementica* needs it more than my bed." Jolen took the bottom of the sheet and ripped it down the center. He was sure Estobán would understand. Material goods were nothing compared to the safety of the ruby tablet.

"Jolen! We need your light," Theodyne called from outside the wagon.

"I'm busy at the moment. Light the torches, and I'll send out what energy I can." Jolen continued to work while pushing the boundary of his essence outward to find the hearts of flames in the guards' torches. He disagreed with the use of light as they moved through open ground. Nothing covered the route to hide the glow from the distance. Any enemy with a spyglass could easily spot their location from a vantage point on the surrounding hills.

Light flashed and flickered. Not from either him or Theodyne, but from above. Jolen leaned over and brushed the wagon flap out of the way and looked up into the sky as a burst of lightning snaked overhead in a brilliant arc.

They had run out of time.

It was best to remain where they were and ride it out. Jolen worked faster, splitting the sheet into strips to make slings for the fragments. With the preparations ready, the pieces could be divided quickly and given to each of the guards in their company. He hesitated doing so now. The iron cask was there to protect and keep the energy from the ruby tablet inside the confines, disabling the necromancers from tracing their party's location by the *Elementica*.

They traveled hard as they dared. Fingers of lightning stretched out as if pointing out their progress through the end of the valley. Rain fell in a hard sheet, drowning the torches. Blind from the downpour and lack of light they couldn't advance in the dark. They didn't dare. Halt was called. Jolen climbed down from the wagon to help secure and care for the horses. He might fear riding the great beasts, but he was more than happy to oblige the others and help tend their mounts.

Icy pellets spit at them from beyond the darkness. Jolen rubbed down one of the wagon horses, while the driver worked the other. The horses shifted nervously as the storm intensified.

Water stood on the ground. Every step Jolen took splashed. His shoes were in danger of sticking in the mud. Motion behind him, a terrible crack of wood breaking under pressure and Jolen turned. In the flash from a lightning bolt he saw the wagon sliding sideways down the hillock.

One. Two. Three steps. He jumped up onto the bed and scrambled in the dark for the strips of bedding and the iron cask.

"Theodyne!"

The wagon continued to slip and slide in the mud. Jolen almost lost his footing. Rain breached the covering. Any water collected on the tarp cascaded inside the bed with the force of a falls.

Drenched, Jolen wiped his wet hair from his eyes and tried to drag the cask to the end of the wagon. The entire vehicle began a slow spin as the wheels lost traction. The brakes no longer worked to keep it grounded in place.

"Theodyne!"

A shake, a rumble. "What are you doing?"

"We need to get the cask off here, or we're going to lose it." Irritated he even had to explain such a necessity, Jolen grabbed one of the handles. "Take the other side."

Together they moved the cask to the end of the wagon. The vehicle gained speed under the rush of flood waters.

"Jump, Jolen!"

Jolen tightened his grip on the handle and leapt for the ground. The wagon swung around, knocking him in the back, sending him crashing into the mud. The momentum brought Theodyne down as well.

Jolen lost sight of his brethren as the wagon passed over him. He rolled into a ball to protect himself from getting hit by the useless wheels when the cart spun again. In the fall, he'd lost his grip on the cask. Only the Gods knew where it had landed.

Damnation! He had to find it.

The wagon rotated in the rising river of muck washing down from the hills. Jolen waited until he felt the wheel brush by then scurried out from underneath, crawling on all fours like a wounded dog.

He lifted his hands, outstretched, palms up, urging the water to recede. It did not respond on the elemental level. This flood served another master.

Rage filled his heart, sent flames licking his blood vessels. Jolen fisted his hands and bent back, shouting at the sky.

"You can hide behind the elements, but I *will* find you. And when I do, I *will* see the Reaper escorts you to the gates of hell."

As if in reply something hit his leg. Hard. The speed and accuracy of the impact caused him to lose balance and once again land in the mud. He felt along the sides of the object and let out a joyful sob. The iron cask.

Jolen used the current to help him move the cask to the horses. Those great beasts were now ankle-deep in the water. They stamped and jerked, trying to be free of their handlers—to flee to safety and higher ground. Animals often showed more common sense than humans.

The world had faded to a black pit of nothingness. The only sensations were the ceaseless rain, the rushing tide of the flood, and the endless fear of dying before journey's end.

A hand on his shoulder startled Jolen. He turned quickly, barely making out Theodyne's face as a cloud cleared from the moon.

"We need to move to higher ground."

"Help me with this. We can't leave it behind." Jolen pulled it closer to the frightened horses.

Theodyne lifted a rope he wore like a bandolier. "Here, use this, and you can drag it behind."

With much haste, they worked to set the rope through the handles and give it enough lead to drag behind the horse without tripping the animal.

Lightning flashed and thunder crashed as if the very earth had rammed the sky straight on. Theodyne shouted something at Jolen, but the words were lost to the squall.

Jolen paid no mind. The time had come to bid the valley farewell. He climbed upon the horse—his heart in his throat. His hands shook as he threaded his fingers through the mane. The scenario was worse than he thought, no saddle, no reins. He had to do the best he could to stay on the animal's back. Luckily his fear of horses had not meant he lacked skill. He'd gained the skills long before he'd learned the fear.

He leaned over the horse's neck and gave instructions. The ears twitched, feet stamped. Jolen gave the animal its head and held on with prayers to both Gods and elementals to see him safe.

ESTOBÁN ARRIVED at the Lancor villa with heart aching and worry burrowed deep in his soul. He'd not be easy again until he had Jolen back in his arms. He didn't fear his lover unable to care for himself—Jolen had just been through so much as of late, and no one knew nor could guess the direction of the necromancers' next attack. He had to trust that Jolen, Theodyne, and the Medovin guards were capable enough to take care of any trouble that arose.

Not being able to see what happened ate at him. Along the line of their connection, Estobán lived all of Jolen's emotions. At present, he felt nothing but despair and fear. Uncertainty. His own sense of hopelessness waged a battle within.

Viola met him in the courtyard as he dismounted. Magus Gaius stood behind her in a protective gesture.

"Brother?" She opened her arms and took him to her bosom, as a mother would a child. When she pulled away, she looked deeply into his eyes. "We had word that Cesare is dead. Is that true?"

Estobán ran a hand down her beloved face. Tension and doubt clouded her eyes. He never wanted to see that look and know he was responsible for putting it there. For him it was but another sin against him. "It's true. Killed by my own hand."

Strain left her, and she placed her hand on his shoulder. Estobán felt her knees go slack. He lowered his voice so only she overhead his barked command. "Strength, love. Strength. Do not let our people see you weak. Ever."

She straightened her spine, a perfect mask of indifference on her face. "I understand."

"Cesare was only one part in our problem of succession. I mean to have it out with the others." Estobán moved in the direction of the villa proper. He wanted a soak in a nice cool bath and to dress in something more comfortable than riding leathers.

Oppressive heat baked down on the villa as if caught in a tidal pool in hell. He rubbed his neck. Sweat wet his hand as if he'd been rained on.

He turned to first Viola, then his magus. "I want you both to meet me in my office in an hour. We have much to discuss and many plans to make. The entire landscape of the court is going to change, and the better we prepare, the less of an upheaval it will make in our lives."

Viola shot a glance to the magus before addressing Estobán. "Are these changes for the better?"

A warm rush filled him at the thought of bringing Jolen here and sharing his life, bed, and home with his lover. "Yes. I believe they will be."

Viola gave a decisive nod. "We will await your audience."

Estobán gave some instructions to his guards and then headed for his suite. He glanced back to watch his sister and the magus and caught the subtle touch of their hands. For some time now he wondered if Magus

Gaius and Voila had become lovers. If they were, the affair was carried out with as much discretion as one could expect in the small social circle of the Medovin court.

As a brother, he'd never presume to tell Viola where to place her heart—the Gods knew that she had never interfered or judged his relationships, except to counsel him during the end of his relationship with Theodyne. However, he may need the bargaining power of her hand in order to secure a future alliance. He'd not meddle unless things became more serious between them.

He'd leave it for now. He had much bigger, more pressing issues with which to deal.

Even as he entered his suite, the servants were busy preparing his bath. Clothes had already been placed in the dressing area. He might love his villa at Gusan, but it was good to be home. The rhythm of the Lancor estate ran so differently than the residence in the holy city.

He allowed the servants to assist him in the removal of his riding leathers. They moved silently in their work, gazes fixed to their tasks rather than at him. Not that they were in the habit of looking directly at their master—as the Medovin it would be considered an insult. A childish smile and guileless eyes flashed in his mind.

Wendro had not stood on such ceremony. He'd been as open and honest a life force as Estobán had ever seen. A vital and promising child. Jolen and Theodyne had both seen potential in the lad, and it angered Estobán that such a bright light had been lost to necromancer evil.

It was up to him and the rest of the *prolates* to ensure that did not happen again. Protection of the citizens under their care was paramount. All the more reason for the move against the Agia. The time had come to bring new blood into Delaneux.

He stepped into the bath. Water swirled around his legs. An instant vision of fighting the cold wet and working against the forces of nature held him in a vengeful grip.

*Jolen!*

"Your Grace?" Silas held his arm out for Estobán to steady himself. "Are you all right?"

"Please, contact Master Nico and tell him Masters Jolen and Theodyne's party is in trouble."

Silas's eyes widened. He turned a stricken look to another of the servants. "Tell the magus to send the message immediately. I'll stay with His Grace."

The servant bowed and left the room.

Estobán leaned his head back against the tub rim and closed his eyes, trying to find Jolen's location. He searched for anything that might give a location and failed. The momentary connection severed—all but the basic emotions remained.

*Oh, love. I swear I will send help. Please hang on a little longer.*

The musky scent of horses wafted up to tickle his nose. Not surprising after his long journey in the saddle, but the tinge of fear clung to his body. Yet the scent did not come from his emotions.

The longer he sat in the bath, the more he wanted to jump from his flesh. A crawling sensation, like the trek of bugs moving along the surface of his skin, began to radiate outward. He scratched at the sensation.

Tingles ran through the roots of his hair. He slid under the water and sluiced his fingers through the short strands. Itches sprouted everywhere, and he only had two hands and not enough fingers to take care of all the spots at once.

What the hell was going on?

Was it some reaction to the soap? A contagion in the water? Perhaps he'd gotten bugs from the horse. He'd have Silas contact the stable master to discover if any of the mounts had mites. Though if he didn't know better, he'd swear that the irritation came from the inside, working its way outward.

No longer able to take the feeling, he pushed up to a standing position. Silas readied a towel and wrapped it around Estobán's torso. The nap of the fabric felt good against the sensitive areas. He pulled the linen taut and chafed it across his back.

"Summon Havero. I need a salve to stop this blasted itching."

"Yes, Your Grace."

Another servant left the room to complete the task. Silas stayed and helped Estobán into a robe, then escorted him into the bedroom.

He didn't have the time to lounge around waiting for an itch to go away. As a matter of fact, he needed to change and meet Viola and the magus in his office. If he missed the meeting, she might take it into her head to search for him. He saw no reason to make her worry.

"Bring me the crimson doublet."

"Yes, Your Grace."

A knock sounded on the door as Silas turned away. Havero entered the room. Concern pulled his brow into a severe frown.

"You asked for me, Your Grace?"

"I need something for an itch."

"Please remove your robe so I can examine your skin."

Estobán stood and did as told. Red welts rose along his arms and upper chest where he'd scratched.

Havero shook his head and clucked his tongue in a disapproving manner. "I will give you a salve, but you must not scratch. That will only irritate the area further."

Estobán raised a brow. "You try not scratching with an itch so powerful, and see if you don't succumb."

"I have a sedative to take off the edge, if you'll allow me to administer it."

Estobán shook his head. "No."

If he really had tapped into his connection with Jolen, all the hells would have to plunge into the depths of ice and snow before he'd wish to sever it. Not with Jolen far away and under attack. If, Gods forbid, anything happened to Jolen, Estobán wanted to know immediately. And yet, it pained him so much to share the emotions on a visceral level. To realize his lover was in trouble and he—Estobán—was across the expanse of Dominical unable to give either aid or comfort.

Havero began to apply the topical ointment. Irritated with the slow progression and lack of instant relief, Estobán snatched the bottle from the physician's hand and tipped the contents up into his palm.

"Your Grace, it should be used sparingly."

Estobán waved his free hand at Havero. "Thank you for the remedy and your instructions. If I need anything further, I'll send for you."

Havero bowed and retreated. When the door closed behind him, Estobán began a vigorous application of the salve.

He glanced up at Silas and raised a brow. "Do you have a comment to make?"

In typical stoic fashion, Silas held his hands before him in a supplicant manner and said, "Perhaps you should follow the physician's instructions, Your Grace."

If that advice had come from anyone else, he might have barred them from his presence. Silas had not once given him misdirection or ill counsel in all the years of his employ, so Estobán gave him more latitude than the other servants. He doubted any of the others would dare to speak so forward, even ending the sentence with "Your Grace."

Estobán watched his servant for a moment before returning to his task. The barest film of salve had made a vast improvement on his symptoms. It did not calm the pit of fear open under his heart. He doubted any kind of remedy could cure that ill. Only Jolen's presence would make a difference.

Estobán waited a few moments before he sat on the edge of the bed. "Help me dress. I will not keep my sister and the magus waiting."

"Yes, Your Grace."

Clothing felt foreign, scratchy. The finest silks and softest wools were as rough as steel across his tender skin. And he was cold. So awfully cold.

The crimson velvet doublet did nothing to quell the chill. The fabric akin to icy pellets hitting his back, chest, and arms. The undershirt proved no protection against the chafe. Silas pulled the jacket closed and set the brass hooks into place.

"Is there anything else, Your Grace?"

Estobán shook his head.

He ran a hand down his torso and took a deep breath, trying to shake the feeling of doom that persisted.

It wasn't easy by any stretch of the imagination—and why should it be? He'd seen things during the last few weeks that were beyond the human brain to comprehend. But they had happened, and his life would be forever changed by the experience.

Estobán moved through the back hallways and corridors to arrive at his office. Viola and the magus were already inside. Their heads bent together, whispering.

"My apologies for keeping you waiting."

Viola turned to him with a gentle yet worried smile. "Please sit and let me pour you some wine."

Estobán waved away the offer. "I need to stand." He walked over to the drinks table and lifted the pitcher of water. Didn't Jolen always say he liked a clear head?

As he poured, he began the conversation he dreaded. "The other *prolates* and I have decided to ensure the safety and security of Dominicál by any and all means, starting with the reinstitution of court alchemists."

Viola and Magus Gaius exchanged glances.

"You have reservations about the appointment?" Estobán raised a brow and then felt a sudden stab of guilt. As his heir, Viola had every right to disagree if she believed the city-state might be placed in jeopardy.

"Your Grace, I only mean to caution you to select your appointed alchemist wisely."

It took Estobán a moment before he realized why she was so concerned. He let out a breath. "I can assure you it will not be Master Theodyne. While I respect his talents and owe him more than I can ever repay for his recent assistance in Gusan, I would not bring him to court."

Viola relaxed a bit. She turned her head to the side. "Then who have you selected? Are you going to allow Master Nico to decide and then abide by his appointment?"

"His name is Master Jolen Meripen, and he was instrumental in exposing the necromancers in Gusan. If not for his aid, the country would now be in serious peril."

"Estobán." Viola drew his name out with a weary sigh. She stood, came to him, and placed her hands on his velvet-clad arms. "Guard your heart, Brother. I can tell you are in fair danger of losing it to this Master Jolen."

Estobán glanced from her to the magus and back again. "Fine advice from a woman who is in love with my magus."

Viola drew in a sharp breath, covering her mouth with her hand. Magus Gaius stood. His hands out and palms up in entreaty. "Your Grace, we meant no disrespect."

"Nor have I taken any. I only meant to say that we cannot always give our hearts where we want. Sometimes love is stronger than the power to overcome its grasp." Estobán rapped a knuckle on the table and stepped away, moving behind his desk as if in need of the furniture as a barricade against his emotions.

"The other topic is something I need you to keep in strict confidence. It is not to leave this room, not even after the eventuality occurs."

Viola frowned. "Then why tell us? Isn't it better if we not know?"

"As my heir, you must be involved in all decisions that will affect our city-state. It is how you learn to rule, and if something should happen to me, it will be a more seamless transfer of power."

Viola rubbed a spot over her heart. "That is the worst thing about being your heir, knowing that to take my place as the Medovin, you will be gone. I don't think I want to even contemplate such a pass."

Estobán looked to his magus. "Surround yourself with those you can trust and eliminate the ones you cannot."

The specter of Cesare's death hung over the room. Estobán still had not given Viola the entire story, and he struggled with how much to tell her. Surely he had no need to give her all the details, even as his heir.

"As you have done?"

Estobán nodded. "I did what was necessary. Cesare not only betrayed the family but all of the city-states by siding with the necromancers. He made his choice. I made mine. I could not take the chance he'd continue to allow them to influence him."

"I understand."

Estobán looked into her eyes and realized she spoke the truth. She wasn't telling him what she thought he wanted or needed to hear. "And soon, if our plans come to fruition, the Agia will follow."

"An assassination? Estobán... Your Grace... it sets a very bad precedent to oust a family long-standing in a *prolatial* seat because you disagree with their politics." Viola stood and walked around the side of the desk, taking Estobán's arm.

He rested his hand atop hers. "The Agias are the necromancers' strongest allies. We have to eliminate them in order to secure all of Dominicál. It is the only way."

Viola turned troubled eyes to her lover. Magus Gaius gave a nod of confirmation.

"So much bloodshed."

"Better those who would see us living under the yoke of death dancers than to lose honest citizens who abide by the laws put forth by the Gods." Estobán had never been a particularly spiritual man, but he'd rather trust in the deities than to leave his fate up to those who lived a shadowy half-life. At least this way he had a chance at an afterlife.

"Who did you have in mind to replace the Agia? Surely the other *prolates* have discussed this elevation as well."

Estobán rubbed away a tingle on the back of his neck. The chills had not subsided since the conversation began, they'd only increased. "There is no consensus yet in that quarter. We are to reconvene in a month for further discussions. Nothing is yet decided on the assassination either; it is at this point only a possibility."

If he thought the wrangling for the *demigogal* position was cutthroat, surely when the whole of Dominicál learned of the Agia's downfall, it would be chaos.

Estobán finally sat. "Now, tell me what *you* have planned for the clerics."

# Chapter Twenty-Three

JOLEN REINED in the horse by a tug on the mane. They had cleared the most treacherous part of the flood, but the storm continued to chase them into the mountains.

It had also been several days since the front of the storm moved across the valley. Their tiny band had hidden in caves and crevices at night, trying to stay warm and holed up from what Jolen felt was an impending attack by the necromancers.

The fact they had traveled for as long and far as they had without seeing any of the death dancers had put him on edge. Every snapped branch and rockslide had him tensing in preparation for an attack that hadn't come. At this pace, he'd be frayed down to his last nerve before ever reaching the pass onto the school's land.

Jolen touched the pieces of the *Elementica* nestled close to his stomach to ensure they remained secure. He'd divided them up the first night of their escape to higher ground.

Theodyne pulled up alongside him. The mount beneath him danced in nervous steps. "What's the matter?"

"I don't know. A subtle change in the air. It's not right. Not for this area."

Theodyne frowned. Sunlight crested the hill, breaking through the constant clouds. He had not spent a lot of time in the area, didn't know the feel of the mountains the way Jolen did; therefore, he couldn't detect the minute changes that might mean trouble up ahead.

Captain Fessen doubled back. He pointed to the ground with the tip of his drawn sword. "There have been movements through here recently. Within the past hour or two. The tracks are fresh, though I can't tell what manner of animals were used."

Both Jolen and Theodyne dismounted and bent down to the soil. It remained damp from the recent rain. Where the tracks were, solid casts formed as if each step had been molded under both heat and pressure. Jolen held out his hand and ran it above the impressions. He closed his eyes, sensing the type of animal that had passed this way, and it was none of his experience.

A beast with great hard hooves, separated into three distinct cloves carried a rider on its sleek back. The legs were long and powerful, larger than a draught horse. Its great head swung from side to side, sniffing the air in search of its prey. The rider on its muscular back, Jolen couldn't quite make out with his senses.

He glanced up at Theodyne with a frown. "Can you see him? The rider?"

Theodyne's jaw hardened, nostrils flared. "Yes, and I've seen him before. He was with the Agia the first time I encountered them."

Anger burned its way up Jolen's throat, leaving an acid bath in its wake. He pushed to a standing position. "And he's come this way for a reason. Is he tracking ahead of us, leading us into a trap, or is he fleeing pursuit?"

"There is no doubt in my mind he's leading us." Theodyne lifted his head and stared off into the distance. Wind ruffled the hair around his face.

Laughter burbled from behind Hazrael's scold's bridle.

Jolen turned and speared the death dancer with a look. "I'd as soon throw you off a cliff than keep you with us and risk being caught by your master. Remember that."

The laugh didn't die out as much as change to a menacing growl. The sound carried, echoing down the hillside and beyond. It penetrated the wind and trees, vibrating every rock and mountaintop.

"Shut him up!" Jolen struck out with a hand raised. Power shot from his palm, sending a charge through the metal cage covering Hazrael's face.

Captain Fessen swatted at Hazrael at the same time. The combined attack had the desired effect, and the man lost consciousness.

"Come on, we need to move fast now. The bastard's alerted his brethren. We haven't much time before they're on us." Theodyne was already in motion, jumping up into the saddle, then kicking his horse to a gallop through the pass.

Jolen climbed onto his horse. They didn't even have the choice of going back the way they had come. The distance was too far to double back and find a new path onto the school grounds. Once they'd entered the pass, they were committed to the endeavor.

Jolen nudged his mount with his knees, urging the animal to move faster. Horrible screams, a choir of banshees, filled the air. The cacophony surrounded and blanketed the riding party until it threatened to smother. The angry wails were enough to cause eardrums to rupture and bleed— though looking around the party, Jolen saw no outward sign of injury. A small relief. In battle a soldier's hearing was one of his greatest tools. Not to mention a quick way for the necromancers to disable the men who rode beside them.

With renewed purpose, Jolen urged his horse faster. If riding headlong into the bastards saved even one of Estobán's men, it was well worth the sacrifice. They knew the objective was to deliver the *Elementica* and Hazrael over into the school's keeping. Anything less was failure.

Jolen was in a mind to ride straight through the ambush to have it over and done. He saw no point in dragging out the coming battle. The best approach was to fall into the breach so the victors might move on.

"Jolen. What are you doing?" Theodyne called out from behind him.

Jolen didn't answer. If he died springing this trap, so be it. He'd die a hero or at the very least a valiant.

"Come back!"

Jolen's heart pounded, his throat closed in fear. He squeezed his knees close to his mount's sides to hold on and lifted his arms.

*"Oh Gods and ancient ones, help me, please! Don't let this be the stupidest thing I've ever done!"*

Fear did a serpentine in his guts. The horse beneath him galloped faster. His mind screamed in terror, but his resolve was absolute.

He opened his hands and seized the wind.

The body of the elemental caught within his grasp twisted and turned, bowed upward and outward, gaining mass and momentum. He hurled the gust like a lance at the covering foliage. Trees shook and rocks became projectiles. Branches broke and snapped. The area became a barrage of activity as the necromancers charged.

A murder of crows rode the wind. Their black silhouettes merged and formed into a great, gaping maw. They swooped as one, diving to catch Jolen and swallow him and his mount whole.

Jolen slid to the right and dived for the ground. The horse screamed. It reared as the crows attacked. It thrashed its hooves, trying to get at its winged foes. Jolen threw up a hand, pushing the air current used by the crows and forced it backward. They squawked and cried, then dropped from the sky, grounded by that mysterious force recently discovered and named gravity.

Theodyne was off his horse and ran to Jolen. He hunkered down beside him. "Are you all right?"

"I've drawn them out. Now we confront on our terms."

Necromancers poured into the clearing. Their mounts were more terrifying than even Jolen had imagined. Spawned from the lower rungs of hell, they dwarfed the Medovin horses. Large heads were covered in scales and shaped more like pictures of dragons from ancient children's tales. The nostrils were as big as a man's fist and glowed red. Steam shot out with every exhalation, burning the surrounding foliage with acid.

Tattered gray robes floated on an otherworldly wind, slower than the movement of the wearers suggested. Cowls covered the faces of their attackers. Jolen would rather know his enemy and look him in the eyes— even if those were sightless sockets in a fleshless skull.

The world began a crazy slide and tilt, as if the necromancers spun the clearing on a potter's wheel. Jolen held onto a rock, to Theodyne, to anything he could reach. His head whirled. All notion of up or down ceased. He tried to find the others to see if they were as affected as he.

Guards struggled to stay upright, their weapons useless against the coming tide of death. Jolen pushed to his feet, closing his eyes to fight the spinning sensation.

"Jump into the ether with me, Theodyne."

Jolen didn't wait for an answer but allowed his consciousness to hover above the ground and watch the battle from afar. It also allowed him to control his body, without being a part of it or feeling the pain of his injuries.

Luckily they weren't great at this time. The distinct advantage to fighting from such a position was that the necromancers' tricks to disrupt his equilibrium had no effect. However, if his mortal body were destroyed, he'd be trapped in the ether for eternity.

It was a chance he had to take.

Theodyne lifted his hand, swinging it in an arc. Dirt rolled, cresting like a giant wave composed of earth, rocks, and debris. The hellbeasts reared, trying to jump over the crumbling wake. They screamed in terror as the wave broke, burying them along with their unholy burden.

Jolen circled the site, waiting for survivors to climb from the rubble. He doubted the amount of dirt would keep them at bay for long. They'd crawl their way out if they had to dig with their feet.

And there, right at the very edges of the pile, tri-cloven hooves scrabbled their way up from the grave. Skeletal hands reached up toward the light. Jolen harnessed a passing static charge and diverted it just in time to ignite the robes of the first death dancer to break the surface.

A chorus of angry shouts rose to the heavens. A choir of demons cursing a creator who showed them no favor.

A ripple in the fabric of reality shuddered, then split. Necromancers poured from the rip, as if called forth by their brothers' cries for vengeance. Too many of them exited the portal for Jolen and Theodyne to hold back.

This was the moment where all was given or all was lost. Either way, he doubted any of them would leave this clearing as more than a memory.

Fury became a palpable thing as the necromancers unleashed a thousand years of hate.

Captain Fessen pulled his broadsword from the scabbard on his back and circled it over his head as the death dancers charged him. Heads rolled, and the bodies fell to dust. Tattered robes smoldered, embers left behind after a fire.

One of the hellmounts gnashed at the guards. It ripped a man from the ground and shook him. There came a sickening crunch, and then the man's neck wobbled at a drunken angle, killed by the unnatural animal forged in nightmares.

Jolen moved his astral arm, bending a tree limb back as far as the branch allowed. He let it go, smacking the beast in the face and knocking it backward with a force so great it rolled ass over hooves through the air. It landed belly up in front of Captain Fessen who struck it through the heart. Showers of black blood sprayed into the air.

The necromancers circled the small contingent. Renvic pulled his pistol and shot into the advancing hoard. The ball hit true. An explosion scattered the necromancer's thorax to the four corners. Colored sparks of green and orange spread outward. That was not a normal gun.

*"I'm going back down. Stay here and protect from above."* Jolen entered his body just in time for a hellmount to rear up.

He lifted his arm to block the strike, a reflexive action that gave him little time to prepare a defense. A boulder flew past his body, hitting the beast like a cannonball. Guts scattered, painting the ground in gore.

Jolen tried to keep his feet but fell in the blood-soaked earth. As he landed, he struck out, taking down a few more of the necromancers.

The men fought valiantly, but for each necromancer killed, two more came into the clearing as if summoned by the call of death. Master Nico claimed the necromancers had the ability to fold distances, seeing them now and their never-ending supply of support, Jolen believed.

They were losing.

It was only a matter of time before the last of the guards fell and both Jolen and Theodyne were either captured or killed.

Jolen tried to push the defeatist thoughts away, but it was hard in the face of such overwhelming odds.

He gathered all his strength, pulling it into a tight ball near his heart. Then pushed, using both hands to disperse nothing but pure energy. The blast shot death dancers and hellmounts outward. A crater formed with Jolen as the nexus.

A deathly quiet came over the clearing then. Jolen turned to ensure he'd not killed his friends.

Cheers erupted. Guards thrust their sword points skyward in a show of victory. Theodyne blinked a few times, settling into his body. He gave a loud whoop, then grabbed Jolen, lifting him up into the air.

"You should have seen that from above. It was amazing!"

Their triumph was short-lived.

Tremors started under their feet. The land rolled like a storm-tossed ocean. Air rippled and split. A portal opened, and an army of beings Jolen had never seen before stepped through.

"By the Ancestor!" Jolen jumped behind a rock, dragging Theodyne with him.

Theodyne's breath sawed in and out. "Damn. I don't think I have much more in me."

"Neither do I. We need to link if we're going to hold them off much longer." Jolen rubbed his forehead where sweat threatened to blind him.

Theodyne looked out from their hiding place. He held his hands together, making a circle, then spread them out wide.

A terrible sound of earth moving and the hollowness of a cavern echoed back to them. Jolen peeked out enough to see the sinkhole opening up in front of the portal. Those death dancers who crossed over into the clearing hit the hole and fell.

Alchemists poured into the fray from the opposite direction, charging down the hill like an army of avenging angels. Jolen turned from the fight and watched as Headmaster Oberon and the others engaged the enemy in a clash as violent and final as anything Jolen and Theodyne had set to motion.

Necromancers fell under the lash of power. Their rotted forms returned to powder and sank into the ground.

Headmaster Oberon dismounted and threw off his helm. "Bloody death dancers. When will we be rid of their presence?"

Jolen ran a hand through his hair. Sweat soaked his palm. His hand shook against his scalp. He'd lost a lot of energy today and doubted he'd remain upright for any length of time. Seriously, he was surprised to be alive.

"So, I take it our prisoner is the one in the scold's bridle?" Oberon looked down on Hazrael's miserable form. Eyes flashed from behind the iron bars. "Take that contraption off him."

Jolen hesitated but only for a moment. Something in Headmaster Oberon's expression resembled panic. Color had leached from his skin, leaving him pale. Jolen nodded to Captain Fessen and watched as the bridle was removed.

Oberon fell to his knees, looking directly into the necromancer's intelligent yet dead eyes. "Hazrael? Is that you?"

What was this? Headmaster Oberon knew the necromancer? How was that possible? The knowledge gave Jolen a start. Theodyne's brows rose in surprise.

For once an emotion other than arrogance shone in Hazrael's eyes. Confusion pulled his brow low. "I know your face."

"We thought you were dead." Oberon lifted a visibly shaking hand and smoothed Hazrael's hair from his face. "We searched. *I* searched." His voice cracked and broke.

Hazrael shook his head. "I don't remember. Only the death and rebirth by my masters."

Oberon's jaw worked back and forth. His mouth formed a straight line, compressed. He stood and helped the necromancer to his feet. "We will discover the entire story, I assure you."

Jolen watched helplessly as Oberon escorted the man responsible for Wendro's death away as if he were the victim. Judging by the tight expression on Oberon's face, perhaps Hazrael was that and more—but it didn't make it right. It did not absolve him of his crimes.

"Headmaster, Hazrael must answer for the death of many, including an innocent boy under my protection and that of the Medovin."

Oberon turned sad eyes to Jolen. "Perhaps, but not today."

Theodyne shook his head, coming to join Jolen's defense. "No. Maybe not, but Nico will hear of this, and his decision *will* be the final word."

Oberon placed Hazrael on his mount. "I have no doubt Nico will be as surprised as I am at this turn of events and will decide accordingly." With that cryptic remark hanging in the air, he mounted behind the necromancer and turned his horse to ride from the pass.

"What did he mean by that?"

Theodyne moved to catch the reins of his own horse. "I don't know, but I'll discover the meaning. I won't let Wendro's death go without answer."

Jolen didn't plan to either, but it appeared that Headmaster Oberon had taken a protective stance over the necromancer, and that had to be explained to some degree, or the confidence the school had in him in a position of authority might be questioned.

"Do you think Master Nico knows Hazrael?" Jolen hedged. He watched Theodyne's face for any tells but came up with nothing. Theodyne appeared as shaken by the news as Jolen.

"I have no idea what Oberon meant, but if Nico does know Hazrael, it explains why he was so adamant that no harm come to him on the journey to the school."

"Then why didn't he tell us?"

Theodyne shrugged. His face was set in hard lines. He was not pleased with the turn of events. "Perhaps he only heard the name mentioned before and was unsure if it was the same Hazrael."

That didn't seem likely to Jolen, though he didn't come right out and say so. Instead he mounted up and rode out with the rest of the alchemists.

# Chapter Twenty-Four

DESAN KARIS hefted his considerable bulk to the front of the court. The fact the man had come to petition the Medovin in the first place was suspicious in the extreme. Most of the Holy See's requests were made in private after court hours. This blatant show of submission did not sit well with Estobán.

Estobán decided to handle the matter with the utmost regard for both protocol and cooperation. He would not have it said that the Medovin flouted church authority or placed his own interests above the Gods' representative. "How may I assist you, Your Eminence?"

"It is my extreme and humble honor that I offer you this token of esteem and gratitude from His Holiness." Desan Karis held out a scroll to the magus, who took the offering with a nod and inspected it before bringing it before Estobán.

A look to the Desan's face told an entirely different story. He wasn't pleased to be the messenger in this case. As a matter of fact he looked in danger of developing an acute case of dyspepsia.

The magus unrolled the official *demigogal* proclamation. Words appeared at the top of the page in an elaborate and artistic hand.

*"By decree of His Holiness Demigoge Alexandro III of that name, on this six day of Prinum, in the year 1547, His Grace, the honorable Estobán Medovin of the House of Medovin, prolate of Sadonia, is awarded this demigogal seal as the Protectorate General of Dominicál."*

Estobán had no idea what it meant or the significance of such an appointment. Was it in name only, or were there duties and expectations attached to the title? He'd no doubt learn those facts in the future—also he'd make the office into what he wanted.

With a nod of thanks to Desan Karis, Estobán acknowledged the gift. "Please extend our thanks to His Holiness on behalf of the entire Medovin family for this honor. We will take our duties to heart and protect Dominicál against all threats."

The words only made the *desan*'s eyes and mouth pinch in contempt—a fact that warmed Estobán's heart.

Magus Gaius continued to read the document. When he reached the bottom he glanced up. His eyes alight in triumph.

Estobán leaned closer and whispered, "What is it?"

"The final paragraph grants legitimacy to Viola's rights as heir. It has the *demigogal* seal. The appointment cannot be overturned unless by His Holiness's hand. The clerics have no recourse on this matter."

Estobán smiled. "Joyous news indeed. Tonight we celebrate in the grand style of our ancestors."

Even if he did not feel much like celebrating due to Jolen's protracted absence. However, this was a major victory and needed to be marked with all the fanfare of such an occasion.

As a matter of fact, he'd not heard one word on Jolen's whereabouts or the outcome of their travel. He didn't even know if they'd safely reached the school, though he'd not felt the finality as if Jolen had perished on the journey.

Court adjourned after two more cases were heard and adjudicated. Estobán climbed the back stairs to his office to read the correspondences piled there. From now on, Viola would have to be involved in every aspect of governorship. If she wanted to take his place or teach her children to rule when it came time for them to sit on the *prolate*'s seat, she'd have to be prepared, and that meant from the most trying of cases to the painfully mundane.

"I thought that court would never end. Do your petitioners always drone on like that?"

At the voice coming from the corner of the room, Estobán spun around and stood as if his feet were rooted into the floor. "Jolen?"

Estobán blinked a few times, trying to test his eyes to see if they had failed him. But no, Jolen stood there with a smile on his face and hat in his hand.

"Have I changed that much in just a few weeks?"

"No. No." Then Estobán was in motion. He took Jolen into his arms and held him tightly. Nothing had ever felt so good as this reunion. When he'd hugged him long and hard, he took Jolen out to arms' length and studied his beloved face. Something swam in the depths of his blue eyes. "What's wrong?"

Jolen nodded to a chair. "May I?"

"Of course. Please sit. Can I get you anything? When did you arrive? Why didn't you let me know?" Estobán took a place across from Jolen. He'd rather have kept touching him, but there seemed a bit more to discuss than their missing each other.

Jolen put up a hand. "One topic at a time, Bán. It's been a very long journey, and I'm worn to the bone. So much has happened since we last spoke. I'm having a hard time taking it all in. The most significant detail is that our necromancer, Hazrael, is not unknown to the Gold School or its administrators, though I have yet to uncover the connection."

Estobán sat back in his seat, not wanting to believe the possibility. "Did you ask?"

"Yes, as did Theodyne. Even he has been left out of the confidence. I have a suspicion he might at one time have been a student who had gone missing." Jolen rubbed the spot between his eyes. "I've not been able to verify the truth. Neither Headmaster Oberon nor Master Nico is talking about it at this point. However, Hazrael is now under their protections, and I doubt we'll be allowed to question him about the necromancers' movements without them present."

Estobán flicked his hand in dismissal. "Let them deal with him, then. We can't be responsible for the entire country, though it pains me that they will hide information as to his identity from you and Theodyne. If he was once a student, is he beyond the reach of recovery? Can he be saved as were we?"

Jolen shook his head, looking off into the distance as if trying to see all the way back to Delaneux without the aid of a scrying bowl. "I have no idea. We were only under the influence for a short time. Who knows how long Hazrael has been among the necromancers and if such a long-term influence can even be expunged."

"Don't you feel as an alchemist and *aerothant* you at least have to try?"

Jolen returned his gaze to Estobán's. Love warmed the sky blue to the heart of a flame. "Not me."

Heat spiraled up from Estobán's belly. "Oh, and why is that?"

A wild hunger mixed with the heat in Jolen's eyes. "I'll be here in Lancor, stationed in your home as your close, personal court alchemist."

"Then we have no recourse but to let the scenario play out as it will and trust they know what they are doing." Estobán took Jolen's hand and squeezed. "As Protectorate General of Dominicál, I have a sworn duty to ferret out and prosecute our enemies."

Jolen raised a brow. "Is that right? Then perhaps it falls on you to put pressure on Master Nico and Headmaster Oberon."

Estobán pulled Jolen closer and rose, coming around to the other side of the desk. "Yes, it is. But in the meantime…." He stopped the conversation with a kiss.

# Glossary

adept—highest level obtained by alchemical master.

Adepts' Council—body of ruling alchemical adepts who preside over matters pertaining to the Gold School.

*aerothant*—product of union between human and air elemental.

Agia, Ignatius—*prolate* of city-state of Calabris. Head of the House of Agia; also referred to as the Agia.

alchemy—the search for enlightenment through the study of science, theology, and the esoteric, and how it relates to the natural world.

Anjufer—full fire elemental who resides in the Gold School in service to the alchemists.

*aquathant*—product of union between human and water elemental.

Basilica of the Heavenly Throne—capital/seat of chief church of Dominicál.

Bertolini, Oberon—adept-level alchemist; Headmaster of Gold School.

*cardgran*—highest level of cleric in the Dominicál city-states. Make up the council who elect a new *demigoge*.

city-states—provinces/principalities in country of Dominicál. They are as follows: Auflaven, Bellor, Bonsuret, Brixton, Calabris, Devani, Dharakhan, Flurian, Nequan, Pliern, Romanta, Sadonia, Trumolo.

Delaneux—largest town in city-state of Calabris. Seat of the Agia family.

*damsk*—silver coin.

Dante, Mecurian—founder of the Gold School; ancestor of Count Nicodemus de Valencia.

*demigoge*—(pronounced: de mí gōche) derived from the word demagogue; supreme religious head of the Dominicál city-states.

deRosa of Bonsuret, Phillipe—*cardgran* from the city-state of Bonsuret, *demigoge*-elect.

*desan*—A Holy See—highest cleric of a city-state; however, is one step below a *cardgran* in the clerical order.

DiCarni, Juan-Carlo—*prolate* from island of Nequan.

Dominicál—the country that comprises the whole of the city-states.

Donando, Headmaster—deceased headmaster of Gold School; murdered by Agia's guards.

Duard—fist assistant to the Medovin Magus.

*Elementica*—stone tablet made of solid ruby, inscribed with the principles and laws of the elementals. Broken and scattered during the Great Purge.

*Eye of Truth*—sacred text of the alchemists, a book of immense power. Contains both codex of laws, spells, and incantations, and rubbings from the original Emerald Tablet—the basis of all alchemical study.

*etherealthant*—product of union between human and spirit elemental.

Fessen, Captain—head of Estobán Medovin's house guards in the Gusan villa.

*gint*—Brass coin.

Grand Matter—also called Prime Matter; universal substance of which everything springs; origins of life.

*guitern*—instrument, cross between harp, guitar and mandolin.

Gusan—city were seat of the Basilica of the Heavenly Throne is located.

Hazrael—necromancer—in employ of the House of Rinni as Magus.

Heavenly Throne—actual throne where the *demigoge* holds religious court.

Holy See—See *desan*. Highest clerical authority in a city-state. Terms Holy See and *desan* are used interchangeably.

Karis, Desan—head of local archdiocese in city-state of Sadonia.

Krutarch, Master—adept who wrote keyed primer.

Lancor—largest town in city-state of Sadonia; seat of the Medovin family.

magus—chief advisor for a *prolate* or *prolatial* house wholly unconnected to the family by blood.

Magus Gaius—magus/chief advisor to Estobán Medovin and House of Medovin. Viola Medovin's lover.

Medovin, Cesare—Estobán's cousin.

Medovin, Estobán—*prolate* of Sadonia; head of Medovin family, also referred to as the Medovin. Theodyne Thespacian's ex-lover.

Medovin, Viola—Estobán Medovin's sister; named heir to the House of Medovin.

Meripen, Jolen—master alchemist of the Gold School.

necromancers—also called death dancers; can raise or speak with the dead. Greatest foes of the alchemists.

necromon—title of esteem and respect given to head necromancer.

*plazo*—small garden or gathering place within confines of an estate, usually decorated with colorful stones.

*prolate*—ruler of a city-state, also head of his family.

*prolatial* courts—courts where *prolates* decide matters of state and preside over local civic and criminal matters.

*pyrothant*—product of union between human and fire elemental.

Renvic—young guard in the employ of Estobán Medovin, who distinguishes himself in service to his *prolate*.

Rinni, Claudio—*prolate* of city-state of Bonsuret; held in thrall by the necromancers.

seal of Devani—seal wore by officials of that city-state to denote them as dignitaries; seal used in all official city-state correspondences.

*slew*—copper coin.

*spagyrics*—alchemical term; act of breaking down a substance then putting it back together in its highest form.

*terrathant*—product of union between human and earth elemental.

The Great Purge—war between necromancers and the elementals one thousand years before Alchemists and Elementals takes place. The Great Purge saw the ousting of the necromancers from Dominicál and elementals taking lesser role in the affairs of man.

Thespacian, Theodyne—former thief, now an apprentice in the Gold School.

*tonza*—gold coin.

Valencia, Count Nicodemus de—alchemist adept. Direct descendant of Mecurian Dante, head of Gold School.

Wendro—servant boy employed at Medovin's Gusan villa. *Etherealthant*.

CASSIE SWEET lives and works from her home office in the New Jersey Highlands, where she shares space with her overaffectionate Golden Retriever and artist husband. Her writing takes her to many destinations, both real and imagined. You can catch her on Twitter under her other writing personae @MKMancosKScott and on Facebook under Kathleen Scott/MK Mancos Author Page.

http://www.mystickat.com/

Alchemists and Elementals Series

http://www.dreamspinnerpress.com

UNION

ANNABELLE JACOBS

http://www.dreamspinnerpress.com

FOR **MORE** OF THE **BEST GAY ROMANCE**

*Dreamspinner Press*

DREAMSPINNERPRESS.COM

www.ingramcontent.com/pod-product-compliance
Lightning Source LLC
Chambersburg PA
CBHW071005280626
47160CB00015B/1371